8/98

in search of snow

BY THE SAME AUTHOR

Across the Wire: Life and Hard Times on the Mexican Border

in search of snow

A NOVEL

luis alberto urrea

HarperPerennial
A Division of HarperCollins*Publishers*

A hardcover edition of this book was published in 1994 by HarperCollins Publishers.

HarperCollins books may be purchased for educational, business, or sales promotional use. For information, please write: Special Markets Department, HarperCollins Publishers, Inc., 10 East 53rd Street, New York, NY 10022.

First HarperPerennial edition published 1995.

Designed by Alma Hochhauser Orenstein

The Library of Congress has catalogued the hardcover edition as follows:

Urrea, Luis Alberto.
In search of snow : a novel / Luis Alberto Urrea.—1st ed.
p. cm.
ISBN 0-06-017089-1
1. World War, 1939–1945—Veterans—Arizona—Fiction. 2. Arizona—Ethnic relations—Fiction. 3. Friendship—Arizona—Fiction. 4. Men—Arizona—Fiction. I. Title
PS3571.R74I5 1994
813'.54—dc20 93-37050

ISBN 0-06-092598-1 (pbk.)
95 96 97 98 99 ❖/ RRD 10 9 8 7 6 5 4 3 2 1

This book is for Lyn Niles:
your friendship is an oasis
in this desert.

my father tucks his hands
into his back pockets
and searches for the Big Dipper
in the wrong part of the sky

Lauren Shakely

CONTENTS

PROLOGUE

YEARS AGO, TWO YOUNG MEN STOOD IN THE DESERT watching the moon rise through the prehistoric ribs of a darkened Texaco station. An amber snake of high-octane gas shimmied across the gravel, its hose lazily disgorging a gallon a minute on the drive above them. A thin rivulet made its way to the tips of their boots and eddied. Mike McGurk turned to look at the slender Chicano beside him—he seemed like smoke in the dark.

"Listen to the cricket, Bobo," Mike said.

It worked its tiny ratchet in the weeds.

A greasy-looking cloud smeared across the moon, and a chromatic flood of blues descended over the badlands.

McGurk could hear Bobo trembling when he spoke: his voice rattled on his lips. Bobo said, "After we find your mother we can look for snow."

"I'd like that," McGurk said. "Maybe California. They got snow in California?"

"Sure, Mike. California, Mexico—they got snow everywhere."

"Not here," said McGurk.

Bobo shivered.

"It makes everything nice and white," McGurk said. "Covers it all up."

"Pinche frío, man. It feels like snow right here."

"Naw. This isn't hardly cold enough," said McGurk.

Bobo rubbed his forearms.

"We'll go up in the mountains someplace, Mikey," he said. "Find all the snow you want."

McGurk nodded. He flipped open the lid of his father's old Zippo with his thumb, clacked it closed with his forefinger: *snick-snick-snick*.

"Got a smoke, Bobe?"

Bobo stared at him for a moment in the gloom, then he dug in his pocket for his Chesterfields. He shook one out of the crumpled pack, extended it to McGurk. McGurk lipped it out of the pack and tasted the delicate tang of unlit tobacco. It mixed with the scent of gasoline. The fumes twirled up his nose and stung the center of his face.

"Well," he said, "let's go."

He could see Bobo's smile glowing in the dark.

"Why not."

McGurk spun the spark wheel, watched the spark fly off the flint, catch the wick, then rise in a comfortable yellow wedge of flame with a blue center. It seemed to drip up into the air.

"You ever notice how fire looks like water sometimes?" he said.

"Not really," said Bobo.

McGurk lit the cigarette, took a deep pull, imagined the smoke circling in his lungs—twin silver whirlwinds flanking his heart. He dropped the cigarette at the edge of the small puddle of gas. A squadron of little flames launched itself from the edges and circled the puddle. The two men stepped back.

Bobo giggled.

They heard a cough and a hiss as the snake of gas ignited and the fire rushed up the drive to the deeper pools of ethyl. The flames united in one brilliant streak and billowed in a mushroom around the pumps. In that instant, before the explosion, Mike heard these things: the cricket chirruping beside the road, the low moan of desert wind cutting the small erosion cliffs down to sand, the impossibly delicate sound of sand on blacktop, the rattle of creosote bushes, a clock ticking, the subtle *cling* of the Texaco sign tapping against the screws on the whitewashed pole.

Bobo grabbed McGurk's shirt and spun him away from the station. They ran across the highway, crossed the two lanes laughing, shouting. Bobo flapped his arms like some wild Quetzal. Mike shouted, "God!" and the pumps ignited, the tanks went up, the hill erupted. McGurk's Texaco launched itself into space.

The thunder slapped McGurk and Bobo flat to earth; Bobo's big motorcycle tumbled off its kickstand and keeled over. They had their arms around each other as the hot shock waves rattled their shirts on their backs. They jabbered silently, weeping at the thrill of the explosion.

Then the boom echoed away across the flats.

They sat up slowly, staring as the landscape collected itself around this new orange sun. The hilltop roared as the flames churned in the air. "Cool," Bobo said.

Flaming pieces of siding, aluminum, wood, iron fell back to earth, trailing arcs of smoke. Terrified vinegarroons stampeded out from under the wrecked cars scattered behind the station. They ran for their lives on scores of desperate legs.

McGurk and Bobo knew there wouldn't be a siren for hours.

part one

big dipper

1

Mike McGurk groaned and rolled over in his bed. The iron springs groaned louder than Mike did. He could hear his old man already at work, banging away at an engine block in the work bay on the other side of the thin wall. Everything at McGurk's Texaco smelled like oil. It gave Mike a headache.

He dragged himself out of bed and held his boxers open in front of the fan.

He'd trailed his gas-impresario father all over the Southwest, as helpless to break away as if connected to the old man by a tow chain. Out of boyhood Oklahoma, across the flatlands of Texas, into the hottest corners of New Mexico and Arizona. At the wheel: Wallace McGurk, aka Turk McGurk, aka Texaco Turk McGurk, self-proclaimed hero of trench warfare, a widower with a shaved head and an extravagance of mustache that swept out and up, giving him the aspect of, well, a Turk in a light opera. These whiskers were echoed by heavy eyebrows that exploded over his eyes in a manner that reminded Mike of two direct head shots with a .22.

Turk's own boyhood seemed to have been one perpetual brawl. He'd vowed to thrash anyone who called him "Wally," a nickname altogether lacking in the kind of heft Turk required. Over the years, he'd developed his sandlot fighting skills into a career as a certified star in the underground bare-knuckle boxing circuit. They fought in storerooms, behind factories, in secret places, and they had all the glory of fighting dogs, only these dogs stood on their back legs.

Turk's first professional fight was in Shreveport, against "Rock" Hardessey, a fading alcoholic who was starting to slide into fighting's version of a geek. Nobody bet on Rock anymore, and he was usually there to spray blood in the "B" fight that warmed up the crowd for the real bruisers.

The fight took place in a railroad roundhouse. It was not called a "bout" or a "contest." It was strictly a *fight.* The canvas was a cement floor carved into a vast turntable crisscrossed with track. The ring itself was a tightly packed phalanx of screaming men. It was not the first time Turk thought about how ugly people could be. "C'mon, ya mug," someone was shouting.

Hardessey's nose looked like a big buttermilk biscuit with veins in it. Turk was staring at this disaster of cartilage when Hardessey launched a right uppercut that clacked Turk's jawbones back into his ears and dropped him flat. The "referee" used his long stick to pry Hardessey away from Turk, then turned Turk over so the blood wouldn't choke him.

Later, Hardessey drove his car into a bayou and drowned.

Turk made twelve dollars.

The ref said, "Don't gripe, McGurk. Look at it this way—sometimes the fighters don't never get up."

Turk looked at the ten and two limp ones, then replied, "I'm never going down again, and you can tell those sons of bitches I said so."

His subsequent ferocity gave him a reputation that struck terror in ol' boys' hearts across three states.

Turk had visions, not in any way focused, involving gasoline and grease and Serv-Ur-Self islands and Mike.

Mrs. McGurk had been taken by "consumption" when Mike was seven. She'd been packed off to a clinic, which Mike never saw. Mom seemed to have been spirited away by magic—she'd started to cough, to get thin and pale, then she went to a hospital in Oklahoma City. When she got better, it was Phoenix for a while. Then, Turk had put Mom on a train west, and she didn't come back. Turk never spoke about it, aside from taking Mike aside and telling him, "Boy, there comes a time in every man's life when it's necessary to grow up. And we have that opportunity here now."

From this oblique comment in the kitchen, both of them sitting uncharacteristically at the table, Mike understood that Mom had died. Turk had donned an ill-fitting suit, the same suit he'd been married in, and drove for two days, showing up at the funeral drunk. Mike waited for Turk's return in the house of a waitress in Las Cruces. He'd met her once before, when Turk had taken him to a bowling alley. Her name was Jenny. Turk had led Mike to her door late at night, Mike saying, "I want to see Mom!" and Turk saying, "Nothing doing." Jenny came to the door in a tattered bathrobe. She wore lipstick to bed. They stood on the porch and watched Turk speed away.

One night she called Mike into the bathroom while she bathed and showed him her breasts. He was seven and a half. He hated her.

There was a little bit of life insurance money. After Turk took down all her pictures and threw away her dresses and underwear, he put the insurance and his fighting wins into ratchet wrenches, calendars, a tow truck. They started near Amarillo with a small Texaco. Then Turk dragged Mike to Tucumcari, New Mexico, where they opened an Esso station. There, Turk shattered the cheekbones of a young fighter named Billy "Upside" Downs, from Fall River, Massachusetts. He took home a cool five hundred dollars and another thousand in bets. Downs, however, lingered in a coma for three nights, then a bone fragment that had been working its way into his head lodged in his brain and killed him. Mike awoke halfway to the tow truck, wrapped in his blankets.

Turk picked up another Texaco franchise, in east Arizona, where his father, Carroll McGurk, had once policed the Apache in the company of Tom Horn, the notorious "regulator." Over the years, Turk's restlessness drove the McGurks west, where they drifted from fight to fight until Turk settled on this little station some miles northwest of Tucson, in the heart of the desert. One of his boxing buddies, Red Lewis, had run the station for ten slow years, "without one goddamned moment of regret." But Red was tired, rounding on sixty-three, and frankly couldn't stand the thought of one more head gasket. He was ready to put up his feet in his little trailer and "watch my television twenty-three hours a goddamned day!"

Red took Turk aside one night and told him there was a rumor floating about that this stretch of two-lane was going to turn into a major federal highway project "any day now." Turk's Texaco, on its low hillock overlooking one hundred twenty straight miles of road, would be a "sure bet" to bring in cascades of dough.

"Why, all's you need," Red enthused, "is for them tourists to start pourin' in—and that's all she wrote!"

World War II—known as the "The Big One" in those parts—had been over for 10 years, and optimistic ideas were flying. Turk imagined a life high on the hog. He mortgaged himself up to the eyeballs, bought out Red Lewis, took on six fights on the California docks, and settled in. At night, under the light of the vapor lamps, Turk sat in his chair and dreamed of V-8 engines.

"Roadmasters, Hudson Hornets, Impalas. Son," he'd confide, "nobody's got anything left to do but *drive*."

Mike, however, dreamed of snow.

He had been Turk's packmule since his mother died. It was as if Turk couldn't let Mike out of his sight. Mike hauled drooling hunks of Ford and Chevy around on his shoulders; Mike skinned his knuckles on the unyielding teeth of Oldsmobiles; Mike chain-winched rebuilt Nash engines into the pickups of suspicious Apaches. And all the time, he hated the brittle desert heat, the rocks inside his nostrils when the sweat-sucking wind dried him out. He hated the blue stink of exhaust, the grease soaked into the back of his underpants.

He kept an eye on Turk's eternally dangling Lucky Strikes too. The ground around the station was so oil-soaked that it had turned black and repelled even the bellicose scorpions. Mike half hoped a tossed cigarette would spark an eruption, send the whole thing sky-high in spinning flakes of aluminum siding. Sometimes he caught himself hoping it would go up with Turk in it.

After Mike's mother died, he was suspended from school six times in the first year. He slugged it out on the playground five times, and once he punched a teacher in the nose when the teacher tried to spank Mike for drawing snow-capped mountains on the inside cover of *My Primary Reader*.

Turk was so delighted that Mike slugged Mr. Hathaway that he gave Mike his first beer that night.

"I was afraid you might be a little limp, if you know what I mean," Turk said. His head, against the light, looked monumental to Mike as he gulped his beer. "But by God, you bloodied that powder puff. A tiger at eight years old! I guess he'll think twice before he tries to paddle a McGurk!"

In the absence of his wife, Turk's usual military frame of mind devolved into chronic war mania. Though Mike could remember little of his mother, he remembered many of his father's diatribes against every race and ethnic group that didn't have the good fortune to be a McGurk. Turk's focus skipped throughout the day, frying as it passed the Limey, the Hun, the Frog, the Pepper-Bellied Greaser, the Bolshevik, the A-rab, the Eye-talian Papist. He saw conspiracy all about him, from the land-grubbing Navajo to the Zionist bankers "controlling" New York and Hollywood. He hated both unions and scabs, hated the Ku Klux Klan and decried the "Negro invasion" of white northern cities. He roundly denounced the church in all its manifestations, quoted pointlessly from the Bible, insulted both housewives and "loose women," called the United States Government the "gooney-mint," and delighted in the foibles of Harry "S for Shithead" Truman. The only apparent solution Turk could see was immediate bombing, followed by arduous hand-to-hand combat.

Pearl Harbor had gone off in the McGurk household like an

errant bomb. Mike wept at the radio. Turk pounded the tabletop and jumped to his feet.

"Isn't it just like a bunch of swabbies to get caught with their pants down!" he bellowed. "Put in a half-dozen doughboys, and by Christ we'd see a different outcome!"

Turk marched outside, kicked savagely at the dirt, then stomped back inside.

"The Jap! This isn't what I expected at all. Your rice-eaters aren't motivated like your meat-eaters. To be bushwhacked by the Jap. Jesus H. Who'd of thought?"

As soon as Mike neared draft age, there seemed to be no choice. Turk marched him into the recruiting office and lied about his son's age. It was 1944, and Mike was only sixteen, but Turk wanted a McGurk to "bloody the Hun."

The Hun was easier to face than Turk.

While swearing to trounce the Wehrmacht and the Fascists, Mike secretly dreamed of the Alps. Among his mother's many old book-club hardcovers was an atlas of the world. In it, blue Alps were topped off with vanilla-colored snow. He'd hunted down the Matterhorn, and it remained in his thoughts as a vast snow cone, God's ice cream sundae. To Mike's undying horror, as soon as his papers came through he was whisked off to Fort Chaffee, Arkansas, home of the chigger. There, aside from the realization that he had made a dreadful mistake, Mike learned about *humidity*.

On the first day of boot camp, D.I. Burton Thibedaux, a fire hydrant in a tight uniform, so demoralized the men that three of them cried as the sarge bellowed up their noses. *He's no Turk*, Mike decided. Still, he was a drill instructor. "One hunnert pyush-yups!" he'd scream, and the boys would hit the sizzling tar and start grunting.

They were roused at four-fifteen the next morning, D.I. Thibedaux shrieking like a demon as he paraded between the bunks banging garbage-can lids together. Mike could not decipher what he was yelling, something like: "Hyarl be hyooggin by gol-dagged hyoorney, and I mean *now!*"

They assembled in the showers, bare-assed and bald-headed. Sarge stood atop the lockers, glowering down at them.

"Pa-thet-ic," he whispered.

Of course the sarge knew there were boys in this outfit who had never worked a flush toilet or bathed more than once a month.

"Youse jest a bunch of pig-humpin' pud-knockers. Or am I lyin'?"

"No, Sarge!"

"Whut jou say!"

"No, *Sarge!*"

"I cain't *heeryoo!*"

"No, SARGE!"

"Uh-huh."

Thibedaux paced, his feet causing the sheet metal of the lockers to clang as it buckled.

All the troops were finding subtle ways to hang their hands in front of their crotches so nobody could see their equipment. Their secrets were safe, however. They all stared up at Thibedaux, slack-mouthed with dread. There was clearly nothing below which this man would not sink.

"Boys!" he shouted. "I do not—I repeat *do not*—'spect to see no soldier lookin' at no other soldier's dick! Dew yew *comprende* me?"

"Yes, *Sarge!*"

"Uh-huh."

Thibedaux produced a thin white towel, as if by magic.

"Now, boys," he reasoned, "this here is a towel. You hillbilly cornholers ain't usin' no flour sacks to dry yourselfs with in this man's army."

They all nodded.

"You are the best equipped and cleanest army on earth."

He raised the towel above his head like an icon.

Their heads swiveled up, all eyes on the cotton.

"This here," he intoned, "is for dryin' yourseff with after your shower. Do I make myself clear?"

"Yes, Sarge!"

"Said I cain't *heeryoo!*"

"*YES, SARGE!*"

"I," he proclaimed, "do not want to see no soldier dryin' his butt with my towel and then dryin' his face!" He shook his head incredulously. "Dry your butt and *then* your face? With the *same towel?* Boys?"

They all shook their heads.

"Doggone right, gennermen! We wipe our face and *then* we wipe our butt."

As they pondered this insight, D.I. Burton Thibedaux lowered the towel. Then, with a short chop of his hand, he summoned hot water from the nozzles. Steam rose in coils, slowly obscuring him as he silently wrung his towel.

An operatically vomitous ocean transport deposited Mike in North Africa.

Mike had hoped to see darkest jungle—hot, sure, but shady, green, full of secret pools and bare-breasted native women. As he struggled down the loading net into the landing craft, he stared at the endless sand dunes arrayed across the horizon and considered shooting himself in the foot. Once on shore, he was loaded on a truck, and he and about twenty other grunts were sweated through a long convoy to a base at an "oasis" that had a name nobody could pronounce, though it sounded like "Wadi Dead Salami."

There, Mike dug latrine holes for a week. He ate dates off the one palm tree that hadn't been broken by tanks backing up. He tried to ride a camel. He cleaned his M-1 about ten times in a week, until somebody told him to stretch a rubber over the mouth of the barrel to keep the endlessly sifting sand out of the works.

Then peace was declared.

Slowly, Mike McGurk made the pilgrimage in reverse.

Turk couldn't believe it. He paced around the station with the WELCOME HOME MIKE banner stretched above the pumps and the twenty-seven American flags hung from every edge of the building. He'd put on his old uniform and stood at attention as Mike got off the bus. Father and son saluted each other, then slapped each other repeatedly on the back as they sort of embraced.

He couldn't comprehend that Mike hadn't killed anybody.

In the days to come, he'd try to sneak it out of Mike, as though it were something Mike was just refusing to share. "You mean to say," he said, "you didn't croak one piddly German?"

Then, coy and wheedling, Turk said, "Come on now, son, Goddamn it. You killed at least one Kraut. Am I right?"

This went on for a decade. To make matters worse, during these interrogations there always seemed to be bruise-colored mountains in the distance, riding the heat waves. They appeared to be levitating above the horizon: purple bruises that taunted Mike until mid-spring with worms of snowpack squirming on their spines.

Mike often hid in the cool men's toilet, a bunker from which he tracked Turk's incoming barrage of automotive outrage: "This sumbitch car drives like two pounds of shit in a one-pound can!" for example.

Mike sat on the throne drinking five-cent Cokes and reading paperbacks he traded drivers for at a gallon a book. He also studied Turk's various EC comics—*Crypt of Terror, Two-Fisted Tales, The Haunt of Fear.* Sometimes he worked.

One of his jobs was to scrub the graffiti off the walls. According to Mike's informal research, American men enjoyed drawing the male member on all available surfaces, as though they needed to be reminded once in a while how handsome a deal it was. The stalls were invariably graced with at least one whanger (Turk's word), drawn so it looked like a wobbly V-2 rocket rising from a launching pad in a scribble of black smoke. Various offers and boasts floated about these drawings, strident as the come-ons of wholesale furniture salesmen. HONEY PET THE DOG! was typical.

And under BLOW ME SWABBIE!: YUM YUM BEEMAN'S GUM!

Or: GRAB MY SHIFTER AND PUT ME IN FIRST!

The inevitable Real Men dropped in to quip: HOMOS!

Kilroy was greatly in evidence on the walls, as were impassioned opinions about Negroes and Messkins and Indians. The local racists, hard put to spell a whole word, made do with KKK.

On rare occasions, some toilet Michelangelo would go to the trouble of drawing his version of the female form. Mike, for a while, gave them the benefit of the doubt. Later, he started to worry about them. It was starting to look like all these desert studs had never really gotten a good look at a woman's body. Certainly not enough to draw anything recognizably human: the most Mike ever saw in these drawings was what appeared to be a tornado in a bird's nest.

BEING A MAN, he wrote, MAKES ME FEEL ABOUT 100% FOOLISH.

Turk pounded on the door.

"Son, you've been constipated for a month! Eat some prunes, for God's sake—there's work to do! Gas to pump! Pinch that loaf and get to work!"

Mike walked out into light so strong it blanched all color out of the world. He slammed the gas nozzle into the mouth of a Studebaker and imagined he was driving, driving, going up out of the desert glare, looping through the Coronado Mountains or the Sierras, plowing into a snowbank so high he could look down on the backs of flying eagles.

The ladies' room was another world entirely. It hardly got used, for one thing. Turk's Texaco catered mostly to long-haul truckers, cattle ranchers, and bored B-17 jockeys, old from WWII or, later, crazy from Korea, burning up their muster pay in cross-country jaunts. So the ladies' room went largely unused. In fact, when Turk was in the men's room, Mike used the ladies'. This, in Turk's eyes, was a sin so perverse as to render him silent on the matter.

Mike cleaned the room only once a week. Even then, with this small peek into the Secret World of Women, Mike felt he was amassing a detailed and precise body of knowledge, in case he ever should need it. For example: women urinated too—only they never missed the toilet the way men did.

Their bathroom was intimidating. He could never escape the sense that he was doing something somehow naughty when he swamped out the floor with the mop or scrubbed the bowl with the huge old brush. He was always careful to wipe the Life Saver–colored lip marks off the mirrors so not a smear was left, though sometimes he couldn't help himself and placed his mouth on the cool glass where their lips had been. He could feel the thin coat of lipstick come off on his mouth, and he ached inside. Then he licked it off his lips.

When it was time to empty out the tin trash cans, he'd rush out to the fire and dump the embarrassing mysteries into the flames. Tissue rosettes curled black in the flames. Their edges glowed bright as neon.

Once, he retrieved a pair of silk stockings, one of them run from the heel up to the back of the knee. He held them to his face—they smelled of lilac and sweat and shoe-leather. He'd never felt anything so smooth; in his opinion, their texture fell somewhere between a horse tail and a garter snake, only slippery. He balled them up in his back pocket, then hid them under his bed, where they emitted female X rays that set his bones aglow with indescribable longing.

2

THE BACK END OF TURK'S TEXACO WAS A WARREN OF jerry-rigged living quarters. The kitchen took up a second, unused work bay. Turk had laid a heavy sheet of plywood over the hydraulic lift and disguised the whole setup with a noxious grease-soaked green carpet. Mike had to be careful not to hit the control lever, sticking up beside the propane stove, or the hidden car lift would rise from under the carpet, toppling chairs and lifting the floor until the table was crushed against the ceiling. He had actually seen this happen one morning when Turk was hung over; his mother's table was reduced to kindling. The only piece of her furniture not now broken or sold off was the double bed Turk still slept in.

The "family room" was a slat toolshed they'd hauled down from Clifton. They had a little round-screen Motorola television in there, with foil wrapped around the rabbit ears. About all it was good for was picking up bullfights from Mexico, Uncle Miltie—which Turk refused to have on in his house—and the occasional wrestling show from the city. Turk had never recovered from his simmering hatred for Gorgeous George, who had sullied the Manly Science. The nearly supernatural physique and wickedness of Nature Boy Buddy Rodgers, however, restored some of Turk's faith.

Mike's room, in an attached 1928 Travellux trailer, was spare. Aside from his bed, one lamp, and the silk stockings, the room held only books and fossils and bones. He had mounted a coyote skull to one headpost and a crow skull to the other. A weathered steer skull hung above his head. Shelves made from planks and fruit crates held his mother's books and his tattered paperbacks.

He'd had to trade an entire half tank of gas for a textbook on fossils he'd spied in the back seat of a big Plymouth. The driver, a professor from the university in the city, seemed inspired by Mike's sudden interest. He sprung from his car, alarmed Mike by grabbing his elbow, and pointed at the flats. "Arizona," he said, "is an untapped wonderland of fossils."

"Oh?" Mike said, getting his arm out of the other man's grasp.

"A veritable cornucopia of prehistory."

The professor smiled and cleaned his glasses on his shirttail.

Mike thumbed through the book.

The professor stabbed at a picture with his glasses. "There!" he said. "Take a look at that."

It was a petrified clam.

"This, young man, can be found a mere ten minutes from where we're standing!"

"No."

"Yes! And it didn't simply wash up on the high tide!" He gestured—rather pointlessly, Mike thought—at the desert around them. "A brachiopod," he said, peering at the elegantly fluted shell through his bifocals. "A rather jaunty-looking *Tropidoleptus*, I daresay."

Mike peered at the page.

"If I were you," the professor confided, "I'd be on the lookout for *Trigonia quadrata*. As they say"—he nudged Mike in the ribs—"cretaceous bivalves are audacious bivalves!"

He cracked up and delivered a feather-light blow to Mike's shoulder.

"Haw," Mike offered, reading the text. Then: "Now wait a minute. This is a clam."

"No doubt." The professor got back in his car.

"So this was an ocean."

"Quite right."

"There was water here."

"Indeed."

Mike looked around.

"This," he said, "was . . . a prehistoric sea?"

"Couldn't have said it better myself."

"Where'd it go?"

The professor looked out the window. "Well, I suppose it dried up, didn't it? Went on its merry way, wouldn't you say?"

This was a whole new angle.

"How old is this, Doc?" Mike said, holding up the picture of *Tropidoleptus*.

"Well, pard"—the professor leered, starting up his engine—"I reckon, in terms of years, we could say a jillion. Give or take a few."

He pulled out, tooting *shave and a haircut* on his horn.

Turk came out of the office.

"Who's that airy-fairy son of a bitch?"

ATRYPA RETICULARIS, Mike wrote near the toilet. Two weeks later, it was answered by a timid OH YEAH DAMNED MEXICAN.

Mike loaded his bookshelves with trilobites and fossilized fish. The crumbling dirt cliffs to the south broke open under his shovel, coughing out nautiloids and a four-inch shark's tooth. He slept amid petrified seafood. At night, he sometimes thought about how the only things of interest in his world were things dead so long they'd turned to stone.

3

"I WAS EIGHTEEN. EIGHTEEN, SON! WE PUT OUR BOOT to the ass of the Hun, by God! It was some of the ugliest goddamned combat ever witnessed by man, I don't mind telling you!"

Turk was buried up to his shoulder blades in the grimy maw of a Buick.

"Socket wrench."

Mike handed the tool to him.

He stared at the hairy crack of Turk's butt rising out of his blue work pants like a dark and hirsute quarter-moon.

A symphonic racket boomed in there, tools contacting engine parts in crescendos. Turk's vocals soared above the accompaniment: "Shitfire!"

This scene had begun as a discussion of fossils, something that was only marginally more interesting to Turk than doilies. Mike had been in the middle of an impassioned report on the *Cybister*, an astonishingly preserved monster roach from the Pleistocene that, according to the book, could be found on rock in a state so perfect that it appeared to be alive. Turk ambushed Mike mid-report by barking, "My God, haven't you ever read the Bible? The Bible says the world is only six thousand years old. Jesus! This Darwin crap of yours. It's all bullshit." Scatology really inspired Turk. "Piss on it, I say. It's a big pile of crap. Any swingin' dick who read his Bible would know it. Hand me the pliers." Mike had put down the book and gawked. "Trench warfare!" Turk bellowed. "Now, *that* was *war!* Don't give *me* any of that Hemingway twaddle!"

The dizzying plunge through all those topics left Mike stunned. All the while, he'd been planning to sneak up on Turk with the dinosaur-roach and slyly work his way over to the past, and then to Mom. But Turk had a sixth sense. He was a tactical genius. Outmaneuvered.

"Mustard gas! What you should have seen was mustard gas. By Christ, it took a real man to face the hideous effects of that. It was like staring into hell unleashed from the pit—a solid wall of yellow hell, eating men alive. Don't tell *me* about pantywaist Nazis. I've seen what mustard gas will do to a man."

Of course, Mike hadn't said a word about Nazis.

Turk had this way of offering up grisly blobs of trench warfare to Mike as some sort of male legacy. He'd even stoop to such buffoonery as: "The Warrior has a Code of Death. It's a Contract of Fire written in hell and signed in blood. A soldier's reward is a bed in the halls of Valhalla." (Mike knew perfectly well that Turk had plagiarized this from a *Two-Fisted Tales* comic book.) History: made by men for manly men.

"Dad, look," said Mike. This was a daring thing to do. Once, when he was in his teens, he'd said "Dad, look" and Turk had exploded, "Don't you say *look* to me!" and decked Mike with a roundhouse left. Mike had gone after Turk with a jack handle, and Turk had locked himself inside the toilet, yelling, "I'll show *you* what a thrashing is!" But today Turk was sober, so Mike said it. "What I really wanted to talk about was Mom."

"Connie," said Turk.

The metallic clamor in the engine compartment subsided. "It strips the skin right off a man's face," Turk said. "Did I tell you that? It turns a man's eyes to pudding." He extracted himself and hitched up his pants. The socket wrench seemed welded into his fist. He surveyed the engine, as filthy and byzantine in its hoses and fan belts as when he had begun. "That should just about do it," he said. He wiped his dome with the sleeve of his Texaco shirt. "Let's go in and have a couple of beers."

"Dad," said Mike, "I been thinking about Mom."

Turk wiped his hands on a rag.

"Good for you."

He turned and headed deep into the garage, through to the office, on toward the kitchen, successive curtains of gloom obscuring him until the only evidence of his passing was the clomp of his work boots.

"Dad? Dad! Did you love her, Dad?"

From the kitchen, Turk's laughter. Mike was about to give up, when he heard a beer bottle spit. Turk was going to tie one on tonight.

"Mike," Turk said, "She's dead. Dead is dead. A whole lot of other sons of bitches are dead and buried with her. And we're out here alone. Okay? To hell with the lot of them."

Mike heard the static sounds as the television warmed up. The mountains wobbled in the distance. He watched a red-tailed hawk ride up a thermal, wings flung wide and feathers open as fingers to the wind. It swooped up a thousand feet without a twitch of effort, so high it was a speck as small as an amoeba.

"Thanks, Dad," he said.

For Turk, his son's apparent failure to amount to anything, to leave home for good, to buy into a good Esso franchise, to box, revealed itself as damning evidence of Mike's basic weakness. Turk had tried to whip him into shape with a kind of holy relentlessness, but his son had essentially failed in his McGurkness.

When Turk looked sideways at Mike after a few belts, Mike could read these thoughts on his face. He chose to ignore it. He was so exhausted from bearing the burden of a lifetime of Turk that he could barely get himself out of bed in the morning. He understood, even as a boy, that the Legend of Texaco Turk McGurk—He Eats Lead and Craps Bullets!—had grown so vast, so complex, as to begin groaning under its own weight. Mike had watched Wallace perform Turk continually, from year to year, adding to it as he had added rooms to the gas station.

Mike thought Turk was trying, as though with the shadow of his ridiculous whiskers, to cover up his hidden boyhood, his aimless wandering from state to state, his financial catastrophes, the bloody mud of France, the creeping terror of age, the loosening wattles of his chest, the whanger that sometimes refused to piss, the night he punched his wife in front of the boy, and the lonely little grave in the Texas Panhandle.

In a family with no word for *love,* Mike couldn't easily explain why he had chosen to stay. But without him there, his father wouldn't have survived a week.

4

ANOTHER DAY. MIKE WASN'T SURE WHAT DAY IT WAS. HE filled his bucket with water and soap, threw the brush in, slung the mop over his shoulder, and wandered off to the bathroom.

"That rifle's got a wig on," quipped Turk.

Mike waved absently and went inside.

He scrubbed the stall walls and daydreamed. A vivid series of moments flared up, indiscriminate and bright in his skull. The foaming brush sluiced away strings of words written in different hands.

CHINGA TU MADRE CABRON

There was a dress. Mom's yellow dress. Yellow flecks. Daisies? They must have been flowers of some sort. White background. Pleated skirt that lifted off her knees when she turned around. In his mind, she twirled like a dancer, her face hidden in shadow. The skirt formed what he recalled as a perfect forty-five-degree angle on either side of her legs.

FORD = Fix Or Repair Daily

Under it:

FORD = Found On Road Dead

A tiny dog, a tangle of brown and gray fur. It had a tail like a plume. He stopped scrubbing and saw the tail: the dog held it high above its back. Turk called it the battle flag. What was its name? Mike remembered it attacking a red ball, bouncing with it, claws scrabbling at a hardwood floor. Mike heard the sound clearly: pebbles down a rain gutter? Hail on tobacco leaves? Where had he seen tobacco? The ball was bigger than the dog's head. Turk calling the dog "that overfed rat."

FLUSH TWICE—ITS
ALONG WAY TO MY
KITCHEN

And the fart war! Mike put his head down for a moment, laughing.

At night, when Turk was feeling good, he would come into Mike's room and read to him. Mike remembered Mom—Constance—reading to him when he was little, before she got sick. He could remember falling asleep to the sound of her voice, how it was like floating away on warm water. He could actually feel himself lift up on the sound of her voice and slide away.

Then, when she was gone, Turk tried to take over.

Turk was especially taken with *The Jungle Book, Tarzan,* and "Rikki Tikki Tavi." Mike heard "Rikki-Tikki-Tavi" ten or fifteen times. But Turk reserved his true love for Mark Twain, and Mike requested passages from Twain with the most regularity.

Turk couldn't help himself. Three of four sentences into the reading, a bizarre light came into his eyes, and he rose from the bed and began to act out the roles. The more scabrous and outrageous the scene, the more Turk emoted. The certified hit of the readings was from *Life on the Mississippi,* when Turk would actually climb on the bed and walk in place, hollering, and Mike would bounce about between Turk's feet, laughing so hard he thought he'd pee.

At bedtime, he'd often shout to Turk, "Read the fight! Read the fistfight!" And Turk would perch his reading specs on his nose, crack open the old book, feign an exasperating search for his place—the book fell open to it automatically by now. Then he would say to Mike, "These boatmen are harassing a fellow."

"Yeah!" Mike said.

"And he has reached the end of his rope."

"Yeah!"

"It is time for him to beat the living hell out of them!"

The ritual dictated that they then say, in unison, "He must be a McGurk!"

Turk read: "'Whoo-oop! I'm the old original iron-jawed, brass-mounted, copper bellied corpse-maker from the wilds of Arkansas! Look at me! I'm the man they call Sudden Death and General Desolation! Sired by a hurricane, dam'd by an earthquake, half-brother to the cholera, nearly related to the smallpox on my mother's side.'"

At this point he stood, one fist raised over his head, and did a slight shuffle. Mike mouthed the words along with him, like a kid in church, getting about every third word wrong.

"'I split the ever-lasting rocks with my glance, and I squench the thunder when I speak!Whoo-oop!'"

Mike yelled his delight when Turk put one foot on the edge of the bed, then slowly stepped up, book close to his face, hollering now: "'Blood's my natural drink, and the wails of the dying is music to my ear!'"

Turk bounced rhythmically, throwing shadow punches with his left hand, beads of sweat popping out of his pate.

"'Hold me down to earth, for I feel my powers a-working! Whoo-oop! I'm a child of sin, *don't* let me get a start! Smoked glass here, for all! Don't attempt to look at me with the naked eye, gentlemen!'"

Turk was now trampolining so hard that his head tapped the ceiling above the bed. Mike bucked and flopped, laughing hysterically.

"'Contemplate me through leather—*don't* use the naked eye! I'm the man with a petrified heart and biler-iron bowels! The massacre of isolated communities is the pastime of my idle moments!'"

Turk ended with: "'Whoo-oop! Bow your neck and spread, for the pet child of calamity's a-coming!'" then he flung the book aside and belly-flopped on top of Mike, and they wrestled furiously for a few minutes. Turk invariably ended up on the floor, on his back. Mike would find himself tied in an impossible knot of sheets.

"Whew," Turk would gasp. "By God, *there* is invective!"

"What's that?"

"Boastful insults," said Turk. "Outrageous palaver."

They'd usually make plans to visit the Mississippi. ("I'd like to have at a son of a bitch like that boatman," Turk confided.) It was always going to be "next year sometime," until enough years passed so that Turk thought it improper for a man to read to his son anymore. Ol' Miss was never mentioned again.

The fart war came one night after Mom had left.

Mike remembered the silence of the house with her gone to the hospital. He felt small in his bed, imagined it was Huck Finn's raft on the river. Turk was down the hall in their bedroom. Neither one of them knew what to expect.

Mike could remember the creaking of the roof beams. The detail of his memory surprised him—the smell of the blanket, the rusty shout of tree frogs outside his window. The Milky Way like glowing smoke in the Oklahoma sky.

Turk farted explosively.

Dad farted!

Mike started to giggle. He tried to keep it quiet, but the harder he tried to stifle it, the funnier it got.

"What's so funny!" Turk bellowed.

Mike lifted his knees and squeezed one out:

Bweet!

"Christ almighty!" Turk yelled. "There's a barking spider in the house!"

Then: *Wonk!*

"Guy, Dad!"

"Haw haw!"

"Dad—who let that goose in the house!"

Yonk!

Turk laughed. "No respect!"

Mike shouted, "Beans beans, the musical fruit!"

"The more you eat, the more you toot!" Turk responded.

They were laughing in their rooms, alone in the dark.

"Hey, Dad?"

"Yeah?"

Fweep!

"Mike, that is the most dis-*gus*-ting thing I ever heard. That was green and had legs. I'm proud of you, son." There was a short pause. "But *this* is what a fart should sound like."

Brraptph!

Later that night, Mike awoke to a presence in his bed. Turk was stretched out beside him, lying very still, staring at the ceiling. His sleeveless undershirt glowed pale gray in the moonlight. His arms were crossed over his chest.

"Dad?" Mike said. "Are you okay?"

Turk sat up and sniffed the air.

"Good God, boy," he barked, leaping up. "What have you been cooking in here?"

5

"BY CHRIST, WILL YOU LOOK AT THIS," SAID TURK, STEPping into full sunlight.

Mike hung back in the auto bay of the station, busying himself with clattering tools and greasy tubes of metal. He was timid and wondering basically this: Now what? Lately, his limbs had started seeming unbearably long and gangly. He envisioned himself as some sort of giant praying mantis.

"Mike!" Turk called. "A look at this here is recommended."

Mike stepped forward, squinting before he ever got to the painful desert light. He stared at the back of his father's shiny bald head, the awful turkey skin of age rippling at the old man's collar.

"Yo, Pop," he said.

"Behold," said Turk, pointing.

Rolling slowly toward them came a squat '32 Dodge pickup, its body largely given over to rust. The endless stripe of County Highway 50 was empty behind the truck all the way to the curve in the earth.

Thick black oil smoke curled beneath its chasis, then seemed to leak out from under the truck.

"It's a goddamned abomination," said Turk.

The truck wheezed up the angled drive and seemed to settle in on its springs when it stopped. Inside, an old man as squat as his truck, face an impossible maze of wrinkles. His peppery hair was brushed up off his forehead, forming a gray-black wedge of pomade. Angled sideburns cut down the old man's cheeks. He stared at them through horn-rims. His bolo tie slide was a preposterous chunk of turquoise. Turk bent forward to the open window and wrinkled his nose.

"We don't serve no heathen Apaches around these parts," he said.

The man looked at him and blew air through his lips.

"Looks like somebody's done whupped your ass with the ugly stick," he replied.

Mike stood back, smiling.

Turk scratched his head.

"Look, Grandpa—there are no women here for you to carry off and molest," he said. "And there are no children for you to slaughter."

The old man lit a Pall Mall and squinted out at Turk.

"Must've been some Sioux boys, yeah?" he said. "They come through here already, looks like. Scalped you pretty good. Took your hair up north to hang on the lodge pole."

"By God, you Apache savage. I have a good mind to pound you into the soil. Only you're too old—I might kill you."

"Hey, Chrome Dome, you sellin' me some gas, or what?" the old man asked. He looked over at Mike. "You ever notice how your old man's head looks like a dick?"

Here they go, Mike thought.

"Pull on up to the pump, Mr. Sneezy," he said.

Delbert Sneezy shifted into first and ground his way up to the pumps, gearbox howling.

"Get a horse!" cried Turk. "You obviously can't handle the machinery!"

Delbert Sneezy ignored Turk completely. He leaned his head out the window and addressed Mike: "How was the war?"

"It wasn't what I expected, Grandfather," said Mike.

The old man nodded.

"Been back long?"

"A couple years," Mike said.

"Must seem like a century," said Mr. Sneezy, nodding toward Turk, who was inspecting the back of the truck, kicking the tires and muttering. Mr. Sneezy guffawed. "Ol' Mr. Shitlips himself," he said, puffing on his cigarette.

Turk came forward and stared down his nose at the old man.

"So, Sneezy," he said, starting to grin, "how's Dopey and Sleepy and Snow White doing?"

Mr. Sneezy burst out of the truck—if burst was the word. He did as fast a burst as he could manage, but Turk honored it by raising his dukes and circling around backward. Mr. Sneezy steadied himself by grabbing the open door.

"The massacre of isolated communities is the pastime of my idle hours!" Turk shouted.

Mike felt a small charge.

Mr. Sneezy hung his thumbs in his belt and said, "Mama always tol' me to stay away from the white man." He reached into the truck, got his black cowboy hat, worked it tight onto his head, and spit. "Pitiful."

Turk shuffled in the dirt.

"Don't look upon me with the naked eye, gentlemen!"

"I will show mercy on you this time," said Mr. Sneezy. "You've gone crazy. I can't kill you." He turned away. "Mike!" he said. "Get me a Nehi, would you?"

Turk's eyes glittered as he followed Mr. Sneezy into the shade. Mike thought he looked like an eager dog. Turk was ready to be insulted for the rest of the day.

Mr. Sneezy had ridden on the San Carlos Apache Police with Mike's real grandfather, Carroll. Carroll McGurk, in spite of having a "girl's name," made a good impression on his Apache officers. He was fierce but generally fair and not in the least bigoted toward the Indians—as long as they were "subjugated."

Delbert was his chief officer, and they rode their horses together in and out of the canyons after Tom Horn had moved on. And when Carroll's drinking finally burned its way through his esophagus, killing him in a geyser of blood that emptied him in a minute flat, Mr. Sneezy had delivered Turk to the train station to ride home alone. Turk was ten.

Their ritual had developed by unspoken mutual consent.

One day, Mr. Sneezy had insulted Turk, Turk had insulted him back, and the years had passed in badinage.

"How do you know if a white man's been around the reservation?" Mr. Sneezy said.

"I have an ugly feeling you're going to tell me," Turk grumbled.

"All the graves been dug up and the sheep's all pregnant."

"You're senile! That's the only explanation."

And so forth.

Mike went back to work on the oil pump of Red Lewis's decrepit Hudson Hornet. The car looked like an evil turtle. Mike could remember when Mr. Sneezy had visited them once at the last station, when Mike was still a boy, and in the truck sat a huge and sullen boy, so chubby he had breasts pushing at his tight T-shirt.

"That's my Mexican grandson," Mr. Sneezy said. "Thought you two boys could play. Go shoot some rabbits."

"I'm Apache," the boy said. "I am a warrior."

Mr. Sneezy looked down at him with some affection and said, "Shee-it." He turned to Turk. "Father's a Mexican."

"Pity," said Turk.

"What's your name?" said Mike.

"Ramses Castro," the boy replied, glaring at Turk fiercely.

"Watch it, Baldy," said Mr. Sneezy. "That one's young, but he's a scorpion, I'm telling you."

Turk slapped him on the back and said, "Let's have a soda pop." He glanced back. "Boys," he said, "go kill something."

"I'm an Apache. I'm not Mexican," Castro said.

He stared at Mike so intently that Mike looked away.

"I didn't say nothing," he said.

"Mexicans are the enemy of the Apache," Ramses said. "After the white man."

Mike shuffled his feet.

"Uh," he said. "Okay."

They stood there.

"Wanna do something?" he said.

"Let's play cowboys and Indians," Ramses said.

"You're kidding," said Mike.

"C'mon," said Ramses. "Let's go."

They charged out into the desert, *kapowing* at each other with extended fingers until Ramses disappeared. They were in a wash, and Mike lost track of him around a bend and then couldn't find him at all.

"Ramses?" he said.

He looked under bushes, around boulders.

"Not funny!" he shouted. "Where'd ya go?"

Suddenly, Ramses launched himself from a stand of brush on the high bank of the wash. He descended on Mike like a one-man avalanche: twigs, sand, clods showered around him as he slammed into Mike. He wrestled Mike flat into the dirt and held him down.

Then he staked Mike out, spread-eagled, tearing strips of Mike's undershirt to tie him to the creosote bushes.

"Cut it out!" Mike yelled. And "Knock it off!" and "I'm telling!" To which Ramses Castro said, "Ooh!"

Mike thought: *He's crazy.*

He yanked at the knots, rattling the bushes. It was going to take hours to work them loose.

Ramses walked off then, leaving Mike to bake.

"Oh, great," Mike said.

"Come back here!" he called.

Silence descended, and Mike lay there on his back. He'd started to sunburn when Ramses came back with a bottle of Pepsi and sat down a few feet from him. "Think about it," he said. "We're coming back."

"Not when I get through with you," said the Son of Turk.

"Oh, right. Big white man talks tough. You're staked out, butthead."

"I'll get loose."

"Will not."

"Will too. And I'll find your house and burn it down with you in it!"

"Huh?" Ramses said, and took a gulp of soda.

"I'll wear your teeth for a necklace!" Mike spit.

Wow! Ramses thought. He almost liked the white boy.

"Look," he said. "We used to cut open your guts and pull stuff out, twirl it around a big stick and let our dogs eat it."

Mike craned his head up and stared at Ramses.

"Good for you," he said.

"Huh?" said Ramses.

"I said good for you. Cut me open, and my guts'll wrap around your pencil neck and strangle you!" The McGurk blood had begun to flow. "And when I get loose I'm pounding you straight down a gopher hole, you butt-wipe."

"Huh?" Ramses said.

"The son of calamity is here!" said Mike. "Don't even look upon me with the naked eye. I will melt it out of your head with my stare!"

Ramses smiled.

"Damn," he said.

"I'm a rock," Mike said. "Push me off a mountain, and I'll roll all the way around the world to crush you! Let me up!"

"What are you?" Ramses said. "Shakespeare?"

He cut Mike loose and Mike dove straight into his gut, head-first. They slugged it out for five minutes, snot and tears and nose blood all over them.

Afterward, they trudged back to the station, never looking at each other once. Something seemed torn in the world, and Mike couldn't get hold of the edges of it. They maintained such a perfect distance from each other that even their shadows did not touch.

Turk and Mr. Sneezy had wisely kept silent when the dirtied boys stomped into the shade and sat on the cement. Mike wiped his eyes; Ramses stared straight out into the desert.

"Grandfather," he said, "when can we leave? This place smells like chickenshit."

Mr. Sneezy cuffed him once on the back of the head.

Then they got in the truck in an awkward silence. Mike watched Mr. Sneezy reach out and take Turk's hand for the first time. They shook. Then the truck backfired and pulled away.

Turk said, "I hope you taught him who the McGurks are."

"There's nothin' to learn," said Mike, then went to wash his face.

It was late afternoon. Mike wiped the grease off his hands and tossed the rag onto the workbench. Mr. Sneezy was leaned back in his chair, the chair tipped up against the wall, as he listened to Turk tell a dirty joke about old men.

"No respect," Mr. Sneezy said. "These damned kids today. What're you going to do with them?"

Mike shrugged and grinned and sat down beside him.

"Mike," said Turk, "do you remember that psychotic Mexican grandson this old fart brought around that time?"

"Boy howdy," said Mike.

Mr. Sneezy cranked his head around and glared at Mike.

"What the hell's *that* mean?" he demanded.

"Means yes."

"Yes!" He looked at Turk, then back at Mike. "Then why the hell don't you just say yes!"

"Now, Delbert," said Turk, "don't go getting your bowels in an uproar. You might have a stroke."

"I'll dance on your grave, you pale-skinned son of a bitch."

Mike started laughing at both of them.

"I swear," he said.

"As I was saying," Turk said. "Delbert's little beaner fat boy grew up, and guess what he's been doing."

"No telling," said Mike archly.

"Fighting."

Mike stared at him. Mr. Sneezy tipped his head to one side and nodded.

"For money fighting?" Mike asked.

They nodded.

"Bare knuckle?"

They nodded again.

Mike whistled.

Turk said, "I'm thinking about thrashing him."

"I ain't kidding, Mike," Mr. Sneezy said. "I told McGurk not to even think about it."

"Dad, really," said Mike. "I don't think so."

Turk simply looked at them.

"You're kidding, right," Turk said.

"He's bad news," said Mike.

"On two legs," said Mr. Sneezy.

"Who," Turk said, rising, "are you two candy-asses calling bad news?"

"You don't even want to know about it," Mike told him.

"What Mike said," agreed Mr. Sneezy.

Turk nodded, once. He smiled a little disgusted smile. Then he walked into the house.

"Good night," he called, and slammed the door.

"Oh boy," said Mr. Sneezy.

"Maybe Castro will be hit by lightning or something," Mike said.

"Mike," Mr. Sneezy said, "don't let him do it."

Mike looked out across the miles of hardpan.

"How do you suggest I stop him?"

Twenty miles away, he saw headlights switch on. He stood up and looked at them. He couldn't think of a single thing.

"Customers coming, Grandfather," he said.

Mr. Sneezy watched the lights.

"Wonder where they came from."

"Stick around, we'll ask."

Mr. Sneezy settled back in his seat.

"Maybe New York," he said.

"Maybe Paris," Mike said.

"Maybe the Congo."

"Maybe the Matterhorn," said Mike.

Mr. Sneezy was smiling.

Mike put his hands in his pockets and said, "Grandfather? You ever seen snow?"

6

WHEN A FIGHT WAS IMMINENT, TURK HUNG A HEAVY BAG off the lift and concentrated on his mid-body attack. He didn't have the speed anymore to blind them with flurries to the eyes and jaw, so he relied on his strength. He bulled into the bag, no dancing, little legwork at all, actually. He planted himself, presented the hand-smashing cliff of his impenetrable skull, and fired brutal volleys of slugs into the bag. His arms looked like parts of a locomotive; his breath chuffed out of his nose. He fought as though in a trance, focused on his opponent's ribs. His eyeballs were pushed deep into his head. The scars on his forehead, across his brow, over his nose, his split lips, his torn ears, his ragged nipple—ripped loose in Louisiana in '49—throbbed white and hard. The scars stood rigid in his flesh like fossils in matrix. *I'll show them who's too old.* His breasts blurred from the action of the punches. Chuff-chuff. His gut a loose rag fluttering across the muscles of his abdomen. Veins like tinder and twigs in his neck. Knuckles cracking on the bag. His ring finger one joint short. A fleck of cataract encroached on the iris of one eye. Chuff. *Bastards.* Sawdust bled from the bag. Turk's odor like copper, like battery acid. Turpentine. A prehistoric bullet wound, sprawled in the shape of a starfish, writhed on his shoulder blade. His fists invisible now. Red thoughts exploding in his brain. Silver-bright coronas of sweat flung themselves in arcs from his head, his back, the crest of a wild marlin, his halo of rage.

7

MIKE WAS SPRAWLED NEARLY HORIZONTAL IN TURK'S easy chair. Between his toes, the TV screen flickered. He was sipping a beer and eating pretzels as horses swarmed through the pale static and riders shot six-guns that emitted impossible plumes of smoke. It was a "Three Mesquiteer" adventure, though he'd missed the title. He recognized Ray Corrigan and Max Terhune, but he couldn't remember the third guy's name.

The phone rang.

That was a fairly remarkable event in their lives. Turk could be heard in the background, trotting to it and grabbing it on the third ring. Max Terhune was grinning at the camera.

"Do tell," Turk was saying.

And: "You could knock me over with a feather."

And: "I should say so!"

Mike turned up the TV.

Turk signed off with a flurry: "Certainly. You bet. No problem. Cain't wait! Bye now."

He came in the room and tumbled onto the couch.

"Cowboys?" he said.

"Yup."

"That Max Terhune?"

"Yup. Who's that other guy?"

"Ray Corrigan."

"No. The other guy."

Turk peered at the screen as the Three Mesquiteers rode off in a cloud of dust, the lady homesteader waving and the credits starting to roll.

"Beats me," Turk said.

A guy came on, selling cars in Phoenix.

"Who was that?" Mike asked.

"Max Terhune, I said," snapped Turk. "You ever clean your ears, or what?"

He was in one of his moods.

"On the *phone,* Pop."

"Oh. Well," Turk said. "Brace yourself."

"I'm all braced," said Mike, yawning.

"It was that no-account brother of mine," Turk said. "Your uncle *Gideon.*"

No-account Gideon McGurk was a successful doctor on Long Island. Mike had met him once, when his mother cooked a Thanksgiving dinner for Gideon as he passed through on his way to hike in the Grand Canyon. It was a couple of hundred miles out of his way, but Gideon called it a "dogleg." That stuck in Mike's mind as being especially descriptive: he drew the detour on the map, and it did indeed look like the back leg of a dog. He always remembered Gideon as a genius after that.

For reasons unexplained, Turk resented him. It seemed to Mike that Turk couldn't forgive him for being named Gideon.

"Somebody die?" Mike said, sitting up.

"No, nothing like that. Seems ol' *Gideon* has a daughter. Did you know that?"

How would I know that? Mike thought. He shook his head.

"The girl got into college, no less," said Turk. "How the hell many years has it been anyway? I must be getting old."

Then he looked at Mike with that pathetic gleam in his eye, expectant as a dog awaiting a biscuit.

"Not you, Pop," Mike said by rote. "You're never getting old." It was as empty as a memorized prayer in Sunday school.

Turk puffed up a little, regarded his pectorals with barely restrained lust. "I suppose I *can* bench-press my own weight when called upon."

Mike half expected him to bat his eyelashes.

"Anyway," Turk said, stretching it out into the weariest sigh, "Little Brother Gideon is driving her to college. All the way across the country—sort of a little family adventure, he calls it."

"College where?"

"Los Angeles."

Turk rubbed the top of his head.

"Looks like they're stopping by."

Mike did a double take.

"Here?" he said.

Turk nodded morosely.

"Passing through?" Mike said.

Turk shook his head.

"Staying?"

"Yup."

Mike jumped up, paced before the TV, went into the kitchen. Then he came back out.

"There's a *girl,* coming *here,* with Uncle Gideon. To stay."

"Awful, isn't it," said Turk.

"When?"

"Said he'd get here in two days. They're out in Arkansas somewhere. Just crossed over from Memphis."

"Two days," said Mike.

"No big deal. I bet I could drive it in one," said Turk.

"What's her name?"

"Lily, I think he said."

Lily!

Mike wondered if he should get a haircut. He looked around the station: there was some serious cleaning to be done.

He fidgeted through his meals. Ten eggs and twelve pieces of toast, nineteen cups of coffee, seven sodas, five doughnuts, and a jar of Mexican salsa later, he still floated by the table in a cloud of worry: my hair's stupid, I sound like an Okie hick, I don't have a thing to talk about, what should I wear, what's the rules on cousins anyhow?

8

ELEVEN-ELEVEN A.M. *THE PERFECT HOUR,* MIKE THOUGHT.

He hung his left elbow on the top of the first pump and affected a nonchalant droop, right thumb hooked in his pocket, feet loosely crossed at the ankle. He'd tried a cigarette but couldn't get it to hang just right off his lips. He'd trimmed his sideburns extra sharp; they snapped away from his ear and suggested small knife blades about to skin his cheeks. His T-shirt was bright enough to hurt the eye. "Here they come," he said.

Turk scuttled out of the garage and peered into the sunlight.

"Where?" he said.

"Right out there, Pop."

Turk squinted until he finally saw a sparkle of chrome, small as glitter.

"I see 'em," he said.

He absent mindedly wiped his hands on his rag.

"Know anything about her?" said Mike.

"Her!" Turk chuckled. "I get it all now."

"Get what?"

"I can't say that I blame you." He punched Mike in the arm. "I'll be damned," he said.

No doubt, Mike thought.

Turk said, "Well, you're a McGurk. What do they expect?"

"Let's not jump to conclusions," said Mike, thinking: *I sound more like him every day.*

The car was the size of a large beetle now.

"Cadillac," said Mike.

"Wouldn't you know it," spat Turk. "*Gideon* went and got himself a car fit for a New Orleans pimp."

"Now, now," said Mike.

"Probly got a gold tooth too. And a white panama hat."

The car was the size of a rat. Its horn, oddly muffled by the heat, greeted them.

"Thar she blows," said Turk.

And the car rolled forward.

They stood and watched as it pulled up. Gideon, round faced and grinning idiotically, waved at them through the closed window. In the back seat, a limp package of what appeared to be discarded clothes raised a head of tangled black hair and peered out at them with darkly made-up eyes.

Turk, out of the corner of his mouth: "Yahoo."

Mike slumped a little more, going for full-bore James Dean. She looked down his legs at his scuffed cowboy boots. Then back up at him. He smiled sideways, giving her a soulful j.d. effect, or maybe a poet. She crinkled her nose. His hydraulic systems went *zing!* She had fine, sharp features—Mike thought she looked like a painting.

"Got a nose like a gopher," Turk muttered. He wiggled his fingers and smiled falsely. Then he stepped around the car to open Gideon's door. He glanced over the roof of the car once and winked at Mike. And then he was bellowing: "Baby Brother!"

Mike opened her door. He was hit with a tender cloud of perfume, bubble gum, cigarette smoke, and Vicks.

His tongue turned to cheap wood and clacked around in his mouth while Gideon and Turk slapped each other's backs and she stared up at him.

Mike enunciated a greeting: "Mrrbl frbbl, Lily."

She got out. She was in some kind of awful stretch pants with little stirrups going into flat black shoes. She wore a man's big white shirt.

"Thanks, cuz," she said.

Was she grinning? Mike definitely caught a faint glimmer of a smile!

She stretched.

He took in the line of her back, the small breasts barely showing under the shirt, the neck. He liked that neck.

"Say hello to your uncle," Turk was calling.

"Hey," said Mike, then remembered to turn and walk over and shake hands. Gideon's hair was thin on his scalp; the pink skin was mottled with small brown smudges.

"M'boy!" said Gideon.

"Uh-huh," said Mike absently, then hurried back around the car to Lily. "Got a bag or something I can carry?"

For some reason, the McGurk brothers found this funny as they walked to the office. Turk was bellowing: "She's a looker!"

Lily glanced over at Mike.

"That's okay, Bill."

"Mike!" he said.

She flapped the loose collar of the shirt, fanning herself, and grimaced.

Mike made a sympathetic monkey-face.

"Damned hot," he offered.

"Tell me about it," she said.

That scared him.

"Got a smoke?" she said.

"Uh," Mike quipped. "Sure."

He stood there for a second.

"Think I could have one?" she asked.

"Yes! You bet!"

He scrabbled a pack out of his rolled-up sleeve and busted two matches getting one lit for her.

She blew a thin stream of smoke over her left shoulder and eyed him as she picked a flake of tobacco off her tongue with her fingernails.

"Hmm," she said, then turned to look at the desert.

What a hick, she thought as she looked around. And, *What a dump.*

I wonder, Mike thought, *if she has a crush on me.*

"Gotta pee," she said, and walked over to the ladies room.

Pee!

Mike had never reported on his body functions to a member of the opposite sex. She was a sophisticate, all right.

"What am I supposed to talk about?" he said, then went inside to see his uncle Gideon.

9

"HOW OLD ARE YOU, LILY?" MIKE ASKED.

They were sitting around the living room, enjoying the fan. Gideon and Turk sipped at a couple of beers. Gideon was nattering: "It's an unpretentious little Tudor, Wallace. Of course, I use the guest quarters for a personal study. The one—oh—ostentatious touch, I'd say, is the tennis court." Turk's eyes narrowed to lizard slits. "Let's have more beer," he said. Lily sat sideways in Turk's easy chair, one leg dangling loosely. She smoked her third cigarette and inspected her nails.

"Nineteen," she said.

"She'll be twenty in three months," Gideon said.

"Fancy that!" offered Turk.

Mike shot him a warning glance.

Lily smiled at Mike.

"What are you studying?"

"Lit," she said.

"So there I was," Turk said, "about to throw the most devastating punch of my career. . . "

"How's the trip?" Mike asked.

"Fabulous," said Gideon.

"Boring," said Lily.

They glared at each other for a moment, then Gideon looked away and nodded politely as Turk orated.

"Got anything to read?" Lily asked Mike. "I'm dying for a good book."

"Those darned college girls!" chirped Turk.

Gideon said, "You never made it to college, did you Mike." It wasn't a question.

Mike looked at him.

"Mickey Spillane," he said, turning back to Lily. "Rex Stout. Zane Grey."

She pulled a face.

She thinks she's so smart, he thought.

"Mark Twain, Ernest Hemingway, Herman Melville, Jane Austen."

Lily's eyebrows shot up.

Mike was feeling cocky.

"Charles Dickens."

She made an O with her lips.

"Just your average small library," he said.

"Take that, Mr. Hot Shit," said Turk.

"All due respect!" said Gideon, baffling everyone.

"Do you like Stephen Crane?" said Lily.

"I don't know," said Mike.

"Red Badge of Courage," said Turk, showing off now.

"So what," said Gideon, draining his beer.

"I'm reading Crane right now," said Lily. "His poems, of course. They're much more pithy than his prose."

Pithy, Mike thought.

"Pomes!" Turk bellowed. "Girl stuff," he said to Gideon.

Lily looked at the ceiling and blew a thread of smoke. She started kicking her foot again. Mike had to do some salvage work immediately. "I collect fossils," he said.

"Of course, Whitman," Turk confided, "was airy-fairy. If you catch my drift."

"Hmm," she replied.

"They're pretty interesting," Mike offered, lamely.

Turk told Gideon about teeth flying in a "cascade of mouth-blood." Gideon nodding, with a glaringly fake smile plastered on his face, was clearly looking around for more beer.

"Brewski's in the icebox, Unc," said Mike.

Gideon hove to his feet and pounded slowly through the room.

"By God, Giddy," said Turk, "you're like a passing storm front. Why the long face, brother mine?"

He was having a swell time.

"Can I lend you a book?" asked Mike, thinking: *I should have said "May I."*

She looked at him and smiled.

"Really?"

"Sure. I keep them in my room. Come on."

She jumped out of the chair and followed him to his room.

Turk said, "Gidster, old boy. Have I ever told you about mustard gas?"

She bent to his shelves and studied the books.

"Steinbeck," she said. "Romanticized, don't you think?"

"How so?"

"Oh, I don't know. Do you really think white trash has so much . . . *depth?*"

"Gee, I don't know," said Mike, feeling uppity. "How many poor people have you met out there on your tennis court?"

"Woo-woo," she said. "He puts me in my place."

Why did she make him feel like such a dolt?

He watched her bottom, peeking out from under Gideon's shirttail.

"What's this?" she said, fingering a black stone.

"Trilobite."

"How *in*teresting."

He couldn't tell what she was about. Was she serious or making fun of him?

Cling! Cling!

A car had pulled up to the pumps.

"Mike!" Turk bellowed. "Calling Mike McGurk!"

She looked over her shoulder at him.

The car horn beeped once.

"Car," he said. "Gotta work. Be right back. 'Scuse me."

Another beep.

He backed out of the room and trotted through the station, Turk braying, "Get the lead out!"

"Hold your horses!" Mike was yelling.

It was Mr. Sneezy.

"Grandfather!" said Mike.

"Tell McGurk not to do it. I seen him," said Mr. Sneezy. "I seen the boy."

"Bad?" said Mike.

"Bad enough."

"Okay," said Mike. "I'll try."

"You tell him. Don't tell him I said so. But you tell him to stay home."

Mr. Sneezy reached out and squeezed Mike's arm.

He ground the starter and ratcheted down the drive and faded into the distance, smoke angling sideways from the tailpipe.

Mike trotted back inside.

Turk and Gideon were arm wrestling.

"What was it?" grunted Turk.

Gideon's face was sweaty as he strained.

"Salesman," said Mike. "Selling Hoovers."

Turk sputtered an expletive as Mike rounded the corner and reentered his bedroom.

Lily was sprawled out on his bed. The little window beside the pillow was cracked open, and dry wind pushed through Mike's tattered curtains.

"I think," she said, "I'd like to try *Wuthering Heights*." She showed him the book. "I'm in the mood for romance."

He revved up to deliver a brilliant riposte but came out with: "Huh!"

She looked through the small window.

"Shall we walk?" she said. "I'd like to walk. Show me around."

Mike mustered up some gallantry and said, "My pleasure."

In the living room, Turk and Gideon were sparring—Gideon's wild punches missing a grinning Turk by a mile.

They crunched away from the back of the station as the shadows of the western mountains started their imperceptible creep across the desert. Mike said, "If I had my shovel, I bet I could dig you up some fossils. I've gotten pretty good at finding them."

"Oh?" she said.

Why, she thought, looking at his arm, *he has a muscle.*

"See that band of different-colored rock on the little cliff? That's shale. We might find some bivalves in there." He gestured expansively, as if he'd built the whole desert himself. "This was once a sea, you know." Then he stuck his hands in his back pockets and grinned.

"But, Mike," Lily said, "Father says you hate it out here."

"How'd he know?"

"Uncle Wallace wrote him a letter."

"Turk can write?" he blurted, then slapped his knee as he laughed.

"You seem to love the place."

"Well," said Mike, "it isn't much."

"I hate it," she said.

"How can you say that!" he cried, suddenly transforming into a desert-booster.

"It's so . . . *big.* Don't you think? I find it overwhelming. Dead."

"Dead!"

"There's no life here," she said. "That's a pretty classic definition of death."

She smirked.

"Lily," he said, "look over there."

She looked.

"Creosote bushes. Look at how thick and waxy those little leaves are. See? Smell that smell?" He broke off a leaf and bent it in half. She sniffed.

"Yuck," she said.

"It doesn't smell like perfume," Mike conceded. "But it's a good smell." He tossed the leaf and smelled his fingers. His nostrils flared like an animal's. Suddenly, she leaned back and caught him from a new angle. Hair flying romantically in the breeze. Hooded sky-blue eyes.

He closed his eyes and smiled.

"What does it smell like to you?" she said, suddenly hit by a gust of *Far from the Madding Crowd*.

"Smells," Mike said, "wild."

He flicked the leaf away and bent down to study the dirt.

"Pack rat's been through here. See his footprints?"

"My God," she said. "I'm out here with Natty Bumppo."

His belt had rattlesnake skin on it.

"Where'd you get the belt?" she said.

"Skinned it myself," he replied absently. He looked up and watched the distance. She couldn't tell what he was looking at—whatever it was, it was far away and had caught all his attention.

He was savage: his shoulders were broad as the hills.

She circled in on him, thinking and thinking.

"Mike, are you seeing anyone?"

"Yeah. Turk. Haw!"

"No, I mean, you know. *Women.*"

"Naw . . . not really."

He stood up.

Lily sidled closer.

"I see several men," she said.

He looked at her with a shocked expression.

"How can I explain?" she said. "I like to be free. I wrote a poem that goes: *If men are free / then why can't we / be?*"

He kicked at a rock.

"That's fair, I guess," he said.

She sure was different from other people.

She was thinking the same about him.

"You make me nervous," he said, moving off a bit.

Shying like a horse, she thought, excitedly.

But still, that neck. He cut a glance at her. She shook her hair back out of her eyes. He looked away quickly.

"Come here!" he said. "Look at this here."

"A cactus," she said, looking up. It was twelve feet tall, its arms raised at angles to the sky.

"A saguaro cactus," Mike said. "Old. Got three hundred

pounds of water inside it, easy. This is a grandfather."

He pointed to two scarred holes on the main trunk.

"Woodpeckers," he said.

"No!"

"Yup. The saguaro makes a little cave around the holes, then these teeny little owls move in there."

She thought: *My own little cowboy!*

Mike sounded the roll call:

Paloverde, nopal, cholla, turkey buzzard, stink gourd, gopher hole.

"There's probably a rattlesnake sleeping in there right now," he said.

She skipped away.

"Crucifixion thorn!" he enthused.

He's a pagan savage, she thought, getting inspired.

"Soap-tree yucca. Indians ate it. Made soap out of it. Liquor too. Hey—a stinkbug."

He smelled like soap, hair tonic, and sweat. Behind his back, she undid her top button.

He chuckled a little, then turned to her and said, "I hope this doesn't sound silly, but I kinda like butterflies."

"They're free," she said, "like me."

"Hoo-boy," he said.

"Think about it," she said.

"I'm thinking about it."

She sprung one on him: "Have you read *Howl*? Ginsberg?"

"Howl Ginsberg?" he said. "Who's he?"

"No. *Howl,* by Ginsberg. It's a long poem. He says 'cock' in it!"

Mike didn't know what to think of that.

"What's it rhyme with?" he said, cracking himself up.

"How old are you, Mike?" she asked, making small talk.

"Twenty, uh, let's see. Eight. Well, nine. I just turned."

Boyish charm, she thought, not altogether charitably.

He plucked the tiniest blue flower off a withered-looking stem. She hadn't seen any blooms at all on the yellow stick. He handed her the flower.

"Magic," he said.

She put her hand on his chest.

"Cuz," she said.

He jumped. He had been about to say: *Indian rice grass.*

She kissed him lightly on the lips.

She flattened both hands across his chest, spreading her fingers. She dug in a little with her nails.

"Wow," he said.

They smooched again.

"Let's," she said.

She cut her eyes to the side, to a shady patch of sand.

"Gosh," he said, then blushed, then stepped away.

Gary Cooper! she thought.

She sat in the sand.

"Do let's," she said softly.

At a loss for anything else to say, he muttered, "I was staked out by Apaches around here someplace."

"Ooh," she said, closing her eyes.

Mike limped away a few steps, desperately thinking about auto parts and hoping his sudden embarrassing development didn't catch her eye.

"Cowboy," she said, eye firmly focused on the precise spot, "why don't you pole-vault over here and teach me a little more about wildlife."

"Yikes," he said.

The sun was arcing down, and the cool shadows poured toward them like purple water. Phoebes and flycatchers darted above them. The first bat of the night jigged overhead: McGurk thought it looked like a leaf or a crumpled page in a strong wind. Venus seemed to ignite. And Lily had pulled open his shirt and kissed his chest and said the things people say on the brink. Then she turned every drop of his blood to powder by pulling off her shirt and bra. He smiled stupidly.

Mike put his hand on her breast and was astonished by her softness, by the tender button of her nipple pushing against his palm. He could barely breathe.

"Lover," she said. "Lover."

But she wasn't his lover. He felt a bolt of shame: what if his mom was out there somewhere . . . *watching?*

He removed his hand from her breast.

He said, "How about we lay here and look up at the sky."

She opened her eyes. She stared at him. She swallowed.

"What?" she said.

"Maybe, sort of, hold on to each other, but maybe, more or less, slow down."

"Slow," she said, "down?"

"It's just that. . . " He lay back and stared at the sky. *Boy, what a jerk.* "We're cousins!" he cried.

"Oh, darling," she said. "Oh, sweetheart."

She bent down to him and pressed his eyes closed with her fingers. He found this rather disconcerting. He was afraid she was looking up his nose.

"I won't tell," she breathed into his mouth, "if you won't."

He had twenty things to say, twenty reasons why he didn't think this was the best idea, but his mind was as blank as the sand. It took him a second, but he finally said, "Golly."

10

He smoked a sullen cigarette.

That was what Lily thought as she watched McGurk, bare butt buried in sand, elbows on knees, smoke rising slowly from his lips. She was going to write a poem about this one. It would be a scorcher too—she was going to submit it to the literary review as soon as she got settled in her dorm. She rolled the opening lines around in her head: *He smoked a sullen cigarette / the love-pulse beaten / silver-sweet between his / haggard cheeks. The taste / of me like cactus-berry wine / a tangled tang on his tarrying tongue. / We were young.*

Yes!

She had to remember to find out if there was any such thing as cactus-berry. But hey—poetic license.

"Got a pencil, Mike?" she said.

He shook his head.

"You're a bit glum," she said.

He looked at her, then looked away.

"Well, gee. I'm glad you enjoyed it so much!" She crossed her arms over her chest and huffed.

Mike held the cigarette in his fingers and rubbed his thumb across his forehead.

Now he'd gone and torn it.

He had to go and make whoopee with his cousin.

"I'm sorry," he said. "I shouldn't a done it."

"Done what?"

"*It.*"

"Don't be silly."

"I'm not being silly."

"Mutual consent," she said. "My idea, to boot."

"No. I'm responsible."

She scrambled to her feet and stood there, hands on hips, glaring down at him. He was disconcerted by her breasts bobbling as she stomped her feet.

"Look here, mister—there's no way you're taking credit for this. I am in charge of my life, and nobody's going to start claiming credit for everything."

"I was trying to be a gentleman," he said, falling back.

"Well, cut it out!"

She plopped back down.

"Christ," she said. "You'd think we'd killed somebody."

But it weighed on him. All he could say by way of explanation was, "But we're cousins."

Lily pulled up her pants and said, "Jeez, Mike. What a square."

She took his chin in her hand and looked into his eyes.

"It's just a taboo."

He actually blinked back a tear.

Thank God I'm blowing this joint in the morning, she thought.

"I'm sorry," Mike said. "It was a mistake."

He cries . . . his tears / salt-sharp as my sweat / caught in the tender goblet of my belly / burn . . . burn . . . burn.

"Cuz," she said, reaching behind herself to hook her bra, "you've got to get with-it."

Gideon was passed out on the couch, a logjam of bottles gathered on the floor. Turk snored loudly in his bedroom.

"You can sleep in my bed," he said, too ashamed to look at her face.

She crossed her arms and sighed.

"Mike, you're sweet, you really are."

She laid a palm on his arm.

"But you're kind of scaring me."

He pulled her hand up to his face and kissed her palm. She felt heat run up her wrist.

"You're not falling in love or anything . . . ?" she said.

He pulled her close and smelled her hair.

"I like your smell," he said. "I'm all confused."

"God, you're strange," she said.

"I know it," he said. "Go to sleep. I'll see you in the morning."

Then he turned and walked out into the night and kept on walking.

11

He gave her a scrap of paper over breakfast. It said:

Your skin all white like snow
Your eyes just like a doe
Your love went by too fast
And now I'm just your past.

Love XXX, Mike McGurk,
Your cousin

For a minute, he wanted to amend another line: *I still got sand stuck in my ass!*

"How sweet," she said, beaming. She kissed his cheek.

He watched her fold the note and tuck it into her shirt pocket, then she tore into her eggs.

Turk and Gideon, both hung over, drooped over their plates.

"The children," Turk moaned, "seem to have gotten along."

Gideon focused on Mike with one blackened eye and said, "Mff."

When Lily was finished, she pulled Gideon's plate over and started in on his food.

She looked at Mike—quite tenderly, he thought—and said, "Got any Tabasco?"

Lily and Mike helped Gideon into the car. He was too ill to drive. Turk stood in the doorway, opening a beer. The bottle cap hit the ground and rolled in little spirals. Mike found himself acutely attuned to every detail of the morning. Five and a half miles away, a buzzard hung in the sky like a fly in a web, for instance.

"I've been dehydrated lately," Turk said. "Gives you a hell of a headache. Beer's the only cure."

"You've been the perfect host, Uncle Wallace," Lily said.

"Sim-salla-bim," he said. "Ish kabibble."

Then he went inside.

"That's my dad!" said Mike.

Lily pulled him off to the side of the garage. They could hear Gideon groaning in the car. One brown shoe hung loosely off his foot, and a horsefly hovered at Gideon's heel, entranced by the fabulous scent.

"Kiss me," she said.

"Don't think so," he said, then kissed her.

"More."

He kissed her again.

"Another."

He lifted her off the ground and kissed her hard.

"I'm the sea," she rhapsodized. "I'm insatiable."

Mike held her.

"Will I see you?" he asked.

She shook her head.

"Different worlds, my darling."

It sounded like the title of a Mike Hammer book.

"Only in our dreams," she said.

He pulled away. He had that sincere look she had started to dread. "I'm—" he started to say, but she put her finger over his lips.

"Remember me," she said.

"Yeah. No kidding," he said.

Then she ran to the car, cranked it, and tore down the drive before Mike could catch her.

He watched the Caddie recede into the still-dark west. He

could smell her on his hands. He could feel God staring at him. He put his hands in his pockets.

"Swell," he said.

On his bed, a small red paperback: *The Collected Poems of Stephen Crane.*

Mike flopped down and cracked the cover, flinching from the love blast that was sure to be in the book.

"Mike," she'd written. "I will write poems about you. That's more than I can say about the others. Maybe it's enough. Yrs, Lily."

Yours.

She had—Mike double-checked—written *Yours.*

Beneath the inscription, she'd written: "Page 44."

He lay on his back and reread her note, sniffed the book to see if she'd perfumed it, and of course she had not. He thumbed through the book until he found page 44. She had sketched a saguaro cactus in the corner. She had written "L + M" beneath it. The poem was Number 41. And it said:

> *Love walked alone.*
> *The rocks cut her tender feet,*
> *And the brambles tore her fair limbs.*
> *There came a companion to her,*
> *But, alas, he was no help,*
> *For his name was Heart's Pain.*

He stared at the page for a while. Then he tucked the book under his mattress, rolled over, and lay facedown. After a time, as the heat swelled within the walls of his room, he began to cry.

12

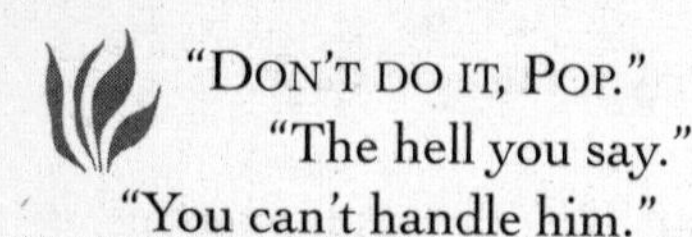

"DON'T DO IT, POP."

"The hell you say."

"You can't handle him."

"Says who!"

"Well, says me, for one."

"Of all the pantywaist claptrap."

"I just heard about him. He's dangerous."

"Dangerous! And I suppose Texaco Turk McGurk is a flyweight—is that what you're saying? Because if you're saying I can't cut it, I'll peel down right here and show *you* who's dangerous, and believe you me, that's a lesson you won't soon forget!"

"Calm down, Pop."

"Calm . . . *down!* I am fucking well calm!"

"Look—"

"Don't you say *look* to me, young man!"

"Father. I've heard bad things about Ramses Castro is all. Shoot, the guy staked me out in the desert once."

"Somewhere, somehow, I failed you as a father. That part's obvious now. Go ahead—blame me. I'm guilty of everything."

"What are you talking about?"

"You should have cut that tub o' lard's heart out. You should have skinned him alive. Like a real McGurk. It's all my fault."

"Don't want you to get hurt. It's that simple."

"Father's always in the shithouse, eh, Mike? It's all Dad's fault."

"People have been talking."

"Like who?"

"Well . . . like Mr. Sneezy."

"Sneezy!"

"He doesn't want you to do it, Pop. He told me."

"Sneezy. Sneaky Apache bastard—of *course* he doesn't want me to fight. Can you imagine? Can you imagine *your* grandson being fed into the maw of these fists? What dishonor. What shameful behavior. And to think you played right into it."

"He loves you."

"He will never set foot inside my house again."

"Dad. Come on now."

"I have a good mind to call him right this minute."

"Let's forget it."

"I'll be goddamned if I'll forget it! My own son teaming up with an Indian behind my back!"

"That's not fair."

"Oh. Excuse me all to hell."

"Listen, Pop. I'm going out for a while."

"Maybe you're not my son. Did you ever think of that?"

"I'm your son, all right, and if you don't shut your mouth, I'll show you who's a McGurk—*old man.*"

"Get out!"

"I'm on my way."

"Don't let the door hit you in the ass on your way out!"

"Get your butt whipped, Pop. I can't wait. Maybe you'll finally die and put yourself out of my misery."

"Sure. Run away. You don't have the stomach for a man's world, Mike, you know it? You don't have the cojones. Go off and think about Lily. Pull your pud while you're at it. That's apparently all you're good for."

"You need a psychiatrist."

"Don't think I didn't notice your little adventure. Doing the deed with your own cousin. I'm calling Gideon! I'll see you go to jail!"

"Thanks, Dad. Lovely chatting with you. While I'm gone, why don't you stick your head in the oven?"

The door slams. The engine of the tow truck roars to life. Turk, spittle on his lips, tears into Mike's room and grabs a book. He's going to rip its pages out and scatter them all over the bed. He stands, panting, book open in his hands. Then he shuts it and puts it back on the shelf. The sound of the tow truck's engine diminishes in the distance to an insect's howl.

"A man has to drink gin around here just to have a little peace. Think you're so smart? I can drink an entire goddamned bottle and still kick your ass from here to Colorado. See if I'm lying, you son of a bitch!"

The doors of the kitchen cabinets bang open. The metal cap of the gin bottle sounds oddly soothing as it is unscrewed. It sounds almost golden. Cool as a mountain stream.

13

MIKE DROVE. THE FIGHT WAS SET IN THE VFW HALL IN Quartzite. As a boy, Mike had often collected chunks of the white and pink quartz that lay scattered around like ice in the desert. Sometimes the quartz had red splashes. Grandfather Sneezy told him, "That's Indian blood spilt on there," and Mike had believed him. At night, Mike had delighted in clacking the rocks together: they threw sparks and lit up inside like crystal flashlights.

He was thinking about Lily. He was thinking about how, when they made love, she'd broken out laughing. She'd laughed uncontrollably. "I always laugh when I come," she'd said. He stored the information in his female data bank: *Sometimes they laugh.* He was also thinking that she wasn't his first. She was his third. But this time it felt like the first two were supposed to feel. He wondered what number he was for her.

Turk sat quietly, watching the landscape.

"I saw a coyote," he said.

As far as conversation went, that was pretty much it.

Turk was feeling bad about what he considered their little tiff. Mike was feeling bad about Lily. Turk thought Mike was feeling bad about him. There was that too. But Mike was also feeling bad about this fistfight. Turk knew it, and it made him feel worse. Plus he was feeling bad about what he'd said about Lily.

As they pulled into the parking lot and Mike wended his

way between dusty trucks and sagging desert sedans, Turk said, "You know, contrary to popular belief, I never much enjoyed being me."

Mike recognized it as a huge gesture, but he wasn't entirely sure which one. It was Turk's way of making peace.

"It's funny," Mike said, parking and setting the hand brake. "I feel exactly the same way."

"There you have it," said Turk. "Proof that we're a family. Right?"

He held out his hand to Mike.

"Right?" he repeated.

He pushed his hand out toward Mike again.

"It may not be much," he said, "but what else have we got?"

Mike took his father's hand and shook it.

"We're a pair," Turk said, "of sorry sons of bitches. We might as well stick together."

They released each other's hands.

Mike shut the engine down. It knocked and shuddered. He got out.

Turk said, "We're it."

Delbert Sneezy stood flat-footed in the dirt, his cowboy hat squashed low on his forehead. He held his arms crossed before his chest and shook his head in regular arcs, like a machine.

"I been waiting all night."

"Here to watch the fight?" said Mike.

"I ain't watching it. No, sir."

Turk stared at Mr. Sneezy, who muttered under his breath.

"Turk McGurk," Mr. Sneezy said, "I'm telling you—pack up and go home."

"Grandfather," said Mike, "I—"

"This is a thing for old men," said Mr. Sneezy.

"Old," said Turk. "I'll show you about *old*."

"Don't go in there."

"I will."

"You can't fight."

"By God I can."

"Don't be no hero, Turk."

"Don't be a coward, Sneezy," said Turk with alarming disdain.

"You're proud, old friend," said Mr. Sneezy.

"Get out of my sight, you dry-gulcher."

Mr. Sneezy held out a cupped hand. In it Mike could see twigs and dry leaves.

"If you won't go on home, burn this."

"What is it?" said Turk, backing away.

"Sage," said Mr. Sneezy. "We'll light it and smudge you—purify you."

"Indian bullshit," Turk sneered. He stepped around Mr. Sneezy and walked toward the building. "Excuse me," he said.

Mr. Sneezy opened the flap on his shirt pocket and put the sage inside.

"Mike," Turk called back. "I'll see you in there."

Mike and Mr. Sneezy stood together, both of them embarrassed. Mr. Sneezy patted Mike on the back. "Maybe he'll win," he said.

"You don't think so?"

"No."

He shook Mike's hand.

"Put money on the Indian," he said. Then, "Good-bye, Mike."

And he was gone.

Ramses Castro stood like a monolith at the far end of the hall. Red-eyed and gleaming with sweat, he wore a red bandanna tied around his head and a long braid hanging down his back. He had with him an entourage of zoot-suiters, Indians, and farmworkers. He locked eyes with Mike but gave no sign that he recognized him.

Turk was light on his feet, joyous, giddy. He threw shadow punches at Mike, bellowed a few tunes, and laughed with his admirers while rising to his tiptoes and bouncing like leaf-spring suspension. Mike, nursing a tepid longneck, did a quick jig when Turk goosed him.

Formations of insects dive-bombed the bare electric bulbs.

Their hysterical shadows grew huge on the walls. Cigar smoke formed a thin veil hanging two feet beneath the ceiling. Mike watched a bug the size of Lily's fist cut through it with a relentless drone of orange wings.

Turk filled the background on the right side of the room. He seemed to Mike as self-conscious as a girl at her first prom. Not that Mike had ever been to a prom.

Mike tipped the bottle to his mouth. He heard Turk lecturing his followers: "Vernon Dalhart. Now, *that* was a *singer*." Mexicans grinned at Mike from their places along the walls. They were dangerous, hopped up with new style—greasy ducktail hairdos and cavernous draped jackets that dropped past their knees. Turk: "Don't *even* bore me with Gene Austin! 'My Blue Heaven'? My Blue Whanger!" Mike patrolled, slowly thunking his boot heels on the boards, circling the room, slyly watching these weirdo zoot-suit greaser pachucos.

"This ain't the monkey house, vato," a voice hissed in his ear.

He veered into the room and turned back to see the source of the voice.

It was a Mexican, slouched against the wall, right hand inserted in his pocket like a knife.

"Or," said the Mexican, "are you taking a beaner survey?"

His partners laughed nastily around him.

Mike took in his double-soled black shoes, baggy pants cuffed in tight at the ankles, gold watch chain looping under pocketed hand, waistband up to his navel. The Mexican wore a sleeveless undershirt. A small cross glowed on his chest. He wore a razor-brim hat pulled low across the bridge of his nose. All his face was in shadow—the only part visible was his mouth.

"Watch it, amigo," the apparition said. "We dangerous."

"Orale, ese," one of the gang said.

"Pinche puto," said another.

The phantom said, "These here Messkins, they carry *knives*, baby!"

Mike was backing away now.

"Dig it!"

They were laughing at Mike.

The Mexican was wearing his belt sideways, the buckle on his left side.

"A Messkin," the phantom said, pushing away from the wall, moving one step toward Mike, "why, he'd just as soon stab you as look at you. It's true. Read your history books!"

"Okay, fine," said Mike.

"And keep them white women away from us! Watch your womminfolk, pard! Keep them brown-backed vermin offen your womminfolk!"

The Mexicans were laughing uproariously, slapping the phantom on the back. He had a thin smile underneath the shadow.

Mike beat it to the other side of the room, into white territory. He maneuvered around behind Turk and the boys, where he cast furtive glances at the Mexicans and the Indians.

"Looks like a powwow in here, doesn't it?" said Turk.

The ol' boys kneaded his shoulders. Castro just stood there, immobile, fists on hips. He pointed at Turk and mouthed: *You're mine*. Then he smiled. Then he blew Turk a kiss.

"Son of a bitch!" said Turk.

Red Lewis said, "I believe that fellow is requesting a date with you."

"Haw haw."

The boys about busted a gut.

Turk said, "I'll tell you what—that 'skin gives me the willies. He's some sort of certified screwball."

"Yessir," said Red. "He's a big 'un."

"By God," said Turk, "you are a master of the obvious."

The Milky Way could be seen, arching above the parking lot from east to west, the spine that held up the heavens. Mike leaned on the round fender of the tow truck, smoking. The light above the back door of the hall was the center of a churning ball of insects. Bats charged into their orbits, huge in the light, silently hijacking gutloads of clear wings and bristly legs.

The door banged open. Out stepped Turk, followed by the phantom. Mike's jaw dropped open, and the cigarette fell to the ground.

Turk and the phantom gestured, nodded, shook hands. Mike gawked. The shadow under the phantom's hat brim had been forced down by the light. It cut a black swath out of his chest. He nodded and stepped back inside.

Mike trotted over.

"Pop!"

"Mike!"

"What's the deal?"

"With that greaser?"

"Right."

"Name's García."

"So?"

"Wrestler."

"No kidding."

"That's right. Wants to fight."

"When's that?"

"After this one. Couple of weeks."

"Should be interesting."

"No doubt. Oh. The boy needs a job."

"Really."

"Yup. I hired him on."

"Whatsie? Whoziz?"

"Said I gave him a job. He's a mechanic. Hell, somebody has to show you how to fix an engine!"

"When's he start?"

"Says he'll be there tomorrow. But you know Mexicans."

Turk waved and went inside.

Things grew more dreadful by the minute.

The rules were simple: The fighters stood in the middle. The rounds were three minutes. No one kept score—there were no points or TKOs. It was a war of attrition. The fight would be lost by submission or knockout. It would go three rounds or as many as it took.

Turk and Ramses Castro squared off. Turk looked up at Castro and said, "I'm sorry, son, for what I'm about to do to you."

The ol' boys laughed real loud.

"Shake," said the ref.

Castro said, "Looks like he's already shakin'."

The Mexicans and the Indians really got a charge out of that.

He and Turk gave each other the most perfunctory of handshakes.

"Luck," mumbled Turk.

Mike was stretched as tall as he could get, looking over shoulders and heads. Red Lewis jabbed him in the ribs and winked.

Ramses Castro smiled his craziest red-eyed smile. His teeth were small and strangely bright against his skin.

"Thanks . . . Grandpa," he said.

The bell rang.

"Don't look upon me with the naked eye, gentlemen!" bellowed Turk. He held one forefinger up in Castro's face, holding him off like a dog. "'I put my hand on the sun's face and make it night on earth!'" Ramses Castro, not a big Mark Twain fan, was getting mad.

Turk leaned in, fists cocked, eyes sinking back into his skull, his inscrutable lizard face going cold and scaly. Ramses Castro waded straight into him—everybody flinched, knowing what Turk had in store for him. Mike thought: *My God—the old man's going to take him after all.* Ramses Castro swung his fist up and over. It came down like an ax blow, straight into the top of Turk's head. *Crack.* The skin of Turk's scalp blew open like an egg yolk. Snot flew from his nose. He fell to his knees. The room was silent. Mike saw a flake of tooth on Turk's lip. Blood cascaded off Turk's head, filling his ears and eye sockets. "Son?" he said, spitting a fine red mist off his lips. "Mike?"

Ramses Castro leaned over him and said, "You lose, asshole."

Turk drifted to the floor, slow as dust, soft as moonlight.

14

RED LEWIS HELPED MIKE DRAG TURK OUTSIDE. THEY couldn't wake him up beyond a kind of groggy whining somnambulism. His heels dug twin troughs through the gravel. Mike was focusing on getting his heart to slow down, his arms to stop shaking.

"She's coming for me," Turk said. "I'm going home."

All around them, cars were revving to life, coughing puffs of exhaust into Turk's face. The Indians were going: "Yip! Aiee!" and the Mexicans were going: "Uy! Uuyy!" and the gringos who had bet on Ramses Castro were going: "Yee-haw!"

"Sounds like a damned zoo," noted Red.

Mike's back pockets were stuffed with wadded bills, tucked in by all kinds of people who mumbled "For the sawbones" and "Good luck." Mike knew Turk would never concede to wasting the contributions on a doctor. He probably would want to burn the money as soon as he was back on his feet.

Turk the Defeated.

They shoveled him into the front seat. Red and another man had taped a wad of bandages to the top of his head. It sat there like a pink-and-red party hat, off center and somehow embarrassing. They closed the door gently against Turk's right shoulder. He slumped against the window, one eye cracked halfway open.

"Luck, kid," said Red. He pivoted on one heel and retreated at a canter.

And that was it. Nobody asked, leaned in the window, ran after them, wept, raised swords. Mike got behind the wheel, leaned over and looked at his limp father, and said, "Don't worry, Pop. I'll get you home. We'll put some ice on that thing. Couple hours sleep—and good as new."

Turk mumbled. It sounded like he was chanting the word *Low*: "Low . . . low . . . low. . . . "

"Maybe sleep all day, huh? How'd you like that?" Mike said. "I got it all under control."

He fired up the truck, wrestled the stick into reverse, eased up on the clutch. "Hang on now." As the truck wheezed back, he glanced out Turk's window to make sure he could clear that rusted-out Packard on his right. The phantom stood there, looking in. His hat brim rose in metric increments. It was clicking like a tool, trimming away the shadow from the man's face, until Mike was looking into startling black eyes.

Mike suddenly deciphered Turk's chant: he was saying, "No . . . no . . . no. . . . "

As he pulled out of the lot, he watched the phantom in the rearview. He stood alone, staring after them, one hand raised, unmoving.

At night, the desert rushes by the windows as though twin turntables of landscape were on either side of the truck, revolving in perpetual motion, the truck a cog upon some small flywheel where these turntables intersect. Hours of blue-gray whirling land orbit around out of the darkness, spin into the cones of light before the truck, and whirl away. The eyes of rabbits, coyotes, foxes throw sparks as the edges of the earth spin.

The only way to get Turk into bed was by fireman's carry: Turk sprawled across Mike's back, toe tips dragging loudly on the floor as Mike struggled under his weight. Turk slid off Mike's shoulder and onto the bed. His body cut a diagonal across the mattress. His head fit perfectly in the intersection of two walls. Mike unlaced his shoes, pulled them off, moved the feet onto the bed, moved Turk's head over on the pillow. He swabbed the blood crust off with a wet towel. Turk opened his eyes.

"Did I win?" he said.

Mike pulled the sheet over him.

"Get some sleep, Dad."

"I have a headache."

"I bet."

Turk's whiskers were black with dried blood.

"Night, Dad."

Mike turned off the light. Turk's door made a soft squeal as he pulled it shut.

"Son?"

"Yes, Dad."

"I'm thirsty."

"I'll get you a glass of water."

"I'd like a beer."

"I think water's a better idea."

"Mike?"

"Yes, Dad."

"I'm hot."

"I'll get the fan too."

"Mike?"

"Yes, Dad." Mike tried to keep the irritation out of his voice.

"Your mother." Turk cleared his throat. "Your mother. I loved her. You wanted to know."

Mike stood silent at the door.

"Quite a bit," said Turk. "Actually, very much. Did you know she was a good dancer?"

"No. I didn't know that."

When there was no more, Mike hurried out to the kitchen, filled a glass with water. He grabbed one of the living room fans and hauled it with him, trailing the cord all through the house. By the time he got back to Turk's room, his father was asleep.

Wind played music on the corners of the house. Mike sat in the kitchen, sipping tequila and rattling trilobites on the table. He imagined they sounded like mah-jongg tiles. *Mom was a good dancer,* he reminded himself. Certain wind gusts rose to a yowl. The windows shook. One of the trilobites was rolled up, caught in the rock and looking like a ridged black marble. He flipped it back and forth—it bounced and skipped across the table.

"Mom," he said to her eternally hovering ghost, "I don't know what's happening."

He got up, switched off the light, and took the bottle by the neck.

"I'm going to bed."

He felt his way down the hall.

In the darkness, his voice could have come from anywhere. He said, "Get me out of here, Ma."

15

It was already one hundred fifteen in the shade when Mike winched the engine out of a Ford truck—the last job left over from before the fight. As far as he could tell, it was the only money they'd be earning this week. If he got to it this early, maybe he'd beat the heat. He was completely covered in a film of sweat. Okay—that Mexican was coming? Let him fix it!

Mike stormed inside for a shower.

Turk was still snoring when he checked on him.

After he bathed, Mike cooked eggs and beans, smothered in vicious Mexican hot sauce. He sat down with a pot of coffee and a stack of corn tortillas. The fan was on the table, turned toward his face and blowing full blast. His hair was completely dry in five minutes.

He finished eating, tossed the plate in the sink, and checked on Turk again. Asleep. Talking, more or less. It could have been French, for all Mike knew. He pulled a kitchen chair into the room and put the fan on it so it was level with his father. In the office, he grabbed an old *National Geographic* and daydreamed about the friendly giant tortoises in the Galápagos.

He heard the phantom coming before he saw him. At first, he thought it was a low-flying airplane. He recognized the sound: a very deep-throated motorcycle. Even from out on the two-lane, it rumbled.

Mike watched through the cheap windows of the office. The phantom roared toward him going seventy, at least. He was on a low-slung, long-bodied hog. Mike heard the engine downshift from the speed of desert riding. The imperfections in the glass made the phantom appear to wobble as he rode by the station, looking at it. He stretched across one window and leaped over to the next, suddenly whole, caught up with himself.

Mike stepped out.

The motorcycle rolled about a half mile, then looped lazily and chugged toward him at fifteen miles an hour.

He thought he wasn't seeing right—a big stick shift rose up beside the white gas tank, and the phantom was working it like the shifter on a hot rod.

The phantom rolled up to the office, gunned it once, and shut it down. Mike was reminded of the aftermath of a thunderclap.

"Qué pasa, Junior?" the phantom said.

Mike gawked at the motorcycle.

"That's some bike," he said.

The phantom put down the kickstand.

"Indian," he said. "Nineteen thirty-eight. Restored it myself."

"I can't get over this business," said Mike, gesturing at the stick shift with his boot. "I've never seen that."

"Standard issue on the Indian Chiefs," the phantom said. "Look here."

He pointed to the fender over the front tire. The little red headlight mounted on it had a plastic Indian's face for a lens.

"I'll be damned," Mike said.

"Best bike on earth," said the Mexican. He pulled off his leather gloves and slapped them down on the gas tank.

Mike couldn't figure out how old he was. He didn't look old, but he didn't look young, either. He could have been thirty or a hundred and fifty. He looked as if he was twenty-one the day he was born. His Zapata mustache hung past the corners of his mouth.

"How's the old man doing?" he said.

"Asleep," Mike said.

"You got that right," the Mexican said. "He's reet beat. Complete!"

Mike gaped.

"Ya estufas con la onda y chale with the chingaderas!" he explained.

Mike shook his head helplessly.

"Tired," the Mexican said. "He's feeling under the weather and lacks pep." He said this with a light curl of the lips.

Mike didn't, in any measurable way, like this guy.

The Mexican dismounted and walked around in a circle, shaking his leg.

"You know when your nuts get caught in the seam?" he said. "I hate that!"

He peered into the garage.

"Hey, Junior," he said. "What you got for me?"

"Ford truck. Engine's blown. And the name's Mike."

The Mexican looked back at him.

"Don't be calling me cute names. I don't like it. Is that a deal?"

The Mexican smiled.

"Tell you what, Ju—ah, Mike. You don't be calling me 'beaner' and all the rest of that shit, and I won't act like a wise guy."

"Right."

"Okeydoke, Mike. We're cool for school."

They couldn't bring themselves to shake hands, so they nodded at each other from ten feet away.

The Mexican laughed.

"Pinches McGurks," he said. "My name's García. Bobo, they call me. Whichever you want."

Mike tipped a finger to his brow.

Real cowboy shit, Bobo thought.

He sauntered into the garage and shouted, "Let's see if you white boys know anything about cars!"

While Bobo worked, Turk slipped into the garage behind them. Mike was sitting on a tool counter, leafing through one of

Turk's *Swedish Nature* magazines: doughy nudists were frolicking on the volleyball court, one grizzled old-timer frozen in midair, flopping for all he was worth. Mike glanced up. "Dad!" he said.

Bobo stood up. "Buenos días, Mr. McGurk," he said.

"García," said Turk. "Mike."

The wadded party hat of defeat had crusted dark brown around the edges. One tail of gauze had worked itself loose and hung behind him like some absurd ponytail. Speckles of dried blood were glued all over his brow. He smelled like meat.

"What happened?" he said.

Mike and Bobo stared at their feet.

Bobo cleared his throat, then looked at Mike.

Turk swayed.

"I'm a little rocky, boys."

"Take it easy, Pop," said Mike.

"That's right, don't strain yourself," Bobo suggested.

"Kee-rist," said Turk. "What am I, somebody's grandmother?"

They shook their heads.

"Is anybody in the state of Arizona still capable of intelligent speech?" Turk said. "Are you girls going to stop dilly-dallying with me or what? What happened?"

"Castro," said Mike.

"Ramses Castro," Bobo added helpfully.

"I didn't kill him, did I? Not another death."

"Not exactly, Dad."

"How many rounds did the fucker last?"

"None," said Bobo.

"Eh?"

"No rounds, Dad."

Turk's face lit up. His smile was hopeful and hideous.

"I took him in the first round . . . ?"

"Uh, no, sir," said Mike.

"What do you mean?"

"Mr. McGurk," said Bobo, "you didn't, exactly, manage to knock him out."

"That's right," said Mike.

It was beginning to sink in, right through the hole in the top of Turk's head.

"Oh my God."

"Sorry, Dad."

Turk started to run his hand over his head but winced.

"Don't tell me that."

Nobody said anything.

"In the first round?"

Mike and Bobo looked at their feet.

The moment stretched out of shape, like a truck seen through the station windows.

"Well, I'll be dipped," Turk said.

Then: "Goddamn me to hell."

Then: "Right in front of everybody?"

"You mean?" he said.

"Do you intend to tell me?"

He glared at them as though they had knocked him out.

Then he turned and staggered back into the house, passing through a wedge of painfully bright sunlight and bouncing gently off the doorframe as he entered.

At five, the desert started to go plum-colored, dark and maroon at the edges. Not a single customer had come in. "Busy place," Bobo noted as he washed up.

He walked over to the motorcycle and settled onto the saddle.

"I've got a sidecar," he said. "You never know who might want a ride."

Mike nodded.

"See ya," Bobo said.

"So long."

Bobo pulled his gloves on.

Mike went over to him.

"Bobo," he said. "Thanks. For helping out with my old man. That was rough for him."

"Hey," Bobo said.

"Yeah."

They shook hands.

Bobo kicked it to life. His vast noise spread all over the desert.

"Tomorrow, vato," he yelled, then burned rubber in a doughnut and peeled out into the lowering sun.

16

MIKE WAS STARTLED TO FIND TURK PRESIDING OVER A large pot of spaghetti. "Mike," he said. "Remember when you used to call this stuff piss-ghetti?"

Mike circled Turk's cheerful mood warily.

"How you doing, Dad?" he asked.

"I've had brighter moments, that's for sure." He peered into a simmering pot of sauce. "Piss-ghetti. What a hoot."

"Haw haw," Mike laughed.

Turk turned his face out of the pot and wrinkled his nose.

"Take a bath, son. You smell like a skunk."

He was shifting gears quicker than an automatic transmission.

"Be right back," Mike said.

He returned from the shower in a clean pair of jeans and a white pearl-snap cowboy shirt with slit pockets. Padding out to the kitchen, he received a cold beer Turk had opened for him.

"Little salt, little lime," Turk said.

"Thanks."

"Those Mexicans, boy. Not much in the effort department, but they make a quality beer!"

Yaarch! Turk belched.

"Say," he said, "what was that García fellow doing hanging around the place today? Looking for hubcaps to steal, I bet."

Mike was trying to handle the old man carefully.

"Uh, I hired him," Mike said.

"Hired him!"

"We needed somebody who was an expert in engines."

Turk shrugged.

"If you say so," he said. "You're the boss."

The sauce bubbled merrily.

"Mexicans," Turk said. "I once did the deed with a Mexican girl in a lavatory on the train from Guadalajara to Mazatlan."

"I didn't know that," said Mike.

"You'd be amazed," said Turk.

. . . *at what you don't know,* Mike finished in his mind, but Turk didn't say it.

Mike licked some salt off the back of his hand, sucked a lime, took a sip.

"That's backwards," Turk said. "You sip, *then* you lick."

Mike stayed quiet.

Turk was moving a little stiffly; Mike noticed that his left hand shook. Not quite palsied, but unsteady. Turk had peeled the wad of gauze off his head. An evil bruise focused itself there, collecting into a tattered black star of flesh on top.

"Keeping that deal clean, Dad?"

"You bet!"

"Let's bandage it up again, what do you say?"

"I thought a little air would do me good."

"How about that bandage, though?"

"I was just saying."

"I heard you, too. But it seems to me some clean gauze would do it a world of good."

"Well, all right," said Turk. "Wouldn't want a fly to come along and get stuck up there!"

Turk was immensely agreeable. It was frightening.

They trooped to the bathroom. Turk sat on the toilet.

"Is this going to hurt?" he asked.

"I'd say there's a good chance," Mike said.

"I can take it," said Turk gamely.

Mike was looking into the wound for . . . he didn't know what, really. Green, brown, fluids, death. Something. He took a square brown bottle out of the medicine chest.

Turk said, "I dreamed my skull was soft."

Yeesh, Mike thought.

"Iodine," he said.

"Not iodine!"

"Sorry, Dad. Iodine."

"Iodine. Shit. How about we just wrap it up and call it quits?"

"No can do," said Mike.

"All right. I'm not worried. Zingo, and it'll be over."

"Now you're talking."

"Don't poke me with that glass rod, though."

"No, I'll just pour some in there."

"That's the ticket! That's my boy!"

Mike dripped some of the iodine in the wound. Turk squirmed, gasped, sucked air.

"Criminy!" he said.

Mike did the best he could with the bandage. When he was through, Turk looked at himself in the mirror.

"I look like an Arab," he said. "Call me Abdul."

He turned this way and that, secretly imagining himself in a burnoose.

"Abdul—is it time to eat, or what?" said Mike.

"Let's do it," Turk said. "And you know what? It's so good you're going to eat till you puke."

"Yum!" Mike enthused.

Turk dropped the first plate he tried to pick up.

It cracked into three thick wedges.

They stared at it on the floor.

"Sorry, Dad," Mike lied. "I didn't dry it."

"Well, Goddamn it. It slipped right through my fingers."

"I'll be more careful next time," Mike said. "Hey—it happens to me *all the time*."

"Really?" said Turk absently.

"Since it's my fault, let me serve you," Mike said. "You worked awful hard already."

Turk sat at the table and watched his left hand wobble. His

elbow knocked several times on the tabletop when he went to lift his beer. With stark terror, Turk regarded this new anarchy overtaking his body.

Mike slopped a bunch of noodles and sauce in the plates and bounced some rolls on a third plate. He got two grape Nehis out of the icebox and said, "We always serve red wine with Italian."

It was one of their old jokes from when Mike was a boy.

Turk smiled quietly and nodded.

"I remember," he said.

Mike tried another one from the old days.

"Good bread, good meat—good God, let's eat! Amen."

Turk chuckled softly.

"Amen," he said.

They ate in silence. Mike kept his eyes on Turk the whole time. Presently, he asked, "You feeling all right?"

Turk glanced up at him. His eyes said: *No, I am not feeling all right, you nitwit,* but he smiled at his son anyway. He bent back to his plate and sucked up multiple strands of spaghetti. Inanely, Mike was thinking: *When the red-red-robin comes bob-bob-bobbin' along.*

"Bare feet at the table, eh?"

"What?" said Mike.

"Bare feet at supper." Turk looked under the table. "I can safely say I have seen it all now. There is not one damned thing I have not seen in the world now."

Mike tucked his feet under his chair.

Turk said, "Okay, Mr. Beatnik. Let's go listen to some records."

He kicked over his chair and rushed into the living room. Mike righted the chair and followed his father, shaking his head.

"To hell with the dishes!" Turk called.

Turk, on his knees as though in prayer, was discovered amid a landslide of scarred LPs and 78s. He bent to the canvas-front box of the hi-fi and fiddled with the knobs. Throwing Mike a ghastly wink over his shoulder, he dropped the needle with a sizzling pop on a Mexican 78. It sounded like bacon frying with some Mexicans singing in the distance.

"'Rencor,'" Turk said. "By Dueto Hermanos Esteves. On the Mexican Columbia label. It's a bolero."

"Wow," said Mike.

"Got it after that train trip." Turk waggled his eyebrows.

Mike settled into Turk's chair and listened. Frankly, it sounded a little anemic.

"The next tune, on the Capitol label, is a 78 by Frank DeVol and his band. It's a waltz, don't you know. Called 'Du Und Du,' believe it or not."

When the record was over, Turk said, "These were songs I loved."

The next record was one Mike recognized: "We're the Texas Playboys from the Lone Star State!"

"Yeah!" said Turk.

"Bob Wills," said Mike.

"Correct."

"I can name that tune in five notes," said Mike.

"You win the Cadillac!" Turk said. "The radio audience everywhere roars!"

"The crowd goes wild," Mike cried.

Turk cranked the knob.

Mike lit a cigarette.

"Like it loud, do you, Dad?"

"Shit, yes."

Hank Williams turned psycho for a minute and threatened: "You're gonna change, and I don't mean pleeeease!"

Turk sang along, top volume.

"Sounds real good," said Mike. "How's the head feel?"

"Hurts! How the hell is it supposed to feel?"

Turk fidgeted with the front of the record player; he lifted the gold-specked material stapled to it and reached inside. He threw Mike a sly smile and pulled out a dusty bottle.

"Mescal," he said. "Puts hair on your chest and then burns it back off." He uncorked it, sniffed it. "Yow," he said, crinkling his nose. "This here will give you visions."

He took a swig.

"Tastes like piss," he gasped.

He pounded the cork back in and tossed the bottle to Mike.

Mike took a swig. He gagged. He coughed. He laughed.

The records wobbled on through the night, heat-warped and noisy as bacon: black skillets full of Texas swing, western, polkas, and Rusty Warren's blue party records.

"What I wouldn't give,"—Turk sighed—"for a copulating session with that woman."

The milky booze had removed most of Mike's vocal cords. Between the records, he enjoyed the welling up of chirping from the insistent and oddly optimistic desert crickets. Suddenly, Turk wrenched the needle off "Gloomy Sunday" and turned to Mike.

"Yes?" said Mike.

"Son, what is this new business of yours?"

Mike took a tentative sip, then decided what the heck and took a full swallow.

"Geeng," he was able to say, then coughed. "What business is that?"

"All this dreamy shit. All this longing-looks-at-the-horizon poetry shit. Not to mention dogging me about your mother."

"Well, Dad, you see"—Mike scooted forward in the chair and leaned his elbows on his knees, intent—"I hate heat."

"Thank God I asked," said Turk. "Everything's clear as a bell now."

Huh? thought Mike.

"No. It's this snow thing I have," he explained. The mescal was not helping. "I want to see snow."

Turk closed one eye and watched him through the other.

"Give me that bottle."

He snatched it and sucked hard.

"Snow," he said. "Snow! For God's sake, you've seen snow! You've seen it in Flagstaff. I took you up there myself."

"But I was a boy."

"And you've grown into a damn fool, let's be honest."

Turk staggered out to the kitchen and dragged a pair of beers back with him.

"Go up to the Grand Canyon at Christmas, if you want snow," he said. "Any damned tourist would know that. Shit, bud—it snowed all the time in Oklahoma."

"Can't recall," said Mike.

"I just don't get it," said Turk. "It's that simple."

The mescal had ignited up and down Mike's spine; tiny rings of flame ran up his vertebrae; Yaqui cactus colors knit triangles in the corners.

"Dad," he said, "you can be a real pain in the ass. How'm I supposed to tell you anything?"

Turk sat on the floor and thought about it. He sucked on one bloated knuckle. Mike readied himself for an explosion.

Nothing.

They held their positions.

"You don't make sense," Mike offered.

Turk maintained his silence.

"You give me a hard time, day in and day out," Mike ventured. What the hell—bet the farm. He pulled himself upright. "And I am real tired of it."

Turk was still awake. Mike could tell that much.

"Goddamn it," Turk said.

He's back!

Mike braced himself.

"Lookit," said Turk. "I'm a profane sack of shit. I know it. I confess." He raised his right hand. "Guilty as charged: God's name in vain, the whole bit."

He emptied his beer bottle, then blew into its mouth: *Hoot!*

"Bartender," Mike quipped, trying to backtrack desperately, "I only drink what causes the greatest harm. But even then, only in excess!"

He couldn't believe how funny this was. He fell back in the chair, snorting.

"Pay attention," Turk said. "God made me an ornery shitheel, and he'll goddamned well have to live with it. But you're my son, and perhaps it's an unwelcome burden. I can live with that, I really can."

The needle was hitting the label of the record, making a dull *scud-scud scud-scud* sound.

"I tell you what, though. I never lie. Do I lie? Have I lied to you?"

Mike shrugged.

"You better believe I don't lie. I'm not about to start tonight: I *am* a royal pain in the ass!"

"The royalest!" Mike barked.

They fell down, laughing.

"I'm a swollen hemorrhoid!" said Turk. "I'm a terminal case of the piles! I'm—aw, fuck it."

They kicked out their feet and clutched their guts.

"I hate you, Dad!" Mike hollered, tears running along his nose.

"So do I!" Turk wheezed, spit bubbles flying out of his mouth. "I stink!"

Mike couldn't breathe, he was laughing so hard.

He could feel the demons from the oily Mexican booze grab the front of his brain and tug it down into a corner of his skull. He imagined his brain was in the shape of a wedge.

"Aw, Dad," he said, retreating at full gallop, "I didn't really, you know, mean it."

"Don't you lie to me, Mike!"

Turk struggled to his feet.

"Don't think I don't know this is all about your mother. Am I right? Of course I'm right. Listen up—what was I sayin'? Ah! The woman's touch!" He put one hand over his heart. "I, as a father, amount to one plug nickel. Don't contradict me, I'm on a roll here. I've been about as useful to you as a screen door on a submarine."

"A rubber crutch," said Mike.

"That's what I'm getting at," said Turk. "Where was I? Ah! The sum total of my expertise in the dad department comes out to be zero. No, no. But me no buts! But hey—if you want a father, Goddamn it, that's what mothers are for!"

This made strange sense to Mike.

"You're not the only abandoned pup in the desert, buster," said Turk. "I sleep alone every night, you know."

He sat back down.

"I did the best I could do, and, uh, I did it."

They sat there in the yellow light, studying their memories.

It could have been fifteen minutes or an hour and a half. The floor of McGurk's Texaco rolled beneath them like the bottom of a rowboat. They thought the service bell clanged, but neither of them got up.

"Fill it yourself!" Turk bellowed.

"Then get the hell outa here!" Mike added.

They snickered.

"Tourist bastards," said Turk.

"Gringo cabrones," Mike replied.

Turk was at an sharp angle, listing to starboard.

"She wasn't no saint, either, you know," he said. "She was nice. She was pretty and I fell in love with her and all. All right? It wasn't all my fault, Mike. Sure, make 'em angels after they're dead, but don't forget they wasn't saints twenty-four fucking hours a day is all I'm sayin'."

Mike could barely talk.

"Thank you, Dad," he mumbled.

He heard the clock, his stomach, the dull whine of the icebox, the chunking of the record needle. Turk smiled sweetly and fell over backward.

"Nhh," he said. "I'd give my left nut to see Connie one more time. . . ."

The bright Yaqui colors came out from the corners in threads, looping around Turk, the lamps, piling on the couch. Mike watched as the colors flared, then faded. Far out in the desert, echoing and faint, his mother's voice was singing: "O Holy Night, the stars are brightly shi-ning . . . " He felt the wool wrap around him and rock him to sleep.

17

MIKE AWOKE, BONES AND TEETH JANGLING, FROM A jarringly colored dream: He'd been making love to Lily. She was wearing silk stockings, and her skin beneath the stockings was also silk, and her pubic hair was foggy and wet. He'd pushed up on his arms and looked down at her, and she'd slowly turned clear beneath him, only her mouth, her teeth, visible. But the fog kept tugging at him, pulling him deeper into itself. Then she was gone, and he was lying naked on a hillside. Six girls from grade school were coming up the hill, and he was terrified they'd see him naked and tell the teacher, who was the sheriff. Crows came down and started to eat him; he had to grit his teeth to keep from screaming so the girls wouldn't see his penis; the crows pulled strips of jerky from his back. Their dry feathers scraped him, slid over him, suddenly became the Navajo blanket he'd pulled over himself in the night as he jerked and fell out of the chair and hit the floor.

Turk had dragged himself to his bed. Mike followed a trail of his clothes through the house: a shoe, a sock, pants, another shoe, a shirt, an undershirt, Turk facedown in bed in shorts and one sock. Mike set up the fan again, then went off to shower. The small tin stall reverberated too loudly, the water hurt. He managed to dry himself and pull on his jeans and stagger outside.

Bobo was at work on the engine.

"Been at it for two hours already," Bobo said. "Pumped two tanks of gas too."

Mike managed a weak wave.

His hair was sticking up like porcupine quills.

Bobo said, "Andas crudo, ese. You got a blue-ribbon hang-over. You been drunker'n shit."

Mike nodded.

"You gonna barf?"

Mike shook his head.

"Naughty naughty," Bobo said, shaking a finger.

"Guh," Mike said.

Bobo led Mike into the shade.

"Tell you what," he said. "I got the perfect remedy for la cruda. It's an old Mexican cure."

"I could use it."

"Give me some money."

"What for?"

"I gotta go buy it, ese. Trust me—you'll love it."

Mike gestured wanly.

"You know where the cash register is."

Bobo went to the office, then trotted out to his motorcycle.

"Cover your ears!" he shouted.

Mike sat on the cool cement and put his hands over his ears.

Bobo rose off his seat, set his foot on the kick starter, and awoke the machine. The rumble vibrated inside Mike's skull. He winced. Bobo kicked up a cloud of dust and white rubber smoke and lit out, seemingly pursued by a muzzy peal of thunder.

Turk was screaming: "Incoming! Hit the deck! Low-flying plane! Shut the hell up!"

Mike rubbed his head.

"I hate machines," he said.

He could feel the pistons pumping inside his head.

There came a crash from the kitchen.

"Who put this table here!" Turk wanted to know.

Mike woke up. He was startled. He'd thought he was awake.

"Oh," he said. "Right."

Bobo's motorcycle didn't wake him when it returned. It took several kicks to the sole of his foot. He cracked an eye.

"Little nap?" Bobo said.

"Naw," said Mike, "just . . . thinkin'. . . . "

Mike focused on the blue tin pot dangling before him.

"What's?" he said.

"The cure."

He took the pot into his lap.

"Menudo," said Bobo. "Got lots of salsa in it too." He dug a spoon out of his back pocket, wiped it on his sleeve, and handed it to Mike. "It'll cure what ails you."

Mike lifted the lid: atrocious steam rose.

"Mmm!" said Bobo.

Mike took the spoon and slurped some of the broth.

He stuck out his tongue.

"See?" Bobo said. "I told you you'd like it."

The colors yellow and gray came to mind as Mike tasted the soup. Fat hominy blobs floated in the red-tinged broth. Pale flaps of what appeared to be human flesh moved in the murk like leeches.

Mike slurped one of the skin flaps into his mouth. It lay on his tongue, limp. He figured he'd better chew it before he gagged. It squeaked on his teeth. Rubber.

"What," he demanded, "is *this?*"

"Tripitas," said Bobo. "Have some more."

Mike ate another scrap.

The hot sauce kicked in and served as a local anesthetic, almost numbing his tongue to the sweaty flavor of the flesh.

"Bobo?"

"Yo."

"What's this stuff again?"

"Tripas, Mike."

"What is it in American."

"Guts. Pig intestines, actually."

Mike spit the wad of meat all the way across the garage.

"Hey!" Bobo cried, deeply wounded. "What's *your* problem! They scrape the shit out before they cook it."

Mike put down the pot and motored to the men's.

"Damn," said Bobo, picking up the pot and the spoon. "Gringos got no manners, ese." He spooned up a load of tripas and hominy and slurped it down noisily. "A toda madre," he said. "This is what I call eatin'."

18

THE ENGINE MARKED THE DAYS. BOBO STRIPPED OFF ALL the grime, oil, carbon. He pulled it apart, soaked it, filed away at the holes, oiled the protrusions, polished the intakes. It seemed that a stark brushed-steel sculpture had risen out of a blob of congealed grease. It hung from the ceiling in a nest of chains. Bobo liked to set it rocking gently and imagined it was a vast spaceship, like the one the Rocket Man flew, moving smoothly across the sky.

Turk had maintained a sulk, listening to his records and riffling through boxes of old letters and photographs. When Mike tried to look, he pulled the box off to one side and said, "Mine."

Mike waited for the phone to ring: surely, Lily would call.

He cleaned the house, went over the hopelessly garbled books in the office and couldn't figure what Turk had spent or earned, took naps, pumped gas. One day, he set out to look for fossils, got fifty yards from home, and gave up and came back. "Did the phone ring?" he asked Bobo. "Anybody call?" he asked Turk.

He saw the details of her naked skin everywhere.

She had a small line of hair running up to her navel.

And then he remembered he shouldn't know about that hair.

He read Stephen Crane. He scoured the book for good love poems, but Crane wasn't that worried about love, apparently.

Mike had a few favorites, though, and he spent a lot of time thinking about them. They were like little windows opening on a new part of the landscape he hadn't seen yet.

He went out to the garage and said, "Bobo. Listen to this." And he recited:

> *A man said to the universe:*
> *"Sir, I exist!"*
> *"However," replied the universe,*
> *"The fact has not created in me*
> *A sense of obligation."*

Bobo stared at him for a moment, thought about it, then started to laugh uproariously. He slapped his knee.

"What's so funny?" Mike said.

"That's a good joke!" Bobo laughed.

"That's not a joke!"

"It's not?"

"It's a poem."

"You mean it ain't funny?"

"No, it ain't funny!"

"Coulda fooled me."

"What the hell do you know!"

"Didn't sound like no damned poem," Bobo grumbled. "Didn't rhyme or *nothing.*"

"Don't you get it?" asked Mike, exasperated.

"Yeah, I get it. That's why I laughed."

Turk came out.

"What's all the hollering?"

"We having a *literary* discussion," said Bobo.

"You girls are lollygagging is what," said Turk.

"Listen to this, Dad," said Mike.

"This here being the text in question?" Turk asked Bobo.

"Simon," said Bobo.

"What?"

"Said sirol."

"Come again."

"Sí."

"By God," said Turk.

Mike read Turk the poem.

"That's it?" said Turk

Mike nodded.

Turk looked at Bobo and burst out laughing.

"Damn!" he said. "That's a good one!"

On Bobo's right hand, a small blue cross slanted between the thumb and forefinger.

Mike watched it as Bobo worked.

"Hey," he said. "Is that a jail tattoo?"

Bobo slid the hand into his pocket.

"Yeah? . . ."

"Did it hurt?"

Bobo shrugged. "You know."

Mike pulled up the sleeve of his shirt and showed Bobo a pale empty heart etched on his biceps.

"I know."

"Who did that?"

"Buddy of mine in North Africa. We were drunk. Suddenly realized we didn't know any girls to put their names in there."

"Army?" said Bobo.

"You bet."

"Me too. Europe, First Cav."

"All right!" said Mike. They shook hands.

"How'd you do yours?" said Bobo, looking at the heart.

"Pretty dumb," said Mike. "We used ashes."

Bobo shook his head.

"Indian shit."

"*African* shit," said Mike.

They laughed.

"Did mine with a pin, some thread, and a bunch of ink out of a busted pen."

"No kidding."

Mike grabbed his hand and looked at the tattoo.

Bobo explained. "You take the thread out of your sock or

the blanket. You wrap it around the pin, so the ink soaks into it and runs down. Then you just start to pokin'."

"Sounds like fun," said Mike, sitting on a pile of retreads.

"Not really," said Bobo. "Young and stupid."

Mike smiled.

"Now we're old and stupid."

"You got that right."

It was one of those days. Nobody felt like doing anything. Even the bees drifted sideways into the shade and ignored the flowers.

"How about a pop?" Mike offered, to break the monotony.

"I like Dr Pepper."

"We got it."

"Then I believe I will."

The two vets marched over to the soda machine, jimmied open its front door, and extracted two condensation-beaded bottles. They went to the office, pulled out their chairs, turned on the fan, and settled in.

"You see any action over there?" Bobo asked.

"No, not really," said Mike. "I got in pretty late. Saw a couple of dead guys. Guy that did my tattoo stepped on a mine. I saw his leg. You?"

"'Fraid so," said Bobo. "'Fraid so."

He sipped his soda.

"I was a mechanic," he said. "Makes sense, don't it?"

"I guess it does," said Mike.

"Fixin' tanks, mostly." Bobo yawned. "But I seen things too."

That was apparently all he had to say on the matter.

They stared out the window. The desert, through the glass, formed a wobbly rhomboid of light. The Texaco's driveway looked about seven miles long.

"Mike," said Bobo, "you ever want to just—I don't know,—*take off?*" He gestured at the highway with his bottle.

"Only about ten times a day," said Mike.

A horsefly entered through the open door, its roar not unlike that of a distant B-17. They watched it circle the room, bob gently into the glass, back off, and fly into it furiously, its head making a loud crack when it hit. "Ouch," said Mike.

"Pendejo!" Bobo shouted.

The horsefly rotated in the air and drifted out the door.

"The way I got into the brig," Bobo said, "was there was this Sherman tank. We were hangin' behind in France, tú sabes."

Mike settled in for a good bullshit session.

"Tell me," he said.

"Them Shermans're ugly, too," said Bobo. "Look like a biscuit somebody left out in the rain."

Mike laughed.

"I hear you," he said.

"So's I'm pretty bored, right? And this one tank, I figure I'll try to soup it up. I figured I'd try to make it into a hot rod."

"You can't soup up a tank!"

"I found that out."

They laughed.

"Man," Bobo continued, "the tank commander fired it up and there was this bang and black smoke filled her up, came out through the firing vents and the barrel and everything. You could hear 'em in there coughing and gagging."

"Shee-it. I guess you got canned for that."

"I guess I did."

Bobo held up his hand.

"This is my little memento."

They watched as Turk went outside, veered around on the tarmac, got his bearings, and moved toward them. He had recently become bow-legged and had a sailor's gait.

"La Motta versus Janiro," he said. "*That* was a fight."

"Yes, sir," they said.

He nodded at them, then went back outside. He gestured once at the highway, then wandered in a circle, then went inside.

"I've seen that before," said Bobo.

"That what? That weirdness?"

Bobo nodded, tapped his temple with one finger.

"No disrespect," he said. "But it's his brain. It's all twisted up from that shot he took. He's chingado in the brain."

"Chingado?"

"Totally."

"I see."

"Sometimes it goes away," Bobo said. "Not always. It leaves your brain like a fruit or something. Soft. It don't sit right. If you make a hat out of marijuana and avocado, it helps."

Mike had thought he'd heard everything.

"A hat," he said.

"Old Mexican stuff," said Bobo. "I'll tell you a secret—all these Mexican old-timers you see around, they all know magic. Ain't gonna be no magic left when they're gone. You'll see."

"Interesting," Mike said.

"But then," Bobo continued, "sometimes it kills them."

"The magic?"

"No."

"The hat?"

"No! The injury!"

"Ah." Thinking: *Sometimes it kills them!* "Did you learn this from the old-timers?"

"Naw. I learned it in the ring."

"The ring."

"In the squared circle, ese. Where you been? Wrestling!"

Mike turned in his chair.

"You wrestled?"

"Sure."

"On television?"

"Pues, sure."

"When?"

"Every Saturday."

"On 'Welsh's Oldsmobile Wrestling Showcase'!"

"You ain't lying."

"Bobo García. *Bad* Bobo."

"That's me."

"Bobo of Borneo."

"I'm your man."

"Master of the Bobo Bop."

"Also known as the Red Devil."

"You were the Red Devil?"

"That's why I wore the mask, vato. I was a good guy in the beginning and a bad guy in the end."

Mike stood up and shook Bobo's hand. "Dang!" he said. Then he sat back down.

"You're famous," he said.

"Right," said Bobo. "That's why I'm fixing engines in McGurk's Texaco out in the middle of Shitsville, Arizona. No offense."

Mike, to let Bobo know he was not offended, waved his hand over his head and said, "Pah!"

"They retired me," Bobo said.

"I saw you get hurt that one time, but I thought it was fake."

"Nope. Real blood and everything."

Bobo bent down and pulled his thick hair apart. There, sprawled just behind the thicket of his hairline, were the old white arms of the starfish of doom.

"Looks like Turk's head."

"I know it. Head butt," Bobo said. "Went sour."

Mike recalled the patently false Bobo Bop that sent full-grown men goose-stepping around the ring in feigned brain damage, arms flapping, until they bounced off the ropes and slammed to the mat while the announcer shouted, "Whoa, Nellie!"

Mike looked at him.

"Did you, you know, get like Dad?"

"I did."

The fans whirred.

"Sometimes—it's funny—I forget where I am, what day it is."

Bobo was staring off into the desert.

"Sorry, Bobo," Mike said.

Bobo shrugged. "They took me off the circuit. I went to Chicago, L.A., all them cities. Had girls too. But not no more."

He sighed.

"Not no more."

❦ ❦ ❦

Mike went out to the men's to think.

There was a new note on the wall:

FOR HOT FUN CALL

naMe	numBer

Under "naMe," someone had written: "Your Mama." Under "numBer": "You know the number."

Mike's final decision was: What a world.

19

DAYS AND DAYS. A WEEK JUST ROLLING BY; ONE HUNDRED ten degrees average temperature, dropping to fifty degrees every night. The moon went full in the impossibly clear sky. Emerald-colored meteorites fell unseen before each dawn. A stray cow, dead in a cholla cactus thicket, fed a small coyote pack. They were moved to melancholy hysteria by the swollen moon rolling through the dark. They cried out, singing the oldest American folk song: *Yippee-tay-ay-yay.* On Wednesday morning, sixteen inches from the back of the gas station, an adolescent rattlesnake made the mistake of moving while a roadrunner dawdled in the shade. The bird darted in, bobbed, weaved, laughed, and snagged the snake behind the head. A frenzy of rattling didn't help the snake one bit. The roadrunner snapped him like a whip, shorting his brain with a sharp crack. The ember of the snake's thoughts blinked out. Ants spent the afternoon transporting scales and flakes of dried skin under the station. Meanwhile, Bobo's motorcycle acquired its crimson bullet-shaped sidecar and consumed one tank of gas. Turk's wound refused to heal. It leaked water day and night; in the mornings, he'd chip off little crystals of pale orange color. He heard a continual buzz, and the top of his head swooned with each movement, as if he had an oil slick under his scalp. On Friday, the patient buzzards saw the coyotes trotting away over a ridge. They'd had their fill. The buzzards tipped down from their fifteen-thousand-foot flights and swooped, chased by their undulating shadows, to the bones.

20

FRIDAY AFTERNOON.

Bobo and Mike decided to go out.

"I'm bored!" Bobo shouted.

"I'm hungry!" Mike answered.

"I'm horny!" Bobo yodeled.

"You're a dipshit!" Turk hollered.

He came out to the garage, threw three twenty-dollar bills at them, and said, "Clean yourselves up and get the hell out of here. Eat a steak. Visit the cathouse. See a movie."

They were effusive in their thanks, but he waved them off brusquely and went back inside.

"At least I can listen to my records in peace," he said.

They showered, Bobo borrowed a clean shirt from Mike, pants from Turk.

"How do I look?" he said.

"Rotten," said Mike.

"No doubt, in these redneck clothes. Let's go!"

They hurried out to the motorcycle. Mike eyed the sidecar warily. "That thing isn't going to detach, is it?" Bobo made some Mexican noise with his mouth that sounded like *Foit!* He jumped on the saddle of the Indian, and Mike worked himself into the sidecar. Bobo handed Mike a pair of goggles.

"You'll need these," he said.

He started the engine.

"You gonna eat a lot of bugs tonight, vato!" he cried.

They swooped in a wide circle; Mike felt the sidecar try to rise off the ground beneath him. Bobo skidded in the gravel on the blacktop and then fishtailed down the road. Mike's hair combed itself straight back, and a drop of spit exited the right side of his mouth and rolled into his ear.

"Yee-haw!" he shouted.

"We going to Tucson?" he called.

Bobo shook his head.

"Let's go to Benson!"

"What the hell for!"

"Movies!"

"There's movies in Tucson!"

"Not these movies."

Mike imagined a smoky back room with silent loops of blue movies flickering on a wall.

"What movies?" he shouted.

"Drive-in movies! *Twenty Million Miles to Earth*!"

"Oh, come on."

"No, vato! It's the one with the giant monster from Venus that eats sulfur!"

"Get outa here."

"It's good—I seen it."

"Why are we going back, then?"

Bobo looked at him with great solemnity.

"It's my favorite."

"Oh," said Mike.

Bobo added, "Plus he fights an elephant."

"Yeah?"

"Yeah! They fight it out in Rome, man, tear all them ruins to shit."

That sounded pretty good, actually.

"What's it showing with?" Mike said.

"*Them.*"

"Giant ants!" Mike shouted. "I love that movie!"

❦ ❦ ❦

Bobo was holding forth on the merits of Indian motorcycles. The sunset was wild behind them as they looped east. Tucson's lights looked strangely melancholy against the purple of the desert dusk.

"You know the Wall of Death?" Bobo said. "In the circus."

"I've seen it," said Mike.

"Them riders all ride Indians. Use 101 Scouts—to a man."

This was supposed to impart some of the mystical wonder of the Indian, but to Mike, any idiot willing to ride a motorcycle around the inside of a giant barrel had bigger problems than what kind of bike he rode.

"Okay," Bobo reasoned, "so the three-speed crash-box trannie stinks. The flat-head's undercarbed too. But so what?"

Mike tuned him out and watched the hills. He could imagine Lily writing a poem about them. He realized fully that he was never going to see her again. He felt guilty and he felt stupid, in equal measure. He turned to Bobo.

"Bobo," he confessed, "I slept with my cousin."

"Oh, yeah?" said Bobo. "What's his name?"

He laughed so hard that he veered into the oncoming lane.

They pulled into the crunchy parking lot of the Chief's Four Feathers Oasis Steakhouse.

"Don't worry about it, Mike," said Bobo. "I done it a million times. Besides, I want a big hamburger. You'll forget your woes."

"Maybe . . . ," said Mike, "a chocolate shake."

"Now you're talkin'!"

"Maybe a malt. With a scoop of chocolate ice cream thrown in."

"A chocolate-chip malt," Bobo said as they headed for the door.

They pushed in and scanned the booths. Five old white guys scattered around, two young couples on dates. They smelled the exquisite grease of french fries. Mike nudged Bobo. Coming toward them, shoehorned into a peach waitress outfit, was the organist for the Victory Bible Foursquare Gospel Outpost up the valley. Mike had never been to church, and Bobo avoided it at all costs, but everyone hereabouts knew Danette. She sometimes played her little Thomas organ on the cowboy movie show out of Phoenix. "Danette Quisenberry," Mike noted.

Her hair was teased and sprayed into a nuclear-test mushroom cloud.

An overpowering billow of imitation French perfume eddied around them.

"Hiya, boys," she said.

"Ma'am," said Mike.

"*Ma'am,*" she said. "My, my."

Bobo said, "Mmm, love the perfume."

"You're kinda cheeky for a Messkin boy," she said. "Booth or table?"

"Booth," said Bobo. "By the window."

"Yeah," she said. "There is so much to see."

As they followed her, Bobo waggled his eyebrows at Mike.

"Down, boy," Mike said.

They sat in the booth as she fanned their menus out in front of them.

"Special tonight, pot roast and mashed. I'll get you some water."

There was a small gold cross at her neck.

"Guess what I want's not on the menu," Bobo said.

"Shh," said Mike.

She came back with two icy glasses of water. Mike could feel her body heat on his arm. He turned and looked up at her. She had lipsticked the skin around her lips to make the lips seem bigger. She had a small fleck of color on her tooth. She smiled at him. He smiled at her.

Bobo piped up again: "I thought you Bible Outpost girls didn't wear no makeup or perfume."

"No, Pancho, we sure don't. And no dancing, neither. And how do you know where I attend fellowship?"

"You're famous," he said.

"I've seen you on television," Mike offered.

She touched her hair once.

"And," Bobo continued, "here you are smellin' like a li'l ol' flower."

"That's church and this is business," she said. "Got to put food on the table, boys."

"Don't we know it," said Mike.

"We'll leave you an extra-big tip," said Bobo.

"Let me go out back and get the collection plate, then," she said.

"Tithes and offerings!" Mike blurted, thinking this was his big joke for the night.

Danette turned her elaborately painted eyes on him and stared, not without pity.

"Be back in a flash," she said, and walked on to the old codger bent over the counter: "Warm up that cuppa coffee, Clayton?"

"I'm an idiot," Mike said.

"You're scoring," said Bobo. "You got her on the line."

"Tithes, I say. Offerings."

"On the line, ese. Just reel her in."

Mike felt a whipcrack of memory: When he was a boy, he used to think beer tasted sweet, otherwise why would Turk drink so much of it? When he found out how bitter it was, he was sorely disappointed. And he'd thought lipstick would taste like fruit gum. But when he made out with a cheerleader, he'd found out it tasted like soap or something. These things were on his mind as he pondered Danette Quisenberry's mouth.

She was at his side again.

"What can I do you for?"

"I'll take a little coffee," Bobo said. "Cream."

"Make that two," said Mike, thinking he sounded real dapper.

"Right, sweetie," she said.

She left again, calling, "Hiya, Pete."

"You're in love," Bobo said.

"Naw . . . I was just . . . thinking. About lipstick."

"I bet."

Danette's perfume joined them at their table.

She landed a squadron of cups and saucers, creamer and spoons. Mike marveled at her ease. She just did things, said Hi to people, like she didn't even have to worry about it. Bobo could do the same. Like they were comfortable.

"So, Danny darlin'," drawled Bobo, transformed into a faux-Texan by some magic, "what you got goin' here is a double life." He nudged Mike's foot under the table. "Your life's full of intrigue."

"Intrigue!" she said. "You make my life sound like the movies."

Bobo was working on some witty comeback having to do with *pretty as a picture,* but he couldn't get it to sound halfway intelligent in his mind.

"You like movies?" asked Mike. "We're going to a movie right now."

"Not really," she said. "I mean, I don't get out to 'em much. I sneak me a cigarette once in a while, you know." She moved her hips, and they said *you know* too. "But aside from that and maybe sneakin' a little dance here and there, I don't get out much."

"Don't that beat all," crooned Bobo "Tex" García. "Y'all's jest a li'l ol' sinner."

"Oh, you," she said.

Bobo twittered.

Mr. Excitement, thought Mike.

"You eatin', or what?" she said.

Bobo sipped his coffee, leaving the moment up to Mike.

"Ma'am," Mike said, "I'd like a hamburger with cheese melted on it, if I could."

"American?" she said.

"Pardon?" said Mike.

"I'm Mexican," said Bobo.

"Very funny, Pancho. I'm about to bust a gut, I really am." She looked back at Mike. "American, Swiss, cheddar, what?"

"Yellow," said Mike.

Bobo snorted.

What a hick, he thought.

Mike continued: "I'll also have a big pile of french-fried

potatoes with ketchup. And some fried onions. And some pickles if you've got them."

"I've got 'em," she said. She scratched away at her pad. "And you, Montezuma?"

Bobo was actually blushing a little.

"Steak."

"Uh-huh."

"Big. Fry me up the whole side of a cow. And lots of toast."

"That it?"

"Chocolate malt."

"Wow," Danette said. "Big night for you boys."

She took off.

They looked out the window at the deepening bruise of sunset. The few cacti and brittlebushes in the parking-lot glare stood out almost white against the dark. They sipped their coffee. They thought their thoughts.

When their food came, Danette said to Mike, "Push over." Then she sat down beside him. "Man, my feet hurt," she said.

Mike fidgeted, while Bobo tore in.

Danette said, "What's your friend's problem, aside from he's Turk McGurk's boy?"

Mike did a double take.

"Didn't think I knew, did you?" she said.

"No, ma'am."

She nudged him one in the ribs. He was smelling her. "Everybody around here knows about the McGurks." She winked at him. He didn't know if she was insulting him or not.

Bobo cut in: "I'll tell you his problem," gesturing at Mike with his fork. "He's lovesick."

"Do tell," she said. She petted Mike's hand. "Is she a Messkin gal, like Pancho here?" She dipped her hair toward Bobo. He ducked.

"No, ma'am," said Mike. Then wild daring lit him up for a second, and he said, "She's a waitress!"

It took her a minute, but when she got it, she laughed nice and loud.

"Lord," she said. "What these boys won't say."

"Love," said Bobo. He shook his head. "It's the worst."

"Some love is," said Danette.

Mike, around a mouthful of burger, said, "It's causing me nothing but trouble."

"Love," said Bobo. "*All* love."

They stared at him. There was a stunned silence. Danette thought of telling him about God's love, but decided against it: let her life be a witness, not her words. Mike wanted to say, *What about family?* But suddenly realized his whole problem was family—even Lily.

Danette closed her eyes for a moment, her perfect lashes intertwining before her green eyes. Mike stared at them and wondered what she was thinking about. He watched the minute flicker of her eyeballs behind her lids.

"I've had the very thing," she said. "Love's heartache."

She held out her left hand.

A wedding ring!

Damn! both Mike and Bobo thought.

"It's not all picnics and flowers," she said.

She got up and made the rounds, pouring coffee into mugs from a glass pot.

"Didn't you notice?" Bobo demanded.

"What, did you suddenly go blind? I didn't see you noticing."

"Maybe she'll cheat."

"Oh, shut up."

She came back.

"Listen," she said. "This is one of the Foursquare Outpost's greatest hits." She laced her fingers in front of her stomach, closed her eyes, and sang: "When we've been here ten thousand years, / Bright-shining as the sun . . ." The old coots at the counter turned and listened. Her singing voice reminded Mike of honey, what it might sound like if honey could sing. He was surprised at the lump that grew in his throat. Bobo sucked on his straw and peered up at her, looking, Mike thought, about seven years old.

When she finished, a couple of the old men clapped.

She said, "You two probably think I'm crazy. Well, I'm not." She smiled. "Someday you boys will think about God, and you'll remember Danette P. Quisenberry. Maybe it'll help." She picked up their empty plates. "Read your First Corinthians, chapter thirteen."

She leaned over to Mike.

"Honey," she said, "sometimes there's something worser than not finding your true love."

"What's that?" he said.

"Sometimes it's worse if you find 'em."

As she walked away, she touched him once, on the back, with her finger.

21

THEY PULLED AWAY FROM THE FOUR FEATHERS, THEIR aching guts distended with beef and cheese and chocolate. Bobo had tried valiantly to pry Danette from the diner. He wooed her by calling her husband a no-account religious fanatic. He thrilled her with promises of adventure and romance. Her only answer was, "I gave my word." She saw them off with a sad smile. She liked them. How many hundred truckdrivers with love in their hearts had rolled in smelly with miles and offered her a new life? How many hands had fallen across her behind? A woman had a real life to attend to: she had work and her husband and the dogs and Sunday school. She didn't have time for the wild boys with their wild ideas, their eyes all full of feeling and lust. But she would remember these two. She'd remember them along with the rodeo rider who went to Anzio and never came back, and the sweet-talking hotrodder who stalled on the train tracks when the freight was pulling through.

Danette made a silent promise. She arranged a contract with God: She'd put these two new boys on her prayer list and remind Him to keep an eye on them. She'd do it once before breakfast, during her quiet time. And then once more, after lights were out and Darryl had rolled over and started to snore.

All God had to do was to make sure nothing terrible happened to them as they ran around the desert, looking everywhere for love.

❦ ❦ ❦

At the drive-in, they parked the bike sideways and sat in the dirt. Bobo loved the monster so much he begged Mike to sit through the movie one more time. Mike surreptitiously wiped away a tear when James Whitmore was eaten by the giant radioactive ants.

22

At 10:00 p.m., Turk awoke from a nap to a fierce itching under the bandage. He was in the big chair in front of the television. The tube flickered. He couldn't raise his hand.

Bobo dropped Mike off at the foot of the drive.

"Good movies," Mike said.

"That monster is reet," Bobo replied, whatever that meant.

"How 'bout that Danette."

"She's a honey." Bobo nodded. "Maybe we'll see her next week." He pulled away.

"Next week!" Mike called.

Bobo waved once. "See you Monday!"

Mike tromped in.

Turk was sitting in front of the tube. Pale cowboys rode.

"Hey, Pop!" he bellowed.

"Ahh," Turk grunted.

Another one of his moods.

Mike went into the kitchen. About six days' worth of dirty plates formed towers in the sink. Mummified scraps of beef stew clung to the edges of plates; cornflakes seemed shellacked to their bowls. "I'm doin' these dishes!" he called out. No response. "No, no!" he quipped. "Don't get up!" And he laughed.

Turk stared at the television. He could see the cabinet but not the picture, just silvery wet flashes flopping and sticking to the screen. *How strange,* he thought. He couldn't hear it—no static, no music. He could hear Mike as though from the other side of a canyon. He heard a dull *crunch crunch* of blood in his head.

His left hand wouldn't move at all. His right hand flopped in his lap. It fell over on its back and twitched. It looked like an animal.

"Oh, Jesus," he whispered.

He became aware, then, of the left side of his mouth pulling down, a drastic half-frown, his lips dead and cold against his teeth. His tongue felt like it was tipping sideways, too heavy on the left. He had a crazy image of a deflating rubber raft in his mouth.

He stared at his hands, ordered them to rise, to flex, to form fists. Fleeting and painful memories of all the things his hands had done seemed to burn in his palms. They were such stupid things. *The feel of a magazine.* He'd always masturbated with his right hand and wiped his ass with his left, because he'd read that the Arabs kept their eating hand clean. *Shaving brush, straight razor, the sandpaper of the whiskers being cut.* He knew he would never again feel the ridiculous things he enjoyed. *Picking my nose, squeezing off the last pint of gas in a full tank, carving a turkey.* How would he ever hold a fork again?

He began to weep.

The phone rang in the kitchen. Mike grabbed it, dropped it with one soapy hand, caught it, propped it up with his shoulder.

"Yo!" he said.

"Mike."

It was Mr. Sneezy.

"Grandfather," said Mike.

The line was crackly.

"How is the old man?"

"He's okay," said Mike.

"I been worried about him."

"No, he's okay."

"You sure?"

"He's in there watching television," said Mike. "Grouchy as ever."

Mr. Sneezy chuckled.

"Kinda cranky, is he."

"You know Turk!"

There was a pause.

"Want me to get him?" said Mike.

"No, that's all right. Don't bother him."

Another pause.

"You sure he's okay?"

"Last time I looked. He was watching cowboys on there."

"You're sure, now?"

"Yes, sir."

"You call me if anything happens."

"Will do."

"Night, Mike."

"Night."

He hung up, then realized he didn't know Mr. Sneezy's phone number. He didn't know anybody's number—Mr. Sneezy, Gideon, Lily. Bobo. What was the word? They were *incommunicado.*

Turk's hands quivered in his lap. His left foot felt like it was two feet beneath the floor. Turk actually strained to look down and see if the floor had a hole in it. The chair was rolling over slowly—he could feel himself slipping to one side in it. If he tried to stand, he knew his foot would fall down the hole and he'd tumble.

"Mike," he said. "Son."

He hung on to the arms of the chair with his elbows, but it was bucking him out. It was time to move, but he didn't know what to do. Part of his mind was still analyzing the situation: *You never think about trying to get out of the chair without using your hands.* Tears heavy as slugs worked down his right cheek—his left was too numb to feel. He was drooling too. He was pretty embarrassed about that.

"Mike!"

He panicked. Cold spurts went off in his body. There was a nozzle inside him somewhere, and it was spraying jets of ice water through his guts. If it hit his heart, it would stop. His eyes bulged as he strained. He knew he was whimpering, but he couldn't help it. The chair rocked forward. He pitched out on his face.

Mike scrubbed away, dreaming about Lily's mouth and Danette's voice. He was going to get out for good. Here he was mooning around like some kid, and he was a man. Pale nighthawks, like fat gray teardrops, swooped past the window. He could imagine their weird, fluty voices.

"Mike!"

What the hell does he want? Probably a beer.

"Mike!"

Let him get it himself.

"Mike!"

"What!"

Nothing.

"Yes, Dad?" he said. *Better be polite.* "You say something?"

Mike listened: silence.

"Dad?"

He started back in on a pot that was apparently painted with charcoal. He froze. From the living room there came a rising moan. At first, Mike thought for sure that a coyote had gotten into the house. The moan rose into a wail, and Mike realized it was his father. He dropped the pot and ran.

Turk pressed his forehead into the floor.

"Please, God, not now."

It was too late for bargains. He knew that. But still. Maybe the Great Spirit would hear a request.

Mike's boots pounded toward him.

"Dad!"

Mike was vividly and forever aware of the details in the room: Turk lay facedown on the floor, a dark stain was spreading across his trousers, the television screen offered a slowly rolling close-up of young John Wayne moving his lips silently.

"Mike," Turk said, "I'm cold."

Mike turned him over. There was spit all over his face. Mike wiped it off with his shirttail.

"No," he kept saying. "Oh no, Dad."

"Move," said Turk. "Can't."

Mike lifted him away from the floor and held him close. He patted his back.

"Dad. Dad. Dad."

"Sorry," Turk said. "Sorry."

He closed his eyes. He seemed to be listening to something far away.

"Hear it?" he said. "Birds."

Mike couldn't hear a thing.

"I hear it," he lied.

Turk smiled.

"By God," he said. "It's springtime out there."

One of his feet kicked.

"Shh, Dad," Mike said. "Come on now."

Both feet started to kick.

"Hurry!" Turk said.

Mike rocked him. He reached behind him and pulled the Navajo blanket off the couch and wrapped his father in it. "Here, Dad," he said. "That better?"

Turk's teeth were chattering.

His feet stilled.

"Did you hear them?" he asked.

"I sure did."

"Meadowlarks, maybe? Bluebirds?"

Mike held him tight.

"Look in the corner," Turk said.

Mike looked. It was empty.

"Look at those dark men," Turk said.

Mike was starting to cry. The first tears hit Turk on the forehead.

"I'm ready for you, you sons of bitches," Turk said.

"Don't go," Mike said.

"Make way, boys. I'm coming through."

"Don't go."

"Blue men, Mike. Dark blue men."

Turk sighed. His body calmed, going limp so suddenly that he slipped out of Mike's grasp.

"Mike?"

Mike leaned down to his father.

Turk said, "The old gray mare, she ain't what she used to be."

He laughed a little.

"Oh, gee," he said.

He reached up and touched Mike's cheek.

"Son," he said.

His head turned to the side, and spit slid out of his mouth.

Turk was dead.

23

IT TOOK TWO HOURS FOR A WAGON TO GET THERE. MIKE had called the highway patrol office and roused a sleepy cop. "Yup," the cop said to every detail. "Yup, yup, yu-up." Mike imagined his voice running across the desert, stretched out thin within the wire, passing through the claws of sleeping ravens.

Turk had lain, cooling, beneath the blanket.

"Age?" the cop had said.

"Don't know."

"Gimme a guess."

"He was getting there."

"Yup."

"Sixty?"

"Yup."

A couple more hazy questions, then the cop said, "Look, Mr. McGurt, be a wagon out there soon's we can get one. You hang in there, hear?"

"Yessir," said Mike.

"Just take her easy, right? These things happen, right? My old man died in the toilet. Think about it."

"Yessir."

"You'll be okay. Right?"

"Right."

"Yup."

Mike sat staring at the body under the blanket. Turk looked like a rolled-up old rug.

When the ambulance crew came in, they did so quietly, looking out the corners of their eyes at Mike. They called Turk "the deceased." Mike knew they were secretly thinking of Turk as "the stiff."

Turk went on a padded plank that they slid onto a set of folding legs on wheels.

"We use the blanket?" one of them said.

"Sure."

They wheeled Turk out through the station. His head bounced at each bump in the floor, as if he was nodding in recognition: yes, there's Connie's kitchen table, there's my favorite chair, there's the nudist calendar.

"Careful!" Mike said.

"No prob," said the attendant.

They wheeled Turk out to their rig. It was a fat Cadillac with a cityscape of lights and sirens on its roof. He would have hated it. The desert was utterly black. The stars were pale as powdered sugar up there. The men slammed the cart into the open maw of the Cadillac; its legs folded against the bumper, and they slid Turk in.

Mike made himself stand still, not jump them and slam their heads against the bumper. He stood still and let the jolt of frantic ice pass through him.

The door had a good solid sound when they slammed it shut. The driver flipped Mike a loose little salute. He was chewing Juicy Fruit gum. The attendant shook his hand, saying, "Where to?"

Mike hadn't thought about it.

"Santucci's Funeral Home . . . I guess."

Santucci was one of Turk's fighting fans.

"It's done, partner," said the man.

The ambulance rolled onto the road. Mike watched the taillights, visible long after the sound of the engine had died. They were two crazy eyes receding, rising up a small incline, winking out.

Mike's hands hung limp at his sides.

The wind pressed itself into his palms, cool and round. He imagined Lily's breasts. He put his hands in his pockets. He thought of the smell of Danette Quisenberry, the smell of Lily's armpits in the sand, the smell of the silk stockings under his bed. He tried to think of a prayer for his father, but he didn't know any. He didn't know if there was a prayer fit for Turk.

Beyond the hills, the moon was preparing to rise. It gave the highest peaks a gauzy halo. It looked, Mike thought, like Turk's spirit, lighting up.

"Good-bye, Father," he said.

24

That weekend, time seemed to melt into smooth waves of light and dark, heat and chill, endless whisper of sand blowing across the walls, cars pulling in, idling at the pumps, honking. Their drivers either gave up and braved the road with no gas or stole a tankful. Tumbleweeds got caught behind the soda machine and trembled, like eager animals, before being freed again by the wind. Long after they'd dropped all their seeds, become lifeless rattling husks, they continued their journeys: Safford, Tucumcari, Amarillo. Impossible distances, breaking down smaller and smaller as they rolled. Dead twigs from here to Oklahoma.

part two

parts unknown

25

MIKE COULDN'T TELL WHAT DAY IT WAS. WAS IT SATURDAY or Sunday? Or was it Monday, and had Bobo not shown up for work? He licked the last drop off the mouth of the empty bottle and threw the bottle on the couch. One thing was certain: he wasn't sitting around this station for one more minute!

He marched outside and placed a cardboard sign on the pumps: FREE GAS—HELP YOURSELF.

He stomped back inside and threw his GI knapsack on the kitchen table. BVDs went in, along with a pair of socks. The last bottle of beer. The silk stockings. Turk's immense Bowie knife. He added a jar of peanuts, a Hershey bar, a bottle of cheap whiskey, a compass. "Oh, sure," he said, "leave the stinking station to me, why don't you." A fork looked like a good thing to pack. "As if I've got nothing better to do than piss away my life around here!" A dictionary. Stephen Crane. Beef jerky. He threw in his fossils, for good measure. "The world's only six thousand years old, he says. Well, *explain these.*"

He jammed his L-shaped green army flashlight in his belt, kicked open the door, and walked west, into the spreading dark.

"Leff! Leff! Leff-rye-leff!" He marched to the Burton Thibedaux cadence, his ridiculous pace carrying him far into the desert.

"I got a gal I call her sugar! Leff-rye-leff! Picks her nose and eats her boogers! Leff-rye-leff!

"Comp'ny, halt!" He jerked to a stop. "Present *harms!*" He pulled down his zipper. "Fire!"

He had an eerie sense, the drunker and farther he got, of the phantom sea towering above him. Columns of ghost water rose for miles. Paltry clouds were transformed into vast swimming reptiles. He waved the whiskey bottle in his fist. "Come get me, you sons of bitches!" He whipped up his flashlight and shot a beam at a passing plesiosaur.

His stomach hurt. He flashed his light back and forth, catching these things in its tube of brightness: barrel cacti, a kangaroo rat hightailing it for the east, quartz chunks, a dark-rusted can shot full of bullet holes. He tapped the can with his toe. A scorpion charged out, threatening to fix Mike's wagon. Mike backed off. He switched off the light. He fancied the dark made a sound as it closed around him. He stood listening.

The dark bulk of a saguaro made itself felt. It was a black cutout against the stars. He stared up at it: thirty-five feet of occult arms and spines, strange shapes lifting gallons of dew out of the sands. *This is what God looks like.*

"Definitely."

Mike undid his zipper to unload some more used beer. The stream spattered on the ground around the cactus. "Live it up," he said. He gave it with great love; the saguaro would store it for the hot season. When he was done, Mike said, "Amen."

He had picked up a companion. For at least a quarter mile, as he'd trudged along, parting the imaginary waves, he'd been harassed. Some small thing zoomed in and, with a cheerful growl, nipped at his pant leg in the dark. He'd kicked at it and missed. "Get lost!" he'd snapped.

He could hear the happy little bastard scampering away and rattling a bush. It yipped, jumping around, daring him to chase it.

"Vamoose!" Mike yelled. "Am-scray, utthole-bay!"

It leaped onto his ankle and wrestled with his cuff.

He listened to it dance away, going, *Yip, yippee!*

"All right," he said. He got the flashlight out of his pants. "Show yourself, you coward."

The light revealed two red flecks reflecting back at him. Big ears. Pointy little tan face. Wide grin.

"Kit fox," said Mike.

Its ears pricked.

Mike sat down in the dirt.

It hunkered down and hung out its little tongue.

It was about the size of a small cat.

"What are you so happy about?" Mike said.

It sprang sideways, running at an angle with its tail fluffed and curling to its side. It frolicked. It played hopscotch in a circle around Mike.

"Okay," Mike said, digging in his backpack. He came up with the compass, stared at it, threw it away. The kit fox dove after it and scrambled around in the dust with it. "No, no," said Mike. He found the beef jerky. "Try this."

He tossed a thin plank of it at the fox, and the fox, suddenly suspicious, sniffed at it while cutting its eyes at Mike to see what he was up to. He got out the bottle and took a swig. The fox grabbed the jerky, shook it once to break its neck, then held it down with its paws while it gnawed away.

Behind Mike, the moon began its rise.

Three miles farther on, Mike stopped to look up at the stars. He tipped back his head, and the ground hit him in the back. He opened his mouth, but only steam came out. He closed his eyes. He didn't dream.

Sniff.

Sniff sniff.

Sniffsniffsniffsniff.

"Away," Mike said.

A delicate scramble, then a cold nose probed his face.

Sniff.

"Damned fox! Trying to sleep here!"

The nose connected again, a wet exclamation.

"Hey!" he said. Then he lay still. A smell came to him. He sniffed it. Strong. Tart. Oddly friendly while nose-twisting. Definite skunk in the air.

He cracked an eye. In the moonlight, he saw a black face with a white Mohawk on its forehead.

"How ya doin'?" he said.

The skunk leaped away, startled. Mike sat up, grabbed his flashlight, and shone a beam at the skunk. Or skunks. It was a big mother skunk with six litttle ones. "Oh," Mike said.

The mother stomped her feet at him in warning, then raised her tail and shook her head. She even sneezed. Just keeping Mike in line.

"No problem," Mike said.

He felt around inside his knapsack and came up with the Hershey bar.

"Yum!" he said to her.

She watched his unwrap it.

"Oh boy!" he said, breaking off a chunk of chocolate and tossing it to her. She stomped her front feet at it, tail raised straight in the air. Then she sniffed it. Being no fool, the skunk settled down to eat the candy. Mike could hear her small jaws working through the chocolate.

Together, the skunks and Mike went through his candy and beef jerky. When they were through, he got up, brushed off his hands, and headed west again. Before he walked away, he left a black arrow made of trilobites, for other ghosts to follow.

26

HOW MANY HOURS IN A NIGHT? MIKE HAD SPENT A hundred hours walking; still, no sign of dawn. The over-inflated moon rolled over the horizon on its way to Hawaii, Japan, China, Mongolia, Persia, Egypt, Greece, England, Greenland, the Empire of New York. All places the child Mike had visited among the pages of his mother's atlas. Down an arroyo, repeatedly sliding backward on the rocky slope, Mike was half listening for the rush of the waters. The ocean was coming back, would refill the Chihuahuan desert, the Sonoran, the Great Basin, the Anza Borrego, the Mojave. Ship Rock in Navajoland would be a pointy island covered in guano. It would look like a glacier. Wavelets would lap at the edges of Flagstaff, Morenci, the West Mesa of Albuquerque, Santa Fe. Glen Canyon would fill, the Grand Canyon, Canyon de Chelly. The ocean was going to roll all the way up the Colorado in a foaming brown wave until it took out Grand Junction. Meteor Crater would be a perfect round bay. He hit the bottle and fished fossils from his bag.

He threw them out, giving them back to the desert, seeing in them seeds of future dinosaurs, drowsing until the saltwater flood kicked off germination. He sailed a nautilus disk, a trio of triangular sharks' teeth, flowery crinoids and audacious bivalves. He unloaded the stony seeds of a million years, divested of history.

Then he powered up and out of the arroyo and tripped on a

lax strand of barbed wire. He had come upon a fallen fence. Ghost cowboys clopped all around him. "You boys seen Turk?" he called.

Sixteen fence posts down, he stood, silent, the flashlight weak now, its beam yellow. A hollowed-out cow mummy leaned into the fence and stared back at him. It was partially wrapped in wire. Mike could not believe his eyes. He circled it, smelling its scent of old shoes. Its stark eyeholes regarded him. He lifted his bottle in toast, swallowed the last of the whiskey, and broke the bottle on a rock.

"To life!" is what he said.

27

TURK, DURING A STATIC-FUZZED BASEBALL GAME ON THE television, the Giants ahead by three in the seventh, Grandfather Sneezy sipping a soda and Turk on his fifth beer, Mike munching the cookies that Mr. Sneezy had brought:

"So this Englishwoman goes to the ball game."

Sneezy: "Where at?"

"What do you mean, where at?"

Sneezy: "What field? She at Wrigley? Candlestick Park? What?"

"Who the hell cares what field! I'm telling a joke here."

Sneezy: "How can I get the joke if I don't know where the story happened?"

"Okay! Yankee Stadium!"

Sneezy: "What teams are playing?"

"It's a joke, for Christ's sake!"

Sneezy: "Got to know the teams, McGurk. What's the use without knowing the teams?"

"Yankees versus . . . the Dodgers."

Sneezy: "I doubt it."

"Just for the sake of argument, all right?"

Sneezy: "Well, I don't like it. I don't think I'll get the joke, most likely."

"This English girl goes to the game, got it? It's her first baseball game."

Sneezy: "They don't have baseball in England?"

"Hell no, they don't have baseball in England. It's England! Now pay attention, Sneezy. This is funny.

"She's sitting there watching the game with her American friends, and she's figuring it out as it goes. You know, what's a run, what's a strike, things like that."

Sneezy: "What inning?"

Turk slams his bottle down.

"Fifth, fifth inning, the bottom of the goddamned *fifth* inning! No! Don't ask! The Yankees are ahead by two!"

Sneezy: "Hmph."

"So the batter gets up—DiMaggio, all right? He's up at the plate, and the pitcher throws a ball. The pitcher throws another ball. The batter gets one strike. The pitcher throws a third ball."

Sneezy: "Not much of a pitcher."

"Listen! So he winds up for another pitch—"

Sneezy: "Is he a southpaw, or what?"

"Right—handed—pitcher!"

Sneezy: "So what's his problem? He throwing high and outside?"

" . . . Right, Sneezy. Anything you say. Now may I tell this joke, or will you spend the rest of the night interrupting?"

Sneezy: "Jeez, if you're going to be that way about it, go ahead and hog the whole night for yourself. Mike and I will just turn off the TV and listen to you talk."

"Sneezy, look . . . he winds up and fires one off—and he walks DiMaggio. DiMag' heads down the baseline to first base, right?"

Sneezy: "That ain't funny."

"I'm not done. Will you—Okay. He's walking, see. And up in the stands, the English girl turns to her host and says, 'Why is that man walking and not running?'

"Her friend says, 'Why, he has four balls.'

"She jumps up and yells, 'Walk with pride, young man! Walk with pride!'"

Turk laughs for about two solid minutes.

Sneezy: "I don't get it."

28

DOWN AT THE FAR END OF THE LONG RAVINE WHERE HE found himself, Mike could see a glow. A red-orange light splashed the dirt walls, vague as a moonshadow. But he'd been in the dark so long he could see it quite clearly. It pulsed like a heartbeat. He moved toward it. Muffled laughter and honky-tonkin' came at him from across the desert.

He crept to the edge of the dirt cliff where the ravine cut out a wide wedge and peered down: recon. Way out there, on a platform of flood-washed sand that opened like a fan across the hardpan, stood a small cinder-block saloon. It was all by itself, not even a paved road for company, blinking in the middle of a gravel lot. Trucks and motorcycles and three horses stood around outside. He could see that at least two of the trucks were up on blocks and had weeds coming out the windows.

He climbed down.

As he got closer, he recognized the sound of Bob Wills on the juke. He got far enough around the front to see the sign. It said "Chikisin" in flyspecked neon: CHI-KI-SIN-SIN-SIN. Mike knew it as old Apache for "brother." An Apache joint. He plugged his hands into his pockets and forged ahead.

There was an audible dip in the noise level when Mike walked in. He was still drunk, but not so drunk he didn't notice the shock wave. He was the only white in the building. Nobody even looked at him, yet he knew he was being watched. He felt against his chest a tender wave of resentment that tried to push him back out the door.

He could hear the clack of pool balls coming from the back room. Mexican voices disputed loudly: "Uy-uy-yuy! This vato thinks he's el mero chingón!" He bucked up and walked as steadily as possible to the battered tin bar and drummed his fingers. He addressed the short woman behind the bar, who regarded him with angry-looking eyes.

"Good evening, ma'am," he said.

She nodded.

"What do you have that's cold?"

Somebody behind him said something in Apache. To Mike, it sounded like "Huh-ho-ha."

She grinned.

"Any old thing will do," Mike said. "I've walked up a thirst."

She turned and flipped open the lid of a floor cooler. There was a sign hand-lettered on cardboard and taped to the inside of the cooler lid. It said: BEER, SODA, ROOT BEER, ESKIMO PIE, SUN TEA (ICE).

Mike peeked in, over the counter.

"Is that an ice cream sandwich? I love ice cream sandwiches."

She flopped the soggy sandwich on the counter. Digging some coins out of his pockets, he handed them to her. He rotated and zeroed in on a corner table and strode through the room, holding his prize aloft. The silver foil, in his mind, was suddenly transformed into a medal of honor. *Me and the Indians,* he thought sentimentally.

He dropped his rucksack on the wet rings on the small round table. He hit the chair hard and hung his feet out before him and leaned back. After a short pause, the noise level around him rose anew. The juke clicked, whirred, and a scratchy record came on. Mike unwrapped the ice cream sandwich. He recognized Bob Wills and the Texas Playboys again. They were singing "Roly Poly." Mike focused on the improbably large Indian shuffling in front of the Wurlitzer, singing along: "Roly Poly—eatin' corn and taters—hungry every minute of the day!"

Oh my God.

"Roly Poly—gnawin' on a biscuit—long as he can chew it, it's okay!"

It's him.

"He can eat an apple pie—never even bat an eye—he likes everything from soup to hay!"

Mike took in the rattlesnake-thick braid hanging down the broad back, so black it shone like oil.

Ramses Castro, in the flesh.

Mike slurped the vanilla ice cream out from between the drooping chocolate cookies, wadding the foil into a tight ball in his fist. He drew a sly bead on Castro, aiming down the side of the sandwich. Where was his knife?

He dug in the pack, looking for it. *Ramses Castro, eh? We'll see about that!* He pulled out a small can and stared at it. It said "Texaco Home Lubricant." Little white houses stood against a red sky, their tiny oily windows lit. The can had a long, graceful spout. Thin letters beneath the house said "The Texas Company." He sniffed the can. It smelled of Lionel electric trains, sewing machines. He stared at the little houses.

"Smell good?"

He looked up. Castro stood across the table, gazing down at him with bleary eyes. Mike was fascinated by Castro's eyes, bloodshot solid.

Castro said, "I don't know, you know? The smell of that chemical stuff chokes up my nose."

He wrinkled his nose, shook his head.

"Wait a minute," Mike said. "Don't go away. I got something here for you." He plunged his hand in the bag, came up with a fork. "Hang on," he said.

Castro hummed along with a Patsy Cline record someone had snuck on behind his back—he'd listened to "Roly Poly" ten times in a row. He swiveled back and forth slowly, thumbs hooked into his jeans pockets. He wore a heavy bracelet on one wrist.

"You ever seen Mount Rushmore?" Castro said. "*I* seen Mount Rushmore."

"Congratulations," said Mike, focusing on the contents of the pack.

Castro said, "I didn't see no Geronimo on Mount Rushmore, you know it? Why didn't they put Geronimo up there, and Crazy Horse?"

"How about Tonto?" said Mike.

"That's cute," said Castro. "You guys have always been so fucking cute." Castro slapped his chest. "You're talking about *my* presidents! *My* popes! *My* heroes!"

Hope I didn't drop it back there with the skunks.

He had a point there.

However—

"Turk died," Mike said.

Castro nodded.

"I heard about that. Word's been goin' around."

He watched Mike.

"What you lookin' for?" he said.

Mike's hand clenched on the carved elk-horn handle. He grinned. He yanked the knife out of the sack.

"This," he said.

Its eight-inch blade hung in the air between them like a bomb. They both stared at it.

"Oh," Castro said. "That."

He nodded as if it were all clear to him. He reached back, pulled a hunting knife out of the back of his belt, and laid it on the table.

"Here, use mine. It's sharper."

Mike, a little confused, said, "Thanks."

"Your old man," Castro said. "He knew what he was doin'. It's the way of the warrior."

"You're full of shit."

"You gonna use that on me?" Castro asked, nodding toward the knife.

"I mean to. Real soon."

"All right."

Castro turned to the room and announced, "Me and him's got a feud. We're gonna fight, but not right now. Later. So nobody beat him up, 'cause I'mo kill him myself."

People all around said, "Huh-ho-ha."

"Okay, Mike, you're safe now. Enjoy that ice cream."

"Safe from what?" Mike demanded, insanely brave for three-sixteenths of a second.

"No offense, McGurk, but me and the People don't want you here." He said it not unpleasantly. "Look at these faces. These here are Navajo and 'Pache faces. No white man comes in here. Why'd you come in here?"

"I was lost."

Castro snorted. "Lost! Whole fucking white race is lost!"

He shook his head. "Shit," he said.

Mike looked around. For the first time, people were smiling at him.

"You know," Castro said, "it's good to have an enemy. I think you need an enemy."

Castro hung his head and thought for a minute.

"You know what I really hate about the white man, Mike?" he said. "You guys blow your noses in a rag—and then you look at it!"

He turned away.

"Your ice cream's melted."

29

Despite what Mike may have imagined, an ice cream sandwich does not, perforce, soak up all the alcohol in your gut and make you sober. The floor surged and dropped beneath his seat. He watched the bar make queasy circuits of the earth, Castro somehow still standing, plugging nickels into the juke.

The woman barkeep came over and wiped down his table.

"I hate it when Castro plays that danged song," she said.

Mike watched her as she went from table to table. She muttered to the guys at the next table. They all looked over at Mike and smiled, raising their glasses to him. Then they laughed at him.

Bladder pressure.

"Roly Poly," Castro sang, "Daddy's little fatty!"

Mike grabbed his home lubricant can and Turk's knife, lurched to his feet, and focused on the door of the men's room. He tooled across the room, only inadvertently waving the blade of the knife under people's chins. The juke, the mysterious Apache language, the pachuco Spanish, the click of pool balls, the clanking glasses, had risen in volume and begun to reverberate.

The sudden silence of the toilet startled him. He set the can and the knife on the edge of the sink and stared at himself in the mirror. "You look like you just crossed a desert on foot," he informed himself. Then he barked once at his own wit.

He bent down and ran cold water over his palms. He brought it slowly to his face, imagining he looked like he was praying or something. He could feel grease under his skin: he was sliding around on his own bones. He cupped his hands. He poured water over his head. He shook water out of his eyes and looked in the mirror. Castro was standing behind him.

"Hey," Mike said.

"Hey," said Castro.

He pushed past Mike and went into the stall, slamming the door. Mike stepped up to the urinal, laying his forehead against the cool tiles of the wall.

Castro said, "Wanna hear a joke Grampa showed me?"

"Yeah," said Mike.

"Why was six scared of seven?"

"I don't know," Mike said. "Why?"

"Because it eight nine and ten."

Ate nine and ten! Mike thought, and laughed out loud.

Castro crashed out of the stall and hit him from behind. His shoulder slammed into Mike's back and splashed Mike against the tile. He ricocheted off and fell to the floor, kicking Castro in the ear as he fell. Castro shook his head. Then he picked Mike up by the shirtfront and heaved him into the mirror. It shattered and accompanied Mike to the floor in a cascade of glass. Castro stood wide-legged, like some mad bear. Mike swam between his feet and threw a kick into the back of his left knee. Castro fell over backward, his head hitting the floor with a grisly *conk.* It sounded like two coconuts crashing.

"Uhf!" Castro said.

Mike wiped blood from behind his ear. A glitter of mirror backing and powdered glass came away on his finger. He stared at it.

Castro rolled over and got to his knees. Mike kicked him on the point of the chin; his teeth clacked loudly. Castro shook it off. His huge fist rose, aimed, fell. Mike slipped sideways, and the punch missed his face, smashing a wedge of wood shaped like the Matterhorn out of the stall door.

Mike scrambled away on his back.

Castro got hold of the knife and stood.

"Oh," said Mike. Every part of his body hurt.

Castro smiled down at him. He put out his tongue and licked the blade. "Mmm!" he said.

Mike was starting to suspect he'd made a serious error in judgment.

"Let's call it a draw," he said.

Castro shook his head.

His immense engineer's boot came down on Mike's chest and pressed. What little air he had came squeaking out.

"I win," Castro said.

Mike locked his hands around Castro's boot and attempted to twist it. It was like trying to pull a tree out of the ground. Castro swung the knife lazily past Mike's bulging eyes.

"Whoosh," he said.

Mike's vision was darkening. He couldn't see at the edges of his vision, so when the bathroom door opened, he could just barely hear it, but he saw nothing.

Castro didn't turn around. He said, "Get lost."

A shiny pair of double-soled zoot-suit shoes came out of the blur and stopped near Mike's face. Mike focused on their sheen.

"Help," he rasped.

"What are you doing, Ramses?" said the man.

"I'm killing this guy."

"Ah-ha."

The man bent down. Mike stared up. It was Bobo.

"Shit—Mike," Bobo noted.

Mike whispered, "I would like to apologize for any imagined or real insult to Castro or the Apache people. . . ."

Castro pushed with his boot.

"Hush up, butt-wipe." He turned to Bobo. "I'mo kill him."

"Come on, Ramses. His father's dead."

"I know *that,*" Castro said, impatient. "He's looking for trouble."

"He's in mourning. He's upset. Let him up."

"I'mo kill him."

"I can't let you do that," Bobo surprised himself by saying.

Castro gawked at him.

"Why not?"

Bobo shrugged.

"I'm not sure. But I can't."

Castro thought about it.

"All right, then," he said. "You get the hell out of here and let me finish him up, then I'll come out and kill you too."

Bobo sighed.

"Right," he said.

His left hand chopped the knife out of Castro's grip. His right elbow hit Castro in the sternum: Castro blew a spray like Moby Dick. His foot rose from Mike's chest as he tried to pump air into himself. Bobo seemed to bow, and his arm whipped around Castro's neck. They spun in a half circle, and Bobo launched Castro, upside down, out the bathroom door. He exploded through in a burst of splinters and landed spectacularly among the tables.

With a delicate pinch, Bobo straightened out the crease in his trousers.

"I learned that one from Dick the Bruiser," he said.

30

THEIR ESCAPE FROM THE BAR WAS ACCOMPLISHED ONLY through dicey negotiations between Bobo and an ad hoc committee of outraged Native Americans. Throughout the debate, Mike drunkenly waved his little oil can around, offering to lubricate them all. "Come on, buddy," he said to one man. "Jest bend over and let me pop this nozzle up your ass, and you'll be good as new!" Once Bobo had backed Mike away from them to his motorcycle, he suspected the Apaches had allowed Mike to live only because they thought he was insane.

He shoveled Mike into the sidecar. Mike had become a bundle of about seven arms and thirteen legs, all of them four feet long and double-jointed. Mike dropped his head and snored as Bobo started up and swung around and out of the lot.

Bobo wasn't sure where to go. He steered with one hand and reached over to drag Mike upright when he threatened to topple out of the sidecar. The wind was as sharp and cold as needles made of ice. Dawn was pushing up the far edges of the sky.

He topped a long rise and looked down the perfectly straight road that sliced open the valley where Turk's dead Texaco lay. Mike leaned out and vomited. "Hey!" Bobo yelled. "Watch the paint!"

The steady *brat-brat-brat* of the idling motorcycle filled the air around them and radiated. Bobo got that feeling again—he was the only one awake in a sleeping world. An empty world.

He was sending his signal, and it went out for miles and miles, over sand and rock, through dark cities, unheard.

"You done?" he said, dragging Mike upright.

They sat on the motorcycle and watched the red light seep across the desert. "And now I'm saving white boys," Bobo said, shaking his head. As soon as the blue wedge of shadow pulled off Turk's Texaco, they wheeled slowly down the grade, morning's scent filling Mike's clothes like Lily's perfume.

31

Bobo dragged Mike in and tossed him down on Turk's bed. "You all right?" he said. "Ummf," Mike replied. Bobo turned on the fan and pointed it at Mike. "I'll make coffee," he said.

"I don't know how to reach my uncle," Mike said. He closed his eyes. He dreamed. He and Turk and his mother were all together, bowling. They rolled and rolled the balls, but never scored a point because the balls were made of ice and the pins were burning. Every ball melted as it rolled. "I'll get it next time," his mother said. She put her hand on his cheek. It was wet and cold from the ice. Turk lit a cigar, looked up at Mike from the score sheet, and called him "Ignatz."

Bobo went through the place. He found the small kitchen and dug a blue-flecked old tin coffeepot out of a cabinet. "Sheesh," he said. "These vatos are cowboys around here." There was a huge red can of grounds in the freezer. Bobo didn't get it; he shrugged and threw a bunch of the grounds in the little percolator basket and poured in water and started the burner. They got gas from a big silver tank outside, and Bobo had to light the stove with a match. Well, it was better than where he was staying. He'd been on the couch of Rigoberto "Mula" Archuleta, former soldier and jailbird, for three weeks.

Archuleta and Bobo made believe they were having fun, drinking the cheapest beer they could find, living off the pickings of three stolen cars sold to the cops in Agua Prieta. A seemingly endless rumba line of Archuleta's pachuca lady friends paraded through the house—all dressed in vampire black, with massive arrays of hair in alarming explosions that half filled the room, and radiating perfume mixes that stuck in the couch for days afterward. La Mousy, La Lu-Lu, La Koo-Koo, La Wall-Eyes and her sister, La Li'l Wino. La Vieja Bear, La Ronni Milpas, La Hootchie, La Ten-Speed Cayetana and her cousin, three-hundred-pound La Flaquita de Tucson, all made their appearance.

El Sixguns was Mula's best friend. He weighed maybe one forty with fifty dollars in change in his pockets. El Six had blue tears tattooed down one cheek, and he drove a '32 Ford, chopped and channeled, that he called "La Mari" after marijuana, which he ran across the border south of Tucson and sold to beatniks and musicians and chukos and weesas. His friends lurked in the shadows, longing to steal things from Bobo but forced to respect him because of the wrestling. They called him "Borneo." A few of them wouldn't have minded trying to beat him up, but everybody was afraid of him.

They were: El Chingas Romero, El Pocho Astenga, El Dreamy, Wacha-Wacha Valdez, and R. "El Chino Cochino" Bong.

Bobo sat there and laughed with them, rutted with their aromatic women, whistled at their various pathetic guns, knives, chains, scars, tattoos. And he hated them all. He itched inside his own skin. At night, he dreamed of bodies in the snow—towers of bodies. In his dreams, he could still smell his uniform, the wet-sheep odor of the scratchy wool fabric in the icy drizzle as he stared at the tractors moving the bodies.

The pachucos told their tales, and he slid his hand up the hard-packed thighs of La Flaquita and thought: *Idiots.*

On certain mornings, he was sure the walls had folded in upon him like the dusty wings of some huge moth, choking him.

Once, he screamed, and El Mula burst into the room with a rusty .22 in his fist.

The only way Bobo saved any dignity was by pulling his pillow over his head and making believe he was asleep.

❦ ❦ ❦

He sat at the table and looked around. He listened to the coffee start to boil. He wiped his hands on his pants. Memories always made his palms sweat.

Mike rolled off the bed and felt his way to the shower. He removed his clothes and stared at the huge bruise on his side. It looked like South America in purple and black. The beaches along the coasts were yellow. His lower lip was swollen.

He turned on the water and sank to the metal floor of the stall. Pulling his washcloth over his head, he pretended he was in a tent in a storm in the Maine woods. He held up the edge of the cloth and peeked out at the drops falling past his nose. The water droplets hit his head like a Gene Krupa drum solo. When he put his fingers in his ears, the sound in his skull became horses stampeding over hard ground.

Bobo drummed his fingers on the table. He looked in the bread box: one crusty-looking cinnamon bun. He took a bite. Shrugged one shoulder. Tossed it back in.

"Babalu!" he sang. "*Baa*-ba-luu!"

Mike crawled out of the shower and dried himself slowly, sort of, leaving running patches of water all over his back and legs.

"Babalu, a-ye! Babalu!"

Mike appeared, naked, in the doorway. "The noise," he said, "must go."

Bobo, deeply offended, cried, "Cover up your dick!"

Mike pulled one of Turk's oily Texaco caps off a peg and covered himself.

"What does it all add up to?" he asked, fully surrendering to post-fight philosophical self-pity.

Bobo shrugged.

"Castro says I'm lost," said Mike.

"Yeah," said Bobo. How the hell was he supposed to figure out the meaning of life for an Okie redneck white boy? "How 'bout that," he said, suddenly sounding alarmingly like his own father. He got down a skillet and lit another burner, scooped some lard into the pan, melted it, started cracking six eggs.

"Them Indians, boy," he said. "They got a spiritual outlook." A bubble of grease spattered onto his hand. He skipped away, shouting, *"Chingado!"*

He looked over at Mike. It was about the most preposterous sight on earth: Mike standing there with his hair poking up off his head and a filthy red cap over his privates. Bobo smiled.

"What?" said Mike.

Bobo chuckled.

"What?" said Mike.

Bobo turned away, then laughed out loud.

"What's the deal?" said Mike.

"I think maybe Castro's right," Bobo said, flipping the eggs.

Mike stared at the eggs.

Bobo snickered.

"Okay, fine," Mike said. "Everybody thinks I'm a mess. Thanks for the information. And by the way, kiss my ass."

He sat down.

Bobo turned around and dug some old bacon out of the icebox. He sniffed it, peeled off a few strips, and dropped them in the grease.

"What's the big problem?" Mike asked.

"You askin' *me?*" Bobo said.

"Yeah."

"*I* ain't got a problem."

"Just asking your opinion."

"You askin' a *Messkin* what to do with your life?"

"That's who I'm asking."

Bobo pinched his chin and thought.

"That's a new one," he said.

Mike looked up at him expectantly.

"As a friend," he said, "tell me what you think."

"Friend," said Bobo.

"Right. You're my best buddy."

"I'm your *only* buddy."

"That makes you the best one."

Bobo wanted to ask someone how he'd gotten into this anyway.

"Ask me no questions, I'll tell you no lies," he said, as a stalling action. He slid eggs and bacon onto two plates and set them on the table. Mike just stared at the food, his gut free-floating up through his body. Bobo sat down and drenched his eggs in Tabasco. Before digging in, he peered at Mike and said, "First thing you can do is put on some clothes, ese. Any of my boys come by for gas and see me in here with you naked—*shit*."

Mike got up, turned around, slid the cap over the crack in his ass, and walked back down the hall. His rear, peeking around the cap, looked like two bowls of vanilla pudding.

Bobo said, "*I* ain't got a problem. *You* got the problem. And he's dead."

Mike pulled on his pants.

"Hallelujah," he said. "It's a goddamned brand-new morning."

Bobo moved through the food steadily, never lifting his head.

"Something like that," he said.

They ate in silence. Mike was sure Bobo could hear the blood-rush in his head. How could Bobo eat with all this bloody crunching going on? But Bobo was still thinking of Turk.

"Yo, Mike," he said.

"Hmm?"

"You havin' a funeral?"

"Sure."

"When is it?"

"What day is this?"

"Tuesday."

"No way."

"It's Tuesday."

"It's not Monday?"

"Tuesday, all day."

Mike just looked at him. The color slowly faded from his face. Bobo watched a film cover Mike's eyes, then fill them.

"It's today, isn't it?" said Bobo.

Mike nodded.

"I think we might be late."

Bobo glanced up at the clock.

"Mike—it's only eight."

Mike suddenly realized he didn't have any fancy clothes. He felt exposed. He felt incapable of movement.

"Bobo?" he said, "Would you go?"

"No problem," Bobo said. "I'm ready."

He wiped his mouth.

"Hell, yeah. Let's do it."

32

TURK COULDN'T BE IDENTIFIED AS AN ADHERENT OF ANY major religious faith. Pete Santucci, director of the funeral home, and a longtime supporter of Turk's, listed "Sun Worship" on the form. Santucci, *the* Santucci of Santucci's Funereal (*sic*) Home and Eternal Rest Chapel, had laid odds on Castro and won big at Turk's terminal fight. He was so remorseful about his good luck that he was doing the burial for free, donating hearse, "funereal," and embalming to Mike. The coffin he discounted 25 percent.

Red and the ol' boys had also pitched in, buying Turk a wreath and taking up a collection to replace Santucci's wife, Flora, on the organ. They hired Danette Quisenberry and slipped her an extra five to play some Hank Williams and make it sound like a hymn. All of them were trying to buy off their sense that they had somehow helped Castro kill Turk. Behind every face in the room, a Wanted poster hung, and it said GUILTY.

About twenty of them had gathered in there. Gradually strangled by unaccustomed neckties, they shuffled around and sat glumly, working their big-knuckled hands between their knees. Santucci himself had waxed and buffed Turk's head: it shone like an apple under the lights. (Santucci had rigged a spotlight above the coffin. It had a color disk slowly rotating before it, casting washes of blue—green—red light over Turk's face. "It's that extra touch," Santucci had confided to Flora, "which we don't got to strictly do, but we do, 'cause we care that deep." Flora, patting Santucci's arm, had replied, "It's a family thing, Pete, that much love." Pete had swelled up a little and said, with great thoughtfulness, "Well." The lights rendered Turk alternately ghastly—putrid—hellish in slow, stately progression.)

Snatches of conversations could be heard over Danette's melancholy noodling. Everything was murmured with heads bent, as if in prayer. "That shitpoke truck of mine's about shot, and now Turk done kicked, who'll fix the bastard?" . . . "Yeah, I got one of them new John Deeres. It's about powerful enough to haul manure. From a rabbit." . . . "So I says, 'Goddamn it, woman, if you think you can handle a cow better than me, then why don't we just put these goddamned pants on you and let me bake the cookies!'" . . . "Psst. Red! Why'd the Mexicans drive three cars to the Alamo?" "I don't know. How come?" "So's they could fit all six thousand soldiers in there at oncet!" "Haw!"

When Mike and Bobo pulled up in Turk's tow truck, they found Grandpá Sneezy standing outside. He was staring across the lot, where Castro had gathered with a small group of followers. They took off their hats and watched Mike.

"Look at that," said Bobo. "I'll tell you what. Don't ever think you got the indios figured out. It'd take you about ten thousand years."

"People are people," Mike said.

"That's what you think," Bobo noted.

"They just don't like me," Mike said. He was suddenly overcome with the desire to be liked—especially by the Apaches.

"Why should they like you? You fucked up their world for them. Killed all their chiefs. Put pinche Phoenix in the middle of the desert to suck up all the water. Those guys been eatin' rocks for ninety years, vato."

"I didn't do it!"

"Go tell *them* that."

Bobo relented—after all, it was Mike's dad's funeral.

"Aw, hell," he said. "They don't like Mexicans, either. We went and killed Geronimo's whole family—kids and all." He opened his door. "Why should anybody like anybody?"

"I don't know," Mike said. "I like everybody."

"You're ignorant," Bobo said.

Mike got out and walked over to Mr. Sneezy.

"Grandfather," he said.

Mr. Sneezy pointed at Castro. Mike looked. "Look at them pants," Mr. Sneezy said. Castro's jeans hung off his tiny buttocks and formed a bag. His gut hung out over the slipped-down rawhide belt.

Mr. Sneezy shook his head.

"Another no-assed Indian," he said.

Mike walked across the lot toward Castro.

Castro had a black eye.

"What happened?" Mike said.

"Grandpa Sneezy," Castro mumbled. "He give it to me."

Mike smiled—he couldn't help himself.

"Thanks for coming," he said. "I think."

Castro nodded.

"I just came out to say How . . . dy."

His warriors all chuckled, murmuring "How" and "Howdy" to each other.

Castro grinned at them.

That danged Castro! What a card!

Mike turned to walk away.

Castro said, "Psst."

Mike turned back.

Castro handed him the big knife.

"We ain't finished," Castro said with no discernible emotion.

Mike stared at the sunlight sliding up and down the blade. He didn't dare look at Castro. He spit on the ground. Castro's warriors stared at the spit as it steamed on the hot blacktop, already going soft in the sun: everyone was deeply interested in that spit.

"I used to chew tar," Castro said. "Reservation chewing gum."

Mike tucked the knife in his back pocket and walked toward the funeral home. He couldn't quite work out his angle on this thing. When he reached his friends, Bobo said, "What did I tell you?"

Bobo and Mr. Sneezy automatically drifted to the back of the parlor, where they stood leaning against the wall. It was an unspoken covenant—they just drifted out of the line of sight. It was the time-honored act of self-preservation that those in the front of the room would call "skulking."

Mike shook hands all around, mouthing and hearing awkward condolences and sentiments: "Tough break, Mike" "Thanks, Red—who'da thought?" . . . "Damn shame, Mike. That Turk—thought he'd whip us all!" "Thanks—hard to believe." . . . "Hang tough." "You know it." . . . "He went out like a man, I'm here to tell you, kid." "You bet!"

Danette did her best to fill the entire room with beauty and somehow drown Mike in sweet melody. Her foot worked that volume pedal relentlessly, swelling the music into waves that swept the parlor. A couple of the ol' boys sniffled as they listened. Mike watched her rump on the bench as her other foot danced across the bass pedals. He wondered what she ate for breakfast, what she wore to bed, what her pillow smelled like.

Santucci stepped up to the podium and recited some Bible at them. He asked for a moment of silence. All the men got to their feet and hung their old sunburned heads. Danette diddled almost silently with the upper-register keys, achieving, she believed, the sound of angels singing beneath the Tree of Life. Perhaps, she thought in a moment of pridefulness, she had somehow mimicked the tinkle of Living Water!

"Those who live by the sword," Santucci summed up, "shall die by the same thing. Amen."

"Amen," they replied.

Mike, Red, and a few of the others took hold of the coffin and hauled it outside. Castro was gone, Mike noted. They loaded Turk into Santucci's big hearse, a car Turk himself had cared for over the years. This idea crossed several of their minds, but none of them knew what to call the feeling they got, like it was some kind of joke but sadder and more mysterious. Danette came out and kissed Mike on the cheek, and he held her close, felt her skirt crinkling against his legs, smelled the secret scent behind her right ear, and he let her go. Bobo squeezed her arm as he passed by. Mr. Sneezy jammed himself into the tow truck with the two of them and rested his cowboy hat on his knee. Turk received a final fanfare of ill-timed engines and loose exhaust pipes, then the whole crew pulled out in a ragged parade: the hearse and the tow truck, twelve pickups, one car. Buzzards, watching from a cool mile above, saw them meander and fade, noisy little boxes, winking out in the hot light.

It was a small boneyard off the highway. Cowboys had been buried there, and their miserable little headstones were made of cement, with crosses drawn in them with wet fingers and names scrawled around the designs: Bill Fitzsimmons; Arnulfo; Tadeusz Sitkowski III.

The desert wind was constant, and though not refreshing, it at least pushed some of the heat off their faces. Mike's hair felt like straw. He had little pebbles inside his nose. Dust lifted off the mounds around Turk's grave and carried on the wind like plumes of smoke.

"Well, sir," Mike said to the grave, "this is where we're putting you." He looked out on the saguaros and the Joshua trees. A cactus wren hopped in the gravel. "Hope it's all right." He wanted some great send-off, some beautiful words. But he didn't know any beautiful words. Lily would have been good for that. "I guess you didn't like Stephen Crane, or I'd say one of them for you." He looked back at the gathered mourners. This whole scene was making him nervous. He could not believe the terrible relief that Turk was gone. "I"—he cleared his throat—"I hope you don't get too lonesome out here. I might not be along too soon to see you, but I'll be thinking about you."

Mike patted the mound.

"Good-bye, Turk," he said.

33

"WHERE TO?" MIKE SAID.

"I don't know," Bobo said. "Where do you want to go?"

"I don't know," said Mike. "Where do *you* want to go?"

"I don't know," Bobo replied. "Where do you—"

"Cripes!" Mr. Sneezy snapped. "You two's dumber than jay-birds."

"I was just asking Bobe where he wanted to go."

"How should I know? *You're* the one driving."

"What, do I have to guess where you want to go?"

"You're driving, all right," Mr. Sneezy said. "You're driving me crazy." He chuckled, nudged Bobo in the ribs. "Get it?"

Bobo considered this quip beneath comment, even from him.

"I'll go wherever you say," he said. "Do I look like I got somewhere special to go? I couldn't care less."

"Let's go to Phoenix," Mr. Sneezy said.

"What for?" said Mike.

"I'm catching a bus for Los Angeles," said Mr. Sneezy.

Mike was shocked.

"Why, Grandfather?" he asked.

"Nothin' left out here—Turk's gone, my grandson's crazy. Hell, I been thinking about it. I never been anywhere, you know it? I never been out of Arizona."

Bobo whistled.

"Hard to believe," Mr. Sneezy said. "So I figure it's time to see the ocean, maybe put in my feet and see what happens. And I heard about this Disneyland out there. I'm going to ride me them rides and eat hot dogs."

Bobo snorted.

"Mmm, hot dogs," said Mr. Sneezy. "I got money."

He pulled a deerskin poke out of his pocket and showed it to them. "It's swolled up with money. Want some?"

"Naw," said Mike. "I got some."

"Don't be proud," said Mr. Sneezy. "I'll stake you two to a month if you want."

Mike shook his head and studied the road.

"Chili dogs," said Bobo.

Mr. Sneezy turned to him.

"Yes," he said, "them are good, all right. And these German kraut dogs sound real good too."

"Kraut dog," said Bobo, pondering it. "Huh. Kraut right on it?"

"Sour kraut and mustard. Plus you can't beat a corn dog."

Bobo put both hands up, surrendering. "Corn dogs. Now you're talkin'."

"You're sure," Mike said.

"About corn dogs?" said Mr. Sneezy.

"About *leaving,*" said Mike.

"Yep."

Mike drove for a while.

"All right," he said.

After five minutes, Bobo turned to them and said, "Nobody asked *me* if *I* wanted to go to Phoenix!"

"Why the hell don't you two just get married," Mr. Sneezy said. "Then you can bicker all you want."

They cut down across the hilly land, dead lava like a shadow around them.

Bobo was asleep.

Mr. Sneezy said, "Stay away from Ramses. One of you McGurks already wouldn't listen to reason, and look at what happened to him."

"We seem to have this feud," said Mike.

"Oh, bullshit."

"It's an Indian thing, right?"

"Christ almighty. Double bullshit. You're both of you so full of bullshit it's dribblin' out you mouths like chaw spit."

"Ramses said—"

"Ramses thinks he's Geronimo's right-hand man. Listen to me, Mike." Mr. Sneezy poked Mike in the arm with a finger as hard as wood. "Geronimo would have took one look at that boy and walked the other way. My grandson's crazy. Period. It's all in his head."

"I can't run," said Mike, feeling the McGurk blood in his veins.

"Sure you can. What the hell did I try to tell your God-damned father? Run! I said. Run, you old fool!"

Mike shook his head.

"Can't do it," he said.

Mr. Sneezy fumed for a while. Beside him, Bobo's nose whistled. Then Mr. Sneezy said, "Well, there you have it. I'm going to California to see if Mickey Mouse has more sense than all of you sons a bitches."

It was night. They stood in the bus station, listening to the echoing announcements. Mr. Sneezy had bought himself a new cowboy hat and a towel. "Got all I need right here," he said, holding up the towel. "Got a towel, pillow, blanket, lunch bucket!" He laughed softly. "Still a little life in the old man."

He handed Mike an envelope.

"There's some money in there. Don't say a word! Take it. Get yourself a hotel. Get some gas. Get a big gun and shoot the hell out of Castro while you got the chance."

The bus came.

Mr. Sneezy shook Bobo's hand, hugged Mike once.

"See you around, Grandson," he said.

Mike smiled bravely. He wanted Grandfather Sneezy to be proud of him. He wanted to be a warrior too.

"Mickey Mouse," said Mr. Sneezy. "Hot dogs."

34

YOU COULD DRIVE FOREVER OUT THERE AND NEVER GET anywhere.

They pulled into the Rode Side Inn. Room prices were scrawled in chalk on a blackboard mounted to the outside of the building. They could have two singles for a total of seven fifty, or a double for four dollars. An old man came out of the office and stood pointing at the board with a shaking hand. His pants were pulled up above his navel, and about five inches of belt hung straight out at them. Bobo and Mike conferred in the truck. When they turned away from the board, the old man's arm slowly fell; when they looked back at the prices, it rose again to point and shake.

"How about the double?" called Mike.

"Oh!" the old man said, apparently startled that Mike was interested. "I don't know!"

"You don't?" said Mike.

"What's it say here?" the old man asked.

"It says four bucks."

"No kidding! Why, prices just keep goin' up!"

Mike and Bobo stared at him through the windshield. He had a corona of moths circling his backlit head.

"A room would be nice," Mike suggested.

"Gosh," said the man. "I don't know if we've got one."

"How do I find out?"

"You'd have to ask Mother about that," said the man.

"Gramps has seen better days," said Bobo.

"Yep," said the man, coming down the steps. It took ninety seconds per step. He ambled over and leaned one elbow in the window. "I ain't got a head for these figures. Did once. Not no more!"

Bobo said, "May we speak to Mother?"

"Gee, I don't know. Is she home?" the man asked. He looked over his shoulder and called, "Mother?" His voice, reedy and delicate, reminded Mike of a bird's. There was no way Mother could hear his call, yet the screen door of the office banged open and she came forth, a tidy little woman in an apron.

"Don't mind Father," she said. "He's in his later years."

"Ma'am," said Mike.

She handed them a wooden plank with a key tied to it with white string.

"Bungalow thirteen," she said.

Mike handed Father the four dollar bills. He counted them carefully, then turned to Mother and said, "Do they get any change?"

"No, sweetheart," she said.

"Okay, gents!" he said. "Thanks for staying with us, and next time you're in the area, well, come back and see us!"

The room was half flooded. They could hear the shower spigot running in the bathroom. Mike walked down to the office and knocked. Mother came to the door.

"Ma'am," he said, "the room's flooded."

"You don't say," she said.

She went inside and came back with a mop.

"Just leave it leaning on the wall there when you go."

Mike walked back.

Bobo couldn't believe his eyes.

"She gave you a *mop?*" he said.

The water had splattered out and soaked the roll of toilet paper. It was swollen to three times its usual size. While Bobo mopped, Mike walked back to the office and knocked again.

Mother peered out at him.

He held up the useless roll.

She squinted and stuck out her lower lip and said, "Young man!"

She went back in and reappeared with a half-used roll. She tore several inches of sheets off for herself and Father and handed the roll out to Mike.

"Try not to use it all," she said.

"Poo-cob don't grow on trees!" Father called from inside somewhere.

The smell of mildew choked them. Mike threw open the windows. Bobo inspected the corners of the room, his feet making squishing sounds on the wet carpet. He squelched into the bathroom and unleashed a torrent into the bowl. He came back out, gingerly holding a multilegged creature that waved its feelers at Mike. Throwing it out the door, Bobo climbed into bed and pulled the sheets up to his chin.

There was a thin newspaper on the nightstand. Mike picked it up. It was a week old. The headline informed him: DOBBS SPREAD GOES BUST. Under a photo of F. J. Dobbs himself, standing before a locked gate, the legend "End of an Era."

Mike's snoring cut short, and he sat up.

Bobo stood beside his bed, staring down at him.

"Huh?" Mike said.

"Where's the hinge?" said Bobo.

"What?" said Mike.

"I can't find that hinge. I had it in the box."

"Bobo?"

"Let's fix that gate. The bodies are coming out."

Mike was wide awake now.

"What are you doing?" he said.

Bobo thought about it.

"I'm waving good-bye," he said.

"You're sleepwalking!"

"No I'm not."

"You are."

"Am not."

"Go back to bed, partner," Mike said.

"Say good-bye to that hinge, then," Bobo warned.

"Go back to sleep." Mike lay back down.

"That truck's not coming?" Bobo asked.

"Not tonight."

"Okay . . . "

"Night, Bobe."

"Okay . . . "

Bobo strolled to the dresser, pulled out a drawer, and stuck his foot in it. The dresser banged against the wall.

"Now what?" Mike said.

"Goin' to bed."

"Not there you aren't."

"Oops."

"Try the bed."

"Roger."

Bobo got in bed.

"Roger wilko."

Mike closed his eyes.

"Over and out," he said.

Bobo started snoring right away.

Mike crossed his arms behind his head and lay there for a while. People around him weren't making sense. Events weren't making sense. Turk had stepped back and yanked the rug out from under the world. Hinges! Castro was bad enough, but hinges was just too much.

Before he fell asleep, he imagined his mother's grave. In his mind, it was atop a small bluff somewhere in Oklahoma near the Texas border. It was on a creekbank, in the shade of a cottonwood. Bluebells grew all around it, trembling in the breeze: almost dancing, kind of reminding him of the excellent dancing he knew his mother had done but he'd never seen. The sun never fully set in his vision, for the thought of his mother alone out there in the dark was unbearable. He didn't mind imagining snow, of course: snow created in his mind a kind of Currier and Ives print, full of wistful mist and soft colors. You could hear the water running under a lacework of clear ice. The sky had perfect, brilliant clouds that were brighter to the eye than neon.

For the thousandth time in his life, Mike McGurk fell asleep imagining those hard, beautiful clouds.

35

WHY WAS BOBO ALWAYS RESCUING PEOPLE? IT WAS ONE of the central questions of his life. He didn't even *like* anybody that much, yet he was always finding some drunk, or some fresh-sprung yardbird blinking at the prison gates. Take Mike, for instance. He didn't like white people. He didn't think he liked Mike. And here he was, suddenly trapped in the confusions of the McGurks. Bobo couldn't figure it out.

Maybe it was Buchenwald—he thought about that possibility—because God knows he couldn't save anybody there. He tried, and he caused a final horror. Yeah, that was some kind of joke on God's part, all right. One last little bit of humor to cap off the experience of Buchenwald. One last thing for those big-eyed ghosts behind the wires at Buchenwald.

It wasn't the thousands on the litters who died because nobody could help them. Bobo had just stared at them like everybody else, urging the Red Cross woman to take pictures because nobody was going to believe *this* shit when they got home. Nobody. He said, "Forget being ashamed. My God—make them look at these poor sons of bitches. Make 'em look!" and she'd shot photographs of things they didn't think anybody had ever imagined before.

He should have left it at that.

But he'd thought he was doing the right thing—he'd found one who was supposed to survive, if the medics could find any time at all to try to attend to him. He'd thought he was the big saint. He wanted to save someone, something. He wanted so badly just to *be a human being* that he stepped into the last practical joke of the cosmos. Back in Buchenwald. One hundred years ago. Last night.

They could smell it from a mile down the hill—the village reeked with it—and when they pushed open the gates, Bobo could see the men ahead stop still, and one fell to his knees. There were two Red Cross Clubmobile girls with them, and they'd been handing out doughnuts and cigarettes to the grunts. They'd joined the soldiers as they all walked up to the gates—there was a certain trepidation about what lay ahead, of course. But also joy—excitement: they were going to let the prisoners go! Phyllis and her little buddy, Cookie. Bobo had his eye on Cookie. He called her "The Cookster," which she found cute. And here she was so nervous she was holding his hand.

Some of the boys had already been in there—Patton himself was raising holy hell with the villagers, who went wide-eyed and innocent and said, *No! Really?* to every atrocity story. And Patton shouting, "Goddamn it, can't you *smell* it?"

None of Bobo's crew knew what to think. They were grease monkeys, mechanics. Sometimes they even fought. None of them had the imagination to picture what was inside the fences.

Cookie's hand: that stuck in his memory. It was hard as a claw, her nails digging into his palm, but he didn't feel pain; he just stood with his mouth open. He stood in a vast puddle of shit and blood and urine. He stood and touched his toe to the side of a corpse so white it could have been carved from soap, its eyes sunken small bowls, its open mouth a black-lipped hole full of flies, its breasts flat envelopes with long leather-brown nipples. It was a teenaged girl. Cookie there, somewhere, crying, vomiting. Faces peering at him from behind wires. Speaking in languages he couldn't understand. None of them seeming to care about it. Why didn't they care?

Bobo couldn't believe she was dead. It was hard to even believe she was real. It was funny, because for some reason, looking down at the dead girl made him blind to the mounds of dead—white walls of dead people. He never even saw them until Cookie and her friend Phyllis pointed them out, and he still didn't see them even when he was looking at them. It took a minute to understand what he was seeing.

Harrison, the only black man in the crew, came running up to him and said, "García, you gotta see this."

Bobo just stared at him.

"We found something," Harrison said.

Bobo turned to Cookie.

"You be all right?" he asked.

She was gray.

She nodded.

He trotted away with Harrison, already adjusting to what he was seeing, already sizing up the barely breathing skeletons still lying around: *He'll live. She's dead already.* He found himself wondering where they'd spend the night. He wanted to slap himself. Then they rounded the corner of a shed.

Babies.

Bobo's squad had found the babies, laid up in perfect cordwood piles, triangular behind a wooden wall, ten babies to a pile, a hole punched in each head—target practice for the guards. And he worked on the tractor engines when the machine wore down from moving the hillocks of naked dead across the haunted parade grounds. Cold flesh—hundred of tons of cold flesh. He was sick for days, for some reason obsessing on cold, thick, stiff flesh. It was the thing that could always put him off a meal. He was even afraid of sandwich meat, afraid forever after that a piece of some child had fallen into the bread somehow, through some dark magic he could never explain. *Cold flesh* was the most horrible thing he could ever imagine. Aside from his one worst mistake.

Bobo couldn't save anyone. He tried to pour water in mouths, and it fell back out. He tried to feed chocolate to a skeleton lying in the dirt, and the skeleton choked to death on the food. The skeleton was named Valentin—he had been able to whisper that much. The scene never left Bobo's mind: He knelt down to Valentin, Valentin's body eroded by an unimaginable flood, his ribs sharp and tall in the light. Valentin touching his own chest and saying, "Valentin. Valentin." He was somebody. And the specters sitting numbly around him, shit in their rags, drool, dying sitting right there as Phyllis shot little pictures and sobbed and Cookie just stood, both hands to her cheeks. Bobo kneeling down beside Valentin, as Valentin gestured and whispered. And the chocolate. And Valentin gestured like a machine, over and over again, touching himself on the heart, and Bobo pushed the candy into the dry mouth, thinking who knows what, just wanting to help, just thinking chocolate would somehow *cheer Valentin up,* chocolate would give him some *energy,* and *Bobo liked chocolate.* And Valentin gulped and choked and his dead eyes still seeing the perfect sky of Buchenwald—birds, birds everywhere, clouds beautiful in the blue—Valentin's still-living eyes going wide and the arm stopping in the air above the heart and Bobo not able to pry open the mouth to save him. Valentin, dry as sticks. Valentin, light as a kite. Bobo afraid to pound his back because he might shatter the spine. Bobo standing back as Valentin suffocated, unable to help.

Not right—nothing right on earth ever again. The men standing and sitting around Valentin watching with no expression as he died. Bobo the savior. This was supposed to be Liberation, Bobo wanted to shout to someone, to Patton, to Valentin, to God—anyone. Not this! Please, Jesus, not this!

And Valentin lay still at Bobo's feet.

And Bobo had screamed until the small blood vessels in his cheeks burst.

You couldn't save anybody in this world. Bobo couldn't anyway. He couldn't even save Cookie, the little blond-haired Red Cross captain from Cape May, New Jersey, a place Bobo had never been. A place Bobo was going to visit after the war, to bask on the beaches with his little white girl: the only Mexican in south Jersey. He was going to present her with a ring as soon as the war was over, right there on the beach in Cape May. She might turn him down, but what the hell—it was worth a shot. She was certainly the only woman who could ever understand what Bobo had seen and done, because she'd held his hand in Buchenwald. And she'd been driving the jeep that killed her.

It was a blackout, and she was driving without headlights, up a mountain road, and she hit a bomb crater in the road that she could have avoided—it was only on the outside edge—a swerve of three feet and she was home free. But she hit it and flipped right off the edge, and they found the jeep, but they never found her. Not a trace. No blood.

Bobo didn't even have a snapshot of her.

And when Bobo came across a lost and wounded German soldier on the outskirts of a small town that had been gutted by tank fire, he took out his k-bar, and he did unspeakable things, finally cutting his throat. The soldier held Bobo's arms as he died, a bright fan of blood opening beneath his chin and burning in Bobo's face. And in the man's pockets, a picture of a woman and a baby girl. A pouch with a lock of fine hair. And a letter in German with pink lip prints above the name: Johanna.

Bobo had come to an hour later, still trying to push the flap of the man's throat closed, still trying to get him to get up and go home to Johanna.

Bobo lit a rare cigarette and sucked the smoke into his lungs. He was shaking again. The end of his penis burned as if he needed to urinate, but he knew he did not. He sat outside with his back to the wall and stared across the parking lot. A battered truck rolled down the highway, back toward Phoenix. He listened to the driver wrestle with the gears. Far, far away, a dog was barking in threes: *Woof-woof-woof. Woof-woof-woof.*

Bobo watched his hand shake.

You couldn't save a single soul.

Not in this fucking world.

36

MORNING HELPED BOTH OF THEM. STANDING IN THE LOT, Bobo spied a jackrabbit peeling out across the ground, and he rose to his tiptoes. "Used to train with rabbits," he said. "When I was wrestling? Used to run after them, zigzagging, to keep in shape. All over the fields, running *hard* too. Best workouts I ever got." He bounced on his toes. To Mike, for just an instant, Bobo looked like a coyote—eyes bright with desire, his limbs quivering, wanting to run.

They drove in silence.

"I'll be dipped," Mike said. "I will be dipped."

While they'd been gone, Turk's Texaco had developed a festoonery of steel chain. The pumps were trussed and padlocked; the doors had loops and crisscrosses of it. A yellow sheet was slathered to the office window with glue. In huge letters it announced:

FORECLOSURE

with a mess of small print at the bottom. Another notice was posted to the door:

THIS PROPERTY
REPOSSESSED
BY CENTRAL ARIZONA
TITLE AND TRUST

Trespassers Will Be Prosecuted

Bobo said, "They can't do that."
Mike said, "They already did it."
Bobo said, "Well, what are you going to do about it?"
And Mike said, "I'm going to break in and make some coffee."
And Bobo said, "That's the spirit!"

Mike cut through the lock with bolt cutters from the truck. They slammed the door open and stomped inside. "Foreclose this!" Bobo shouted, slapping his butt.

They felt unfettered. They were fed up. They rode a huge wave of noise through the place, chasing the ghosts away. They argued, yelled, slammed drawers, belched. Every tool that could clang was clanged. Mike tore open Turk's various boxes: jockstraps, bolo ties, a whetstone, a dried rattlesnake head, a concha belt, bullets, whisker wax, a gold coin, a German pistol, a cowbell, bowling shoes, fool's gold, a collection of French postcards of nude women.

"Look at this," he said. "The old devil."

Then Mike pulled out his baby shoes and held them up to his boots.

Bobo was arguing with him as he looked through the boxes.

"Look, Mike," he said. "I'm telling you, you're full of shit."

"Bobe," said Mike, "there's no stinking rabbit in the moon. It's a man in the moon."

"You're crazy," Bobo hollered. "Anybody can see it's a *rabbit* in the moon."

"Rabbit, he says," said Mike. "Mexicans. How pathetic. No wonder you people eat donkey tacos and sleep under cactuses. You're a tragic race."

"At least we ain't blind, ese. At least we don't hallucinate."

"Bobe, how can I put this simply, so your Latin mind can grasp the concept? Any American will tell you it's a *man* in the moon."

"It's a rabbit!"

"Man."

"Rabbit."

And so on.

❦ ❦ ❦

The photographs were at the bottom of Turk's steamer trunk.

Mike had pulled up old sweaters and a massive pair of swimming trunks. He'd gotten down to Turk's flat, frying-pan WWI army helmet. "Get a load of this," he said, pulling it out.

"Flying saucer," Bobo said. *"Day the Earth Stood Still."*

"Uh-huh," Mike said.

The cardboard bottom of the trunk was humped, as if there was something under there. Mike pried at it with his fingernails. It finally popped, came free, and bent up.

Turk, thick black hair hanging in his eyes, smiled up at him. He was wearing the same trunks Mike had just found.

Mike showed Bobo the picture.

On the back, in ink faded a pale violet: "Summer '29—Gulf/Mex—Wallace."

Next photograph: Turk, with a goatee, in a tight uniform. One of his hands was wrapped in bandages.

"The hero," said Mike.

He grabbed a packet wrapped in wax paper. Gas stations. Turk and/or Turk's father, Carroll, variously grinning and scowling across four decades' worth of gas pumps, model A's, screen doors. Occasionally, Uncle Gideon appeared in the backgrounds, varsity sweaters around his shoulders, foolish college beanies on his head. In every picture, he had the same uncomfortable half-smile. The last photo of this bunch was on tin, of ancestor Wiley McGurk, solid as a stump, standing with his mail order bride, Inga, on the warped steps of "McGurk's Okla Territory Trading Post & Emporium—We Deal in Pelts—Stagecoaches and Wagons Welcome." In smaller print, barely legible, "Axles Greased While U Wait!"

"A long, noble history," Mike said.

A final packet lay at the very bottom. Mike slid his finger under the flap of old paper and pulled out a brown, half-torn photo. His mother stood in the sun, one hand shielding her eyes and another lightly touching her chest.

❦ ❦ ❦

They shuffled back and forth between the photographs. Mike couldn't stop fingering them. Their curling brown surfaces stuck to his fingers. There she was. Mom.

Mom in long shorts and a man's white shirt, tails loose, thick ocean foam around her ankles, and her belly wide with the proto-Mike, slumbering within.

Mom in a dismal muumuu that made her look like a Hawaiian trapezoid.

Mom dressed to kill.

Mom in cowgirl regalia, perched on a fence rail.

Mom in a wedding dress, arm hooked through Turk's, blurred as though an earthquake had hit, one of Turk's eyes flashing insanely, coming up the aisle of what looked like a small country church.

"My God," Mike kept saying, and, "Holy smoke."

He showed the beach picture to Bobo for the tenth time.

"Look here. That's me in there."

Mom in a Mexican dress, about thirteen, in front of wooden birdcages, hair in a thick braid falling to her left shoulder.

"What a doll!" Bobo said.

"She was a looker, wasn't she?" Mike said. "She was real pretty."

Mom sitting in a turtle-shaped Roadmaster.

Mom waving good-bye.

37

BOBO: "I DON'T GET HEMINGWAY, VATO."

Mike: "I get Hemingway. How can you be a man and not get Hemingway?"

Bobo: "All that bullshit. All them bull runs and drinkin' wine from bags. That war shit."

Mike: "What I don't get is Faulkner."

Bobo: "Who?"

Mike: "But Steinbeck!"

Bobo: "Now you're talkin'. I read that *Tortilla* book. I read that Okie one too."

Mike: "I got beat up once in Texas, and I had to lay in bed for a week. That's when I read *Grapes of Wrath.*"

Bobo: "Beat up for what?"

Mike: "I hate lima beans."

Bobo: "Fuckin' hate 'em too."

Mike: "I was on a run for Turk, you know. Some stupid thing—gaskets or three-inch Ford dildos or something. I pulled into a diner, and the guy was basically cooking meat loaf."

Bobo: "You didn't like the lima beans."

Mike: "Not too damned much, let me tell you."

Bobo: "Guy gets offended."

Mike: "Well, yeah. But that didn't start the ball. He was pissed at me, sure, but then these Mexicans came in and he threw 'em out. And I said something about it, and the next thing I knew, we were at it."

Bobo: "And? And?"

Mike: "I had him down and was pounding fistfuls of lima beans into his noggin when the sheriff entered the scene and laid boot leather to my posterior."

Bobo: (Laughing) "Oh, man! The crusader! Defending beaners and protesting beans!"

Bobo: "Yeah, well, you know what I hate? I hate ironing hundred-percent-cotton shirts."

Mike: "I know it."

Bobo: "Once they get a wrinkle. . . "

Mike: "You might as well hang it up right there. Sons of bitches got a *memory*."

Bobo: "Man, cotton never forgets a wrinkle!"

Mike: "I'll tell you my secret. I get the iron hot as she'll go."

Bobo: "Yeah?"

Mike: "I get it cooking away, then I *sprinkle water on the shirt*."

Bobo: "No!"

Mike: "Sprinkle it right on and iron it in. Steams the wrinkles out of the cotton."

Bobo: "But what about them long-sleeve ones, ese?"

Mike: "Long sleeves! Shoot, give up right off the bat. I've never figured out how to iron them. Cuffs, those little buttons. There isn't no way you can iron a long sleeve on a hundred-percent-cotton shirt."

Bobo: "Pinche Mike, that's what I been sayin' all along!"

Bobo put down his coffee. "What you gonna do?"

Mike shrugged.

Bobo said, "Mike—what you gonna do? They took your house. Grampa's gone. Your old man's dead."

Mike fiddled with his coffee, stirring it slowly and watching the milk swirl in it.

"I hate this place," he said.

"But it's still your house!"

"Well," he said, "I guess I've got nowhere to go."

Bobo said, "Whew."

He'd been away from home as much as he possibly could—he'd run off to war, then wandered the country, wrestling in Chicago, in Dallas, in Phoenix, in Los Angeles. He'd been to jail, he'd been to the Statue of Liberty, but he'd always had a home to go back to. The very thought of having no home threw him into a minor panic.

"It could be worse," he said. "But I don't know how."

"Bobe," Mike said. "I never had a home. Not really. Just me and Turk and stinking engine parts. Nothin'. Not even these." He touched the pictures on the table. "I'm the man from nowhere."

"In wrestling," Bobo said, "they'd call you Man Mountain McGurk—Who Hails from Parts Unknown."

"Parts unknown . . . that's me," Mike said. "Especially this part," he said, grabbing his tool.

"I seen it," Bobo said. "No wonder ladies prefer me."

Mike sipped his coffee.

"Maybe I could go to Los Angeles," he said, knowing how foolish it was as he said it, "and find Lily."

"Forget it," Bobo said.

"I know. It's dumber'n snot."

"Exactly."

"I've got to get on with things."

"Egg-zackly."

"Live my life."

"Right. So what you gonna do?"

Mike faded out and stared at the wall. Bobo started fidgeting. When it became obvious that Mike wasn't going to offer any information, he got up and went into the living room. He switched on the television. He hadn't seen a TV for almost a year. He sat in Turk's big chair and stretched out his legs. A pack of Chesterfield Kings danced across a stage, kicking long feminine legs. "Shit," he said.

A dapper gent came on, touting Carter's Little Liver Pills. He was discussing sincerely the miraculous properties of liver bile. He displayed two beakers on a table full of fat globules.

"You got to be kidding," Bobo said.

"Your golden liver bile," the fellow informed Bobo, "breaks fat down into smaller blobs!"

Then the show came on.

"Hey, Mike!" Bobo called. "It's time for Beany!"

Mike came in and sat down on the couch.

"I used to watch this back home," Bobo said. "Me and Pops. Moms usually went out into the garden. Carnations," he said, staring at the screen.

"You have a mom?" Mike said.

"No kidding," Bobo sneered. "Who *doesn't* have a—" He caught himself. He looked at Mike.

Mike was staring at his hands.

"What's she like?" he said.

Bobo sat up straight. "She's, uh, nice. You know."

"No. I *don't* know."

"She's a mom. She cooks stuff. She don't know much. Don't read much, don't speak English. But she does planting and cooking. She raises birds. Got little soft hands." He smiled.

Mike sighed.

Bobo watched him.

Beany nattered on the TV.

Mike leaned back and closed his eyes.

Bobo was watching, thinking.

"Say, Mike," he said. "You wanna come home with me? Meet the momster? Meet Pops García?"

Mike's eyes opened slowly.

He smiled.

"Could I?" he said.

"Why not," said Bobo.

"Let's go," said Mike.

Bobo was thinking: *Why am I always rescuing people?*

They mounted two fifty-gallon drums on Turk's tow truck and pumped them full of ethyl. "I'll show those bastards," Mike said. "It's my gas—I'll take it if I want to."

They packed a few things for the trip. The pictures. Some

boots. Mike dug into his dirty laundry and found the wad of "doctor money" Red and the boys had tucked into his pocket the night of the fight. "Lookee here," he said. He riffled through it. "Three hundred dollars."

Bobo eyed the cash.

"You gonna share some of that?"

Mike tossed him the money.

"You're the bank," he said. "I hate money."

"I love money," Bobo said.

Mike filled Bobo's cycle, topped off the tow truck's tank. Bobo made a couple of sandwiches. He gave Mike the baloney, shuddering a little at the cold meat. He tossed six peanut-butter-and-jam sandwiches into the sidecar.

"Where we going?" Mike asked.

"East. Then north. Going up by New Mexico, around Clifton and Morenci. McQueen, Arizona—the Copper Town."

A pickup came tearing toward them along the highway. They started up their engines, and Bobo said, "Just follow me."

The truck pulled up the drive.

A skinny man was driving, and Ramses Castro sat in the entire passenger side like a load of cement. Bobo got off his bike and moved around beside Mike's truck, just in case.

Castro hung his head out the window.

"What's up?" he said.

"Nothin'," said Mike. "What's up with you?"

"I'm lookin' for Grandpa Sneezy. You seen him?"

"He's gone," said Mike.

"Where'd he go?"

"California," Mike said.

"Disneyland," Bobo called.

Castro raised his eyebrows.

"Huh," he said. "How about that."

He looked around, eyed the bright foreclosure stickers plastered on the station. He pointed. Mike shrugged.

"You goin' somewhere?" Castro said.

"I'm taking Mike to my house," Bobo said.

Castro looked either cunning, stupid, or crazy—it was a

look he cultivated. Mike wished Bobo had said nothing. He'd learned the hard way that Castro was capable of anything.

Castro smiled.

"Okay, boys!" he called heartily. He waved once. "Have a swell time!"

The truck tore down the drive and up the highway, horn tooting about nine times.

"That boy," said Bobo, "is about three arrows shy of a quiver."

Mike lit up a smoke.

"Hey, Bobe," he said, "we going to your house, or what?"

Bobo started to walk to his motorcycle.

"I think you're going to like it," he called back. "We got painted flowerpots!"

part three

everything garcía

38

McQueen, Arizona, was once named May Queen, which the miners found too precious and unmanly—and un-American, since the term had come from an Austrian settler who'd sunk the first shaft and called it the May Queen Mine when he hit a small gold nugget on May 1. The gold soon enough played out, but the Austrian used it to build a small opera house down on the flats, in Safford, and it was called The May Queen and was built to suggest a small Mississippi paddle boat. Ironically, it was washed away in one of the periodic floods of the San Francisco River as it tore down the gaps in the mountains, driven mad by rain. The Austrian, rumor had it, had gone on to San Francisco and performed in vaudeville as a plate juggler.

His original grubstake in the mountains was bought by Ferdinand Ochoa, Hiram Wynkoop, and Clayton McQueen. They had heard there was copper to be had—after all, Clifton and Morenci were already rich in ore. They heaved themselves up the mountains with a mule train skinned by a driver for hire named Malachi "One Ball" Westrick. Westrick, three years later, would become May Queen's first sheriff.

The trio dug around for six months, and it was Ochoa who first found a sheet of copper between two unearthed boulders. The little mine started coughing up all the copper the boys could dig. The three partners prospered. McQueen himself turned a tidy profit in turquoise, selling it to the Apaches and the Navajos and the Zunis. The three partners became town fathers "right simple," as McQueen himself put it. "We pulled the ore from the land, and we pulled the miners *onto* the land, and straightaway we were in a position to form a new society." Which consisted of three wood houses, nineteen tents, a saloon/cathouse, and a dry-goods store. The name change from May Queen to McQueen was simple enough, especially after Ochoa was shot by McQueen in a tiff over Rosy McGrady. Hiram Wynkoop sold his share in the May Queen Mine and the McQueen settlement to Clay McQueen and returned to East Cambridge, Massachusetts, where he fished for alewives until he died in 1931 of old age and gout.

McQueen himself vanished on a hunting trip into the Apaches' White Mountains, leaving the town to run itself, which it did with the help of disgruntled Mexicans from neighboring Clifton and Morenci, fleeing the hard conditions at the big pits and feeling welcomed by Sheriff Westrick, who, in spite of his testicular oddity, married a Mexican woman and sired ten children. He'd painted the famous sign that now hung in the small Historical Museum on Second Avenue: BIENVENIDOS SONSOBITCHES. The Mexicans could read only the first part, and it was the friendliest thing said to them in Arizona for years. And for a while, until the big conglomerates bought it up, they labored together in the "enlightened" May Queen copper pit. But business was business, and the mines were the same all over Arizona, and soon you couldn't tell the May Queen from Morenci.

Bobo, riding ahead of Mike, ascending toward his home like a rocket, saw in the peaks and dry rock towers the most magical place on earth.

The copper country's beauty was quieter than the rest of Arizona. There were no spectacles here like the Grand Canyon, Meteor Crater, the Painted Desert, or the Petrified Forest. The land, rising like a sigh out of the desert, seemed to rejoice with small bursts of trees and splashes of flowers.

You had to cut through Clifton on the Coronado Trail first, then swing northeast, up the San Francisco River, into the tree-line. Most people went from Clifton to Morenci and never saw the smaller town nestled near the New Mexico border.

McQueen's old cowboy hotels and saloons and storefronts had withstood the periodic floods of the river and the endless runoff of time. As Mike drove through, his first thought was that it looked like a town in a cowboy movie. The covered sidewalks and nineteenth-century bank were so well preserved, so alive, that Randolph Scott and Joel McCrea could have ridden down the street with pistols on their hips; nobody would notice.

Every morning, McQueen awoke and went about its business. Men and women packed their lunches, and at the whistle of the mine alarm, they started their trudge uphill, some of them gathered in the backs of trucks and calling out jokes to each other. The new town librarian was attempting to create a collection of books in the recently abandoned May Queen Fire Station. Each day, he sent a platoon of letters forth to benefactors and colleges, publishers and authors, hoping they would donate reading matter. In his spare time, he wrote and printed the *McQueen Mercury,* a four-page newspaper that ran the same three ads for ten years straight: First Bank, Petra's Burritos, The May Queen Food Store. News was scarce, so the librarian often wrote small historical sketches, hoping to educate the populace about its own interesting past.

Feature articles that week included: "Al Farnsworth's Dog Herb Missing: $10 Reward," "Local Teen Going to College," and "Martinez Wedding Huge Success." The subhead read: "Festivities Slightly Marred by Liquor."

That day, the *Mercury* was running a small profile of Bobo's father, Aureliano García. It was in an ornate box, tucked in beside the bank ad because the librarian knew enough to separate Mexican history from the burrito stand.

> García, ferocious hero of battles hard to number in the cataclysmic Mexican Revolt, confidante of Villa, and sharpshooter who, it was said, could hit a dove in the eye at fifty yards, pulled up his war-tattered roots in the unyielding Mexican soil and came forth to the American Promised land.

Unbeknownst to Bobo, it was an auspicious time to return home.

Mike had driven into the dawn, Turk's knife and the Texaco home oil can rattling on the dash, staring at Bobo's hunched back and fluttering hair until he was half asleep. They'd stayed over at El Mula's house—Bobo on the couch, Mike on the floor. Mula had almost fallen over when Bobo brought in a gabacho, a white man. Grumbling, he'd gone into his bedroom and never come back out. Bobo had kicked Mike's foot at four-thirty and said, "Let's boogie, compadre." Cold beans wrapped in stove-charred tortillas for breakfast, and they were gone—Bobo hiding a stack of purloined *Mad* magazines in his sidecar.

They rolled east, through the deadly boredom of the flatlands, but before they got too close to the New Mexico border, they swung left off the main road and went north. Bobo pulled away from Mike as they climbed. Mike dropped it into second and groaned along.

At the edge of Clifton, they'd been stopped by a long, snorting ore train that crawled across the road and meandered up into town. On the left, another track cut down the face of a cliff (Cliff Town!), and three huge blue-and-white locomotives charged down it like dragons. Mike was amazed—they looked as if they were flying. Each engine said P-D on its side.

Bobo rolled his bike back to Mike and said, "We might as well relax. This'll take about twenty minutes."

"What's P-D?" Mike asked.

"Phelps-Dodge," said Bobo. "Los meros chingones—the big dudes. The mines, ese."

Mike nodded.

Bobo was as happy as Mike had ever seen him. It felt like they'd been friends for years. He envied Bobo his eager stare, the way he looked in every direction, obviously loving each rock, tree, glint of broken glass on the tracks. Mike didn't know what to call it. If Lily had been here, he'd have asked her, and she'd have said, *Sense of place.* Something fancy like that. Mike had it: it was *Home.* He didn't know what that felt like.

Bobo couldn't stop smiling. He kept up a continual visual sweep of the landscape, turning his face to it, breathing its smell.

The rusty train cars lurched and crashed, rolling with ponderous heaviness, even though they were empty. The team of locomotives ahead unhitched and rolled on into town. The bright P-D engines chuffed and belched smoke and maneuvered backward into the cars. Everything banged when they hooked on. Then they banged again all the way down the line as the locomotives pulled away, leading the cars up the cliff, and they extended and pulled against their couplings, almost reluctant, then finally succumbing to authority and following.

Mike said to Bobo: "Painted flowerpots, huh?"

Bobo grinned as if this was the most fabulous thing.

"Just wait," he replied.

39

THERE WERE, INDEED, PAINTED FLOWERPOTS.

Up above the edge of McQueen, on a hill-hugging dirt road that leveled out on a mesa that overlooked a stunning seascape of dark desert far below, the García home hid in a stand of olive trees. All along the top of its low cement-block fence stood brightly painted Mexican flowerpots: pots painted yellow and blue; red, yellow, and blue; orange and green; black and yellow. They drooped cascades of ivy, geraniums, fuchsia, spider plants. They raised small stockades of mint, cinnamon, carnations, chili peppers. Blooms of many colors crowded each other by the gate, in the pots, and behind the fence. "Dig it!" Bobo called. "Dig them colors, daddy-o!" He revved his engine and sped ahead.

Mike had never seen so many plants.

He drove up to the house and saw: bees, a hummingbird, small wooden cages with nervous canaries, hung on pegs in the wall.

"Mom grows this shit!" Bobo exulted. "Bananas! Nobody up here can grow bananas!" Bobo pointed to a ten-foot fan of leathery-looking leaves.

He hopped off his bike and came to Mike's door.

"Look down there," he said, pointing to a brilliant quarter-mile rectangle of swaying plants.

"Corn, baby," he said.

Mike was terrified. He wanted to go home. He wanted to

get out of there before the rest of the Garcías came out—he imagined a whole household of pachuco gardeners, all of them with evil little goatees and switchblades, everybody so . . . *Mexican.*

Then all hell broke loose.

The screen door burst open, and six tiny girls in dresses flew off the porch, swarmed through the loudly screeching gate, and dove headfirst into Bobo's gut, screaming, "Tío! Tío! Tío!" Bobo received them with hoots and bellows. Little girls climbed him. Then a small, Indian-looking woman in a faded print dress and an apron shambled out on the porch. She wore bedroom slippers on her splayed feet, eyeglasses on her nose, and a bun of gray-black hair on her head. She seemed to scowl as she wiped her hands on the apron, then she gasped and cried, "Bonifacio!" She flapped her arms as she hustled down the steps, calling back over her shoulder, "¡Muchachas! Apurense! ¡Ha llegado Bonifacio! ¡Córrele!"

She came out on the road and cried, "¡M'ijo! Ay, ¡m'ijito!"

She threw her arms around him, and Mike thought Bobo was going to crack her ribs as he hugged her.

Safe in the vault of Turk's truck, Mike watched her kiss Bobo and pat his face.

To Mike, the Spanish was as indecipherable as machine-gun fire, a high-speed flurry of consonants that sounded like *rraccatta-rraccatta-rraccatta.*

Two women came out of the house together. Mike did a double take. They were twins. One of them wore an old dress like Mama's; the other, work pants and a sharp hairdo. They came down the steps, hands flapping above their heads, and had at Bobo when Mama was through with him. The little girls hung on to his belt, his legs, his waist, and tugged him back and forth. Bobo reached out a finger and touched the cheek of one twin.

Mike watched.

Around the corner of the house, a rugged old man hove into sight. He had a bum leg—it lurched as he walked, yanked around with a slight grimace that crossed his seamed face with every step. A battered gray fedora covered his head, and around his feet, a pack of small dogs eddied and swirled. They spied Bobo and tore out to him at top speed, seemingly ready to bite, but when they got to him, they rose on their back legs and began a small canine square dance.

The old man limped out, removed his hat, mopped the sweat off his brow with a crumpled bandanna, put the hat back on, and waited for the women to get done with Bobo. Mike could hear mourning doves cooing and a parrot inside the house raising a ruckus.

The women backed away, making a clear space before Bobo.

"M'ijo," the old man said, and stepped forward. They shook hands. Then Bobo threw his arms around his father in a fierce abrazo that knocked the old man's hat off. And the old man twisted his face around and kissed Bobo on the cheek.

It was the kiss that did Mike in.

Tears filled his eyes. He couldn't hold them back. His eyes burned as the heartbreak overcame him. He sobbed, and it boomed in the cab of the truck, and they all turned to stare at him. Even the dogs stopped rotating around Bobo and looked. Mike couldn't stop. He heard himself saying "Tu-hur-hurk!" and "Mo-ho-hom!"

Bobo quietly said to his family, "He is my friend. His father died in a fight."

They didn't ask questions—they came to the door of the truck and threw it open.

"*Rraccatta-rraccatta,*" they were saying to him. Soft women's hands were laid on him.

"Pobrecito," Mama said.

They extracted him from the truck and escorted him inside, patting him on the back, on the arms, hands, shoulders, cheeks. Little girls matched his steps as he walked. Dogs sniffed at his feet and his crotch. The screen door slammed behind them, and Mike glanced back to see Bobo, Papa, and the dogs, standing guard.

❦ ❦ ❦

Inside, the García household swung into action: Operation Comfort Mike went immediately into high gear. The twins rushed to the kitchen to begin making coffee and heating food. Mama had the basin in the bathroom full of cold water and was holding Mike's neck in a death grip as she splashed water in his face. Some of the girls still patted him; one held a towel; the others perched on and in the tub to watch. Mama hollered at Mr. García, and he hollered back and slammed the screen. In a moment, he appeared with a glass and a bottle. "Vino," he said, "García."

He uncorked the bottle and poured Mike a stiff four-finger shot of red wine, almost black in the glass.

"I make," Mr. García said. "Me and God!"

Mike took a swig; it was so potent his nose ran.

Mr. García let out an explosive laugh: Ha-*hah!*

"Is good, no?"

"Is," said Mike, "real good."

Mama hustled Papa out of the bathroom, and the towel-bearing girl closed in on Mike's face, scrubbing it dry.

Mama looked tenderly into his eyes and said, "*Rraccattac-cacca.*"

40

THE TWINS LIT THE STOVE AND ATTENDED TO THE ANCIENT task of tortilla production. The Garcías favored flour tortillas—tortillas de harina—over more traditional corn tortillas—tortillas de maíz. They had a large tin tub with damp cloths laid over a mound of raw dough. They removed the cloths, pulled down a flat board and a rolling pin, scattered flour over the board, and pinched balls of dough off the mass. They flattened the balls with the roller, then picked up the pancake of dough and started slapping it firmly from palm to palm; it expanded beyond their hands in a perfect circle. Then they laid the raw tortilla on a hot iron skillet, and as the heating dough blistered up in bubbles, they patted it down with wadded white cloth.

Mr. García poured himself a glass of wine and stood behind Mike, who sat and watched this esoteric process take place. Mike sipped his wine. It was sweet and rich. Pots bubbled around and behind the tortilla pan. The smell of coffee, beans, and sauces filled the house.

Mike was to learn, seated at their big kitchen table, with a huge mug of coffee and a circle of concerned brown faces turned his way, that Mexicans couldn't say "Mike" if their lives depended on it. The closest any of them could get was "My."

Bobo regaled them with tales of Turk. The women clucked at the boxing and the death and patted Mike. He understood by

Bobo's acting out the blows what was being said. When Bobo apparently arrived at the fatal blow, he cried: "¡Cataplúm!" He turned to Mike and said, "That's Mexican for *Pow.*"

"Ah," said Mike.

Mike was starting to recognize another sound amid the rapid firing of the Spanish. Bobo occasionally said, "Yee-ho." This seemed to mix in with the *rraccattas* at varying points and in various combinations, appearing to constitute the entirety of sound in the Spanish language.

Mr. García had removed his hat and set it on the table beside his elbow. His hair covered his head in thick steel-gray curls. His face was deeply etched brown; dark laugh lines bracketed his mouth. His nose was sharp; his nostrils flared. He looked fierce, and the entire household deferred to him, using the formal *Usted* (thou) when speaking to him. He accepted the honor as a given.

He rested his elbows on the table and tore big chunks out of bolillo bread rolls. He dipped the bread in his coffee. He offered some to Mike.

"Supper long time," he said. "We wait"— he wrinkled his nose and shook his head—"too long for. Eat 'em up!"

Bobo nodded to the plate of rolls.

"Try it, vato."

"You like, My," Mr. García said. "Is pooty good!"

Mike took a roll. It looked like a small football.

"Dippy," Mr. Garcia said. "Dippy en you coffee."

He pantomimed dipping the bread in the cup.

Mike did what he was told. The bread came out a soggy mass. He plopped the wad in his mouth. It was delicious.

"Pretty good," he said.

Mr. García laughed: Ha-*hah!*

He slapped his hand on the table and rose. One of the little girls rushed to his hat, lifted it, brushed off imaginary lint, and handed it to him. He settled it on his head, then worked it down tight. He patted Bobo on the shoulder and went through the house, whistling tunelessly, on his way back to the gardens.

Bobo and his mother held hands.

"Damn," said Bobo, leaning back in his chair. "It's good to be home."

"Yeah," said Mike, smiling gamely.

Bobo and the women launched into a long and involved conversation in Spanish. The little girls (Carmen, Juana-María, Lupita, Chata, Blanca, and Umbelinda) flirted with Mike. He, having never been around little girls much, was not overly relaxed in their company. He was alarmed when they alternately batted their eyes at him, scolded him, ignored him. The smallest, Lupita, crawled into his lap, and he repeatedly found ways to scoot her off gently. Then she'd get back on, smiling up at him. She thought it was a game. She smelled like pee.

He stuck out his tongue. They squealed, one of them grabbed Lupita's hand, and they stampeded through the house on a wave of fabricated hysteria. Their black-and-white saddle shoes pounded the floor until the adults took up an outraged cry that followed the girls through the house: women hollered as the girls yodeled, and the canaries in the far back went insane in their cages. Then the door slammed, and Mike could hear the girls receding in the distance, a pagan horde laying waste the countryside. He thought he heard, small as a frog's croak, Mr. García's voice yelling at them too.

The twins (Almita and Florita) were apparently overwhelmed by Mike. He could see no evidence that they were married, and their recon revealed the same about him. They turned their slow dark eyes at him and stared. They came out of the kitchen wafting scents of garlic and chicken broth, and they swung their ample hips near him as they passed. When they smiled, they looked away quickly, covered their mouths with their hands, and giggled. He couldn't keep his eyes off the richness of the color of their arms. Their skin looked soft as butter. There were no angles here, as there were with Lily. The twins kept watch out of the corners of their eyes.

And he watched these people with all their secrets, and he had never felt more alone.

He excused himself by holding two fingers up to his lips.

"Smoke," he said to Bobo.

"Quiere fumarse un cigarro," Bobo said to Mama.

"Pase, My," she said, gesturing graciously with her hand.

"Um," he replied, "gracias."

He walked out the front door and took a profound breath of dry mountain air. "Jeez," he muttered. He dug in the truck for a pack of cigs and fired one up and took a deep drag.

41

THE AIR UP HERE WAS EXCEPTIONALLY CLEAR, AND IT ROSE cool from the ravines. He gazed down at the far desert—it looked like a vast shadowy lake beneath him, and he imagined this small plateau in the winter, an island with snow blowing softly and piling along the base of the rocks. He moved across the front of the house, looking in at the doves in their cages. They preened and blinked, with little collars of dark feathers around their necks. They looked as gray and delicate as ashes. Mike would have been shocked to learn that the ever-practical Mr. García periodically beheaded a bunch of them and roasted them over an open fire.

Hummingbirds whirred along the fence, and one darted near and hovered by Mike's ear to see what kind of nectar he was carrying. Disgruntled, it zoomed back out and got in a spat with another hummer, and they loop-the-looped all across the road. Mike watched fat bumblebees working the fuchsias. He was amazed that he could hear them rattling around inside the blossoms.

He leaned his arms on the fence and launched a smoke ring. Across the road, four crows sat on a drooping phone line, exchanging boasts. He watched them nudge each other, shout, raise their wings, and grumble. All they needed were cigars. "Croc!" they yelled in each other's faces. "Croc!"

They seemed to be keeping watch over the Garcías' corn patch. He moseyed down there to take a look. The corn swished and swayed in the breeze, bright gold tassels shimmering. It smelled good. White butterflies dashed along the rows, tipping up into the sun on high-speed strafing runs. A preposterous stick-and-broom Mexican effigy rose from the corn. Mr. García had exercised some whimsy by perching a faded Mexican sombrero on the scarecrow's head. Its mop-handle arms held out the sleeves of a checkered shirt. Drooping work gloves served as hands, and in each one, Mr. García had pinned bundles of old black socks.

Mike looked back at the crows. They had their heads cocked as they stared at the stickman. Mike laughed. The socks must have seemed like strangled crows to them. They were *worried,* he realized. He imagined the crows coming near every morning to keep an eye on this homicidal Mexican. He blew a puff in the air to get their attention.

"I'm surprised at you boys!" he called. They stared at him. "Afraid of this old thing!"

They blasted off the phone line, flapping madly in a fabricated panic, warning every crow for miles: *Walking thing! It's yelling at us! Croc!*

They swooped down a gully, their complaints audible long after they had flown out of sight. Mike turned and, still smiling, saw Umbelinda staring at him.

"You talked to the birds," she said.

"Uh, well, yeah, I guess I did," he said.

She regarded him with a somber expression.

"Do they talk back?" she asked.

Mike dropped his cigarette and stubbed it out with a toe.

"Not yet."

She nodded.

"Grampa talks to the plants."

About a half acre away, Mr. García stood framed by grapevines that arched over a brick walkway. The other girls, bright flecks of color, swirled down the slopes of the hillside, flashing in and out of bushes that Mike imagined were full of raspberries, blackberries, chokecherries. He knew nothing about berry bushes, of course, but they seemed to go with little girls. He could hear the dogs barking as they scrambled around the girls, chasing each other and wrestling, leaping high, their tails wagging.

While Mike daydreamed of straw baskets full of berries, three of the girls were peeing in a bush. Chata and Blanca had cornered a small garter snake and were poking at it with a stick. Mike might have been pleased to know that while she squatted in her bush, Juana-María did reach behind her and pick a berry and pop it into her mouth.

The grape leaves above Mr. García's head fluttered, backlit by the afternoon sun. They seemed impossibly bright, as if they were plugged in. Electric.

Mr. García looked up at him and waved.

Mike saw Umbelinda staring up at him.

He smiled at her.

She reached out and took his hand and led him down toward the grape arbor.

"Come on, Mike," she said.

They walked under the cool tunnel of grapevines, and Mike became aware, as they passed, of green clumps of baby grapes, small and hard-looking as plastic beads. The same white butterflies he'd seen at the corn patch dodged around his head.

"What are these?" Mike asked.

"Butterflies," she said.

"What kind?"

"White ones," she said, as though he were the silliest boy in town.

"Is buttermilk butterfly," Mr. García said as they approached. "Dile," he said to Umbelinda, ordering her to explain what he'd said. But Mike said, "I understand."

Mr. García nodded expansively and said, "Ah."

Umbelinda went over to an upturned barrel and sat on it. She kicked her feet, banging her heels into the wood. She said Mike's name three times in a singsong: "*Mike*—Mike—*Mike.*" In official Little Girl, this translated as: Mike is my boyfriend.

Mr. García gestured at his garden.

"You likey?"

It was an expanse of fruit trees—some of them in tents of plastic sheeting. Mike was to learn that these were little one-tree greenhouses. There was a thick stand of beaver-tail cactus. "Nopal," Mr. García said. "Nopal," Mike repeated: his first Spanish lesson. Cascades of sweet peas were tied to fences and stakes, their blossoms soft-colored, reminding Mike of tissue paper. Rows of lettuce, rangy tomato vines crawling up chicken-wire frames, wooden boxes grown thick with herbs. Everywhere, the white butterflies, bees, small birds. Mike had never seen anything like it.

Mr. García pointed to a low wooden box jammed full of pink flowers.

"Claveles," he said, then pointed at Umbelinda.

"Um," she said, seeking the word. "Carnations."

Mike nodded.

"Cla . . . ?" he said.

"Claveles."

"Claveles," Mike replied.

Mr. García launched his laugh: Ha-*hah!*

Then he nudged Umbelinda to translate what followed, but Mike understood it perfectly well. Mr. García said, "I likey inside, inside okay, but no too much. Es mucho mejor outside. I like pooty good!"

Mike nodded.

"Yes," he said. "I like outside too."

Mr. García clapped him on the shoulder.

"Cah-mah," he said, which Mike deciphered as *Come on.* He followed Mr. García. Umbelinda followed him. She hooked one finger in his belt loop and let him pull her along, imagining she was water-skiing, something she had seen on the television. Mike glanced back at her and sort of smiled.

Mr. García took them to a dark green bush; its leaves were leathery. From it depended large fuzzy yellow fruit.

"Membrillo," said Mr. García.

Mike repeated it.

Umbelinda beamed proudly: *That's my boy!*

Mr. García said, "You espeakin Espanish, My!"

They laughed together.

They cut loose membrillos and cut out white slices and ate them. The fruit made Mike's mouth pucker. He nodded. He said, "Strange." Umbelinda translated this, and for some reason, it delighted Mr. García. He laughed out loud for so long that he started to cough. Mike was startled when Mr. García pulled a full set of false teeth out of his mouth, spit, licked his gums, and slid the teeth back in. He said, "Puta madre," which Umbelinda's reaction indicated to be obscene.

"Cah-mah," Mr. García said, and Umbelinda grabbed Mike's hand and skipped beside him as they moved toward the next tree.

Inside the house, Bobo and his mother murmured in soft Spanish. She had already begun her campaign on Bobo. She was as relentless as a velvet hammer, gently implacable in her love.

"My son, you have been gone long enough. Why won't you come home to us? Look at your friend Miguel—he has no home."

"Ay, Mamá," Bobo said.

"Isn't it true?" she said. "We love you. Why must you roam like a wild soul?"

She began to weep.

He patted her hand.

"Have I done you wrong, Bonifacio?" she asked.

"No," he said. "Never."

"You don't want to work in the mines, I know," she said. "It was hard for your father, and now it's hard for Almita." Bobo felt guilt, but he also felt the suffocating rage the mines brought up in him. "Come back for the land," she said. "Come back for your father. His hips trouble him worse every year. You could farm together. You could get a goat and win a sweet girl's heart and join us in the house."

Jesus! Bobo thought.

"Mamá," he said, "I am home. For now, let that be enough."

He crossed his arms.

She nodded, recognizing the gesture.

"Yes, my son," she said.

Florita, the simpler of the twins, came up and hugged Bobo from behind. Her arms crossed at his throat and nearly strangled him. Her bust pillowed the back of his neck. "You bad boy!" she growled into his ear.

It was an old game between them, from his childhood. Though the family called the twins "the girls" (las muchachas), they were at least ten years older than Bobo. His "sisters" had been adopted into the family when their widowed father was killed in a mining accident in Morenci.

The two women had each secretly pressed Bobo's teenaged face into their breasts, put their hands down the front of his pants, lifted their skirts to show him their dimpled bottoms and to allow him—on the days when they wore their girdles—to touch them all over. Neither was aware of the other's experiments. Bobo knew that until a husband came along, he would remain their secret love. And he could never manage to replace the feelings he had for them. His most agonizing sexual fantasy consisted of Florita's impenetrable girdle, his fingers bending backward as he tried futilely to work them down under the elastic, all the time praying for just a half inch of clearance.

"But still," said Mrs. García sadly, "it hurts a mother's heart to have her only son forget her."

She looked out the window.

Bobo laid his head back against Florita and closed his eyes.

"I'll try," he promised. "I really will."

Mr. García had three bright green tendrils from a grapevine in his hand. He handed one to Mike and one to Umbelinda, who promptly popped it in her mouth. "Here," Mr. García said. "Chew." He pointed to his mouth.

Mike chewed the end. It was sour—bitterly sour. His nose crinkled. He grinned. It was awful. He loved it.

"Is good," said Mr. García. "Bitter make strong the blood!"

He turned Mike to the wooden frame that held up the grapes. "Look," he said. Then, to Umbelinda: "Tú, niña. Ven aquí." She crowded in next to Mike, banging her hip into his leg.

Mr. García pointed. Mike looked, saw nothing.

"Leaves?" he said.

"No."

Mr. García kept pointing.

"Lookee."

Mike studied the vines, the wood.

Umbelinda nudged him, pointed.

"Ants?" he said.

"¿Qué dijo?" Mr. García asked Umbelinda.

"Hormigas," she said.

"Sí. Ants. Ants." He pointed. He made his way along the frame, still pointing. Umbelinda glanced at Mike and giggled, then shrugged. They followed the gnarled finger, staring at the ants as they ran along the vines and the wood. At a clump of big leaves, the ants vanished.

"Now!" said Mr. García.

He turned a leaf over gently. The underside of the leaf was covered with aphids. Umbelinda craned up to see them. They were bright green and looked like tiny walking grape seeds. The ants swarmed around them.

"Is it a war, or what?" Mike said.

"Look!" said Mr. García. "You no look, you no see nothing, My."

Mike looked. And then he understood. The ants were tenderly stroking the aphids with their feelers. They surrounded the bugs and petted them, and periodically a clear drop of nectar popped out of the aphids' rear ends. Umbelinda made a small breathy sound. The ants carefully picked up these drops and ran back down the length of the vine, carrying the nectar back to the nest.

"Hey!" said Mike.

Mr. García laughed.

"Son vacas," he said. "Is cows." He pointed to the aphids and said, "Cows." Then he pointed to the ants and said, "Farmers."

He led them to the entrance of the ant nest. A small cone of pebbles rose around the opening. "Miners too," he said. "Just like me." He smiled, put his hand on Umbelinda's head. "Thirty-five years," he said. He patted his hip. "No good now, My. Is bust."

He and Mike nodded at each other.

"I'm sorry," said Mike.

Umbelinda reached over and tucked a loose shirttail back into Mike's beltline.

"Is okay," said Mr. García, looking far beyond Mike now, watching the peaks as the lowering sun ignited their tips. "Vivo afuera, Miguel. I live outside." He smiled at his trees. "Outside," he said, "is pooty good."

42

MIKE HAD SEEN ROWS OF LETTUCE LOOKING LIKE THE heads of cavalrymen buried by Apaches. He'd learned the Spanish names of onions, garlic, pears, peaches. He'd learned, through some intuitive sign language and a series of grimaces and guffaws, how Mr. García made beef jerky, then shredded the jerky to make machaca. He'd been shown the ball-peen hammer and the drying racks and the strips of hardened beef. Umbelinda had stolen a piece, and both Mr. García and Mike had pretended not to see her, all three of them enjoying the scandal.

At the compost heap, Mike took a pitchfork and turned the black mulch. He was fascinated with the stuff in there: coffee grounds, eggshells, fruit rinds, onion skins. Feathers.

Earthworms like lengths of yarn wiggled in the dark soil. All the time, Mr. García whistled with no particular melody in mind. He scooped up a fistful of the dirt and showed it to Mike. Mike grabbed his own handful, then Umbelinda got hers. Mike squeezed it hard in his hand; the black loam curled out between his fingers, rich as chocolate cake.

And then it was time for supper.

Umbelinda was in the girls' room, telling the others, "Mike wants to marry me."

They all gasped and giggled; Juana-María pulled a face and made a fart sound with her mouth. "Guácala," she said, which meant "Yuck."

Lupita said, "Can I be your daughter?"

Blanca said, "And I'll be the grandma and sit in the back room all day and knit!"

Umbelinda put her hand out and said, "Wait until you see my ring."

Mrs. García called to them to wash their hands and get to the table.

Bobo sat in his old bedroom, staring at the photographs of himself stuck in the mirror: wrestling as Calamity Claud in Kentucky, as The Butcher of Burundi in Arkansas, with a blond dye job as Lovely Lyle Lollipop in Oakland. A photo showed him innocently proud in his new uniform, among other grinning boys, most of them not destined to return. Beside it, a photograph of one of his lost girlfriends, all dolled up in her weesa clothes, looking all reet and loca.

"¡Bonifacio!" his mother called. "Lávese las manos, m'ijito, que ya es hora de cenar."

He walked down to the bathroom and locked himself in. Then he punched the tile wall as hard as he could. His father had built the wall himself—it was solid as a boulder. Bobo's knuckles cracked against the tiles, the skin split, and tiny lines of blood seeped between his fingers. He watched it fill the creases in his skin. Home. Home again.

In her bedroom, Almita lay on the bed and sighed. She'd put in a short day at the mines today, her feet in her boots too sore to stand on. But it was her belly that really gave her trouble. She'd gone with Angel again this weekend, to one of their "picnics." This time at the cemetery below Clifton. And they'd done things there, and she was afraid. It was a worse sin in such a holy place, but the sin excited her. Her face flushed darker.

Angel said he would marry her, but he had first promised it five years ago, and here she was still waiting. He promised her a honeymoon—maybe all the way to Phoenix. She couldn't imagine it! Tall buildings with many windows. Almita had been only as far as Clifton, and once she'd traveled the sixty miles down to Safford.

Phoenix.

She rubbed her belly and thought of what might be in there now.

She closed her eyes and said the word aloud: "Fénix."

Bobo looked around the bathroom. It was all the same. Everything was in its place, his father's straight razor lying half open on a white cloth beside the shaving-soap mug, the brush propped against the mug, its bristles up. He felt them—they were still damp from this morning's shave. Nothing had moved.

There was the huge barrel for dirty clothes accumulated until the monthly laundry day, when ladies from the village joined Mrs. García in a day-long festival of boiling and scrubbing and cooking and gossip. This barrel where he had first thought to fish out Almita and Florita's underwear, breathing in the forbidden scent of their secrets. They could have been the same exact underpants in there now—big and limp, pale blue and yellow, with vaguely discolored patches.

He knew where every pot was hung, where the twins hid their huge Kotex pads, where the liquor and the mouse poison were. Not even Buchenwald had moved anything. Not even the smell of Buchenwald had removed the medicinal odor of Mr. García's various herbal cures lined up in mason jars on shelves under the sink.

These people did not comprehend a place such as that.

When he had tried to tell them, they nodded gently and patted his hand. But their eyes remained blank. They barely understood who Hitler was. Their imaginations were still riding with Pancho Villa and Emiliano Zapata; their dreams were still circling the royal palace of Cuauhtémoc and the ships of Cortés. How could they understand ovens?

He washed his face.

Mrs. García was clapping her hands together and crying, "Time to eat!"

He looked in the mirror and tried on a smile.

❦ ❦ ❦

Mr. García took his place at the head of the table. Mama García sat at his left hand, at the corner. Down the left side of the table, a fidgety row of girls, ending with Umbelinda, firmly linking her arm through Mike's and smiling passively at everyone. Lupita scooted off her seat and piled onto Mike's lap. On the right side, after they had finished serving, sat the twins. Almita was shy and looked away from Mike; Florita brazenly flirted with him and broke into uproarious laughter at everything he said. She kept asking him, "Favajú?" which in time clarified itself as "How are you?" After saying "Fine" three times, Mike started saying, "I'm still fine," which made her laugh more. Beside her, Bobo crowded in on his father's elbow.

Umbelinda said grace, in English to honor Mike. "Bless us, Father, and these thy fruits, amen."

"Amen," everybody said.

Mike, locking eyes with Mr. García, did a sideways nod, throwing some shoulder into it: *Smart girl!*

Mr. García, with a waggle of his head and a general scowl, replied: *I don't raise no fools!*

Food filled the expanse of the table before him. Three towers of tortillas steamed under white cloths. A plate of onions cut in rings, sliced tomatoes, and chilis. A huge bowl of frijoles de hoya, the beans floating in thick soup. Potatoes cut in wedges and drifting in a clear onion-and-chicken broth. Soft strips of beef marinated in a vaguely sweet sauce. Pitchers of salsa, coffee, milk. Corn on the cob. Butter. Mike gawked.

"Dig in," said Bobo.

Florita said, "My? Favajú!"

Mr. García ate with his mouth open. He chomped away loudly as he directed the table conversation. The things he was saying were apparently quite funny. Mama García occasionally slapped at Mr. García's arm. When she did this, he got a wide-eyed innocent look and stared at Mike, and everybody laughed. Mike had absolutely no idea what he was laughing about. He ate around Lupita, who periodically raided his plate for a morsel.

Umbelinda leaned over to her and said, "Now be a good girl, Lupita. Don't drive your daddy crazy."

"Yes, Mommy," said Lupita in a baby voice.

Mommy! Daddy! Mike thought.

He would have enjoyed keeling over right there at the table and being buried out under Mr. García's membrillo tree.

"I want to be a Mexican," he announced.

This was greeted with several translations and an outburst of joy.

Just when Mike couldn't possibly eat any more, Bobo said, "Wait, there's more."

The twins and Umbelinda cleared the table. The other girls were watching Umbelinda and giggling. Mr. García told them they sounded like little chicks peeping over a piece of corn. This made them giggle more.

Florita produced a gooey-looking thing that was only a half-inch thick but weighed three pounds.

"Ko-flecky pie," said Mrs. García, as though imparting great wisdom.

"Ko-flecky," said Mr. García.

"Yum," said Bobo.

"Ko-flecky?" said Mike.

Mr. García cut a piece and dropped it on a plate and handed the plate to Mike. "Ko-flecky pie, My!"

Bobo was too busy chewing to offer any insight, so Mike just dug in. It was dense, sweet, sticky. *Caramel,* he thought. *Marshmallows. Corn flakes!*

Cornflake pie!

He beamed at them and said, "Mo make mie!"

43

THE EVENING MEANDERED ALONG, AND IT SUITED MIKE just fine. They all gravitated to various couches and easy chairs around the living room and focused on the television. Mike smiled as Fred Mertz flickered, flickered, flickered.

Mike, in his recliner chair, noticed that, at regular intervals, the backyard dogpack tore out en masse, with a hysterical bugle and yammer. They charged around the house and berated the front gate, then could be heard clicking back along Mr. García's walkway, growling in their throats with utter self-satisfaction. Mike could almost hear them saying, What bad dogs are we! Then a car would crunch by in the dirt street, and they'd hurtle back to the gate, demanding an explanation.

Mr. García lounged on the couch, feet in Mrs. García's lap. She absentmindedly fiddled with his toes. The couch itself was indescribable in its ugliness: it had a mid-decade "modern" color, the shade of a very bad color photograph of oatmeal.

Umbelinda brought out her blanket and laid it over Mike.

"Thank you," he said.

She wrinkled her nose at him dismissively.

The twins sat upright on kitchen chairs, Florita watching Mike and laughing softly. Bobo sprawled in an old lounge chair. And in the middle of the floor, in a tangle of dolls and blankets, lay the litter of girls.

Lupita detached herself from the throng. She had a Raggedy Ann in a stranglehold. She walked up to Mike and plugged her thumb into her mouth. "Yes?" he said. She climbed into his lap. She squirmed around until she was comfortable. The top of her compact skull rolled against the point of Mike's chin. Nobody looked. He was frozen for a moment, then slowly relaxed. He put one arm around her. Then the other. After a time, Lupita began to snore softly.

On the television, Ernie Kovacs was caught in a huge rubber band. It launched him three miles into the sky.

44

THUNDER AND LIGHTNING.

Mike was aware, through his sleep, of the fast-moving storm tearing into the hills, the drumroll of hard rain, the jug-band melodies of wind in the eaves. He slept in his jeans.

He awoke to a presence in the bed. For a mad moment, he thought it was Turk. But it was only Umbelinda.

Only Umbelinda!

He sat up—and there were Chata and Lupita too. And Juana-María. Carmen and Blanca lay crosswise over his feet. He was entirely hemmed in by little girls. Their noses whined and snuffled in their sleep. They smelled like feet and wind-dried cotton and bubble gum.

Now what?

He wanted to extricate himself, but he feared waking them and some sort of horrible discovery following: screaming little girls and Mike in the middle as Mr. García aimed a shotgun and Mike said, "I was only sleeping—honest!" He tried to move Umbelinda. She was dense. He imagined a sack of sugar.

Slowly he put his leg over Chata and raised himself over her. He felt for the floor and finally found it. He did a cautious one-armed push-up and held himself as he passed over the child. Just as he was freeing himself from the bed and standing straight, Umbelinda said, "Where you going, Mike?"

"Bathroom," he muttered, backing out of the room.

He bumped through the house and made his way to the living room. He stretched out in Bobo's easy chair and tried to sleep. Later, after he was snoring, Umbelinda came out and covered him with her blanket.

Mrs. García awoke him at dawn. She didn't seem the least surprised to find him sleeping in the living room.

"Buenos días, My," she said.

"Morning," he said, trying to smooth his hair down.

"Ven conmigo." She gestured for him to follow. He got up, wrapped the blanket around him, and minced barefoot behind her as she went to the enclosed porch at the back of the house.

He rubbed the sleep out of his eyes while she pulled cloths off birdcages. Washboards hung from nails above a large iron sink. Mike leaned on the sink and peered into the cages.

"Canaries," he said.

"Sí." She nodded.

He thought the birds smelled like bread. The birds, pondering the sight of Mike first thing in the morning, fluttered and said, "Pete? Pete-pete?"

Mama pointed in the corners of the cages. There, little cardboard birdhouses held nests made in tea strainers. Mike was startled to see tiny eggs.

"Huevitos," Mama said.

She took his hand in her own. She patted the back of it with her small palm.

"My-ito," she said. *Little Mike.*

He was acutely aware of her hands. They were quite like birds themselves. They were so soft he couldn't imagine bones in them. He watched her hands beating against his knuckles as though ruby hearts beat within them.

Beside him, the canaries stared up at him and asked, "Pete? Pete?"

"Yeah, it's nice," said Bobo.

They sat on a bench in the backyard, sharing a smoke. Mike balanced a cup of coffee on his knee.

"But it ain't easy," Bobo continued.

"How so?"

Bobo looked at him as if he were an idiot.

"Money, vato. Where do you think they get the money?"

Money had never occurred to him. He thought the García spread was a magic kingdom, utterly separate from the earth.

"The ol' man got fucked up royal in them mines," Bobo said. "You seen him try to walk?"

"Yes," said Mike.

"You don't get too much of a break around here. Not when you're a Mexican."

Bobo took a puff, grimaced, snubbed the cigarette out.

"I'm gettin' sick of these damned things."

"You send them money," Mike said.

"I *sent* them money. When I was famous."

Mike nodded.

"Now," Bobo said, "Almita's in the mines and I send what I can. The old man can't get around good enough to really farm. They still got to buy meat, shit like that. Can't make no dough off the produce to pay for stuff. Tú sabes. Same ol' same ol'."

"Man," said Mike. "I would give anything . . . "

But he stopped.

He didn't want even to think about it.

If he started to love this place, he knew something would happen.

Something always happened.

It was the McGurk way.

"Maybe," he said, "maybe we can stay awhile and help out."

"Yeah," Bobo said. "Maybe."

Umbelinda came around the corner.

"Mike," she said, "Mama wants you."

"Be there in a minute."

She wrinkled her nose at him and skipped off.

"Those girls," Mike said.

"Buncha monkeys," said Bobo.

"They your sisters?"

"Naw." Bobo picked up a stick and dug in the dirt. "Two's my nieces, from my dead sister. The others are orphans from a mine family. Pops took 'em in. Same as the twins."

"*They're* not your sisters?"

"Shit, no."

Mike couldn't help thinking: *Maybe they'll take me in too.*

Bobo noticed the look on his face but didn't mention it. He said, "You better go see what Mama wants. She's the boss."

Mike got up and drifted around the corner, lost in his dreams.

She wanted help collecting pea pods. She wanted Mike to pick the peas and put them into her upturned apron. Through Umbelinda she said, "Look at these flowers. Don't they look like little dog faces? Watch the doggy stick out his tongue," she said, and pinched the flower between thumb and forefinger, pulling on it until a long tongue popped out of its snout.

"Hey!" Mike said.

As they laughed, Mama stopped and looked over Mike's shoulder. He saw Almita coming home early from work, clutching her stomach. She put one hand over her mouth and hurried into the house.

Mama's eyes were stern as she watched, then she gestured for Mike to start picking, and she impatiently shook her apron at him.

45

Bobo lay back on his bed, arms crossed behind his head. He stared up at the ceiling, at the horse-shaped cracks that seemed to gallop into the corners. The midday noise of the García spread drifted into his open window as the curtains furled: the dogs, the girls, the canaries, the crows, Papa's tuneless whistling, the distant cry of the trains, the clatter coming from the kitchen.

Mike poked his head in the window.

"Hey," said Bobo.

"I've gotta do something," said Mike.

"You bored?" Bobo replied.

"No! I gotta *do* something. I've never done a thing!"

Bobo just stared at Mike.

"O-kay," he said.

Mike nodded, as if they'd traded something intelligent. Then he waved once and left the window.

Bobo shook his head.

"McGurk," he said.

He sighed. He thought about Florita and Almita. Back around when he was twelve.

It all began with that line full of droopy underwear outside. One day, as he ran after butterflies, trying to nail them with a flyswatter, he ducked under the line and various wet panties flapped across his face. He slowed down, stopped, and turned to consider this. He walked back through the panties, letting them slide across his cheeks. He was thinking about where they'd been. And he was thinking that they were on his face now.

He started peeking into the twins' window as they undressed. There was the slightest gap between the curtain and the edge of the window frame. Soon there came the dreadful day when, while Almita was at work, he sat on their big bed, watching Florita powder her face at the round mirror. He watched her bottom, then looked up at her eyes reflected in the glass, then back at her bottom. Every time he looked up, her eyes were locked on his. The huge powder puff blew clouds of powder around her head. She suddenly growled, "You bad boy!" and he was upon her, grappling with her from behind, pressing against her hard-packed rump with all his might. His face reached just as high as the back of her neck, and he had to keep blowing hair out of his way. He reached around her and wrenched her breasts this way and that, while she steadied herself against her vanity table and pushed back against him. She smiled faintly and sucked air through her teeth in a repetitive pattern, as though she had hot jalapeños burning her tongue: "Ssst—ah. Ssst—ah."

Bobo smiled up at the ceiling.

They took to clenching like this often. Sometimes they met five or six times a day, sometimes for ten full minutes, squeezing, pushing, and hissing. Bobo, glued to her backside, tried gamely to see over her shoulder so he could watch her breasts rotate.

Whenever he seemed to be getting too excited, she'd fool him with "Here comes your father!" and he'd unhand her and dive for the other side of the room, where he'd try to look innocent. The ruse worked on him for years, he was so addled with lust. During these reprieves, Florita would take up her pink puff and start in on herself again.

Then, one night, he followed Almita to her room after she got home from work. She'd stepped into their huge closet to slip out of her work pants and shirt—it was closed off from view by a blanket—and she'd said, "Don't go away. I'll be right out."

And Bobo, already feverish with the idea, slipped behind the blanket.

"I don't know," Mike was saying. "I try to do my best. I really do. But I screw things up.

"I let my dad down. I don't know what he wanted, exactly. I couldn't figure it out. Shoot. Turk, I guess—yeah, he was a difficult guy. I'd say that much for him."

He laughed a little. He took out a cigarette, looked at it, and put it back.

"I just want to . . . I just want to *do* something. You know? I just want to get going and do *something*. Go someplace nice. Maybe settle down. Get a dog.

"I don't know."

Umbelinda rested her chin on her fist and listened.

"It's okay, Mike," she said. "Sometimes I want to do my homework, but I gotta go play first. It looks like you did your homework first. Now you got to play."

She nodded reassuringly.

"Really," she said. "I think so."

"Kind of like recess," Mike said.

She smiled at him.

She patted his hand.

"You'll be happy," she said.

He stared at the thin clouds passing above him. *Clouds,* he thought, and the word had more meaning than itself to him. They were sitting behind the membrillo tree. One of the dogs lay pressed against his back. He reached around and scratched its belly.

"You think so?" he asked.

She nodded.

"You live with us now," she said. "We'll take care of you."

She picked a dandelion and blew the tufts away.

For a short moment, Mike forgot everything.

Bobo got up.

All that groping, it was all right for a kid. But he knew it was over now. He would never find it possible to touch either twin again. It had just happened. He suddenly knew, when he got back from the war, that it was finished.

He walked out of his room.

Almita was emerging from the bathroom. Her face was pale and damp from her splashing it with water. Her black hair stuck to her temples. He waited for her in the hall. He put his arm around her shoulder when she came up to him, and she stopped. He laid his head against the side of her face. He could smell her sweat, feel her heat through her dress.

They stood for a minute together, just holding on.

"Ay, Bonifacio," was all she said.

46

It took Mike a week, but he decided what to do. He had said to Bobo one morning, "I'm going to give them all my money." And Bobo had said, "No way." And Mike had said, "Yeah! I have a couple hundred left from the house, got the fight money, got Grandfather Sneezy's money. It's a lot." And Bobo had said, "Look, Mike—there's no way. Pops won't take no money. Forget it."

Later in the morning, Mike said, "Then let's go to town and buy them stuff and say it's from you. From both of us."

"What stuff?"

"All the stuff. Any stuff. Whatever we want to get 'em. Whatever they need. But especially stuff they don't need."

"Chocolates?" Bobo said.

"Dolls," suggested Mike.

"Hats," Bobo recommended.

"Hot-water bottles," Mike sang.

Bobo, looking at him for a long moment, said, "Really?"

He blushed, then started to laugh, then clapped Mike on the shoulder. They found themselves in the tow truck, heading down toward Clifton and Morenci. Bobo's pockets bulged with rolls of bills. The day was spectacular—the sun slanted up from the desert a bright golden-orange, the cliffs radiated light as if from within.

"Look there," Bobo said. "Mine shaft."

Mike craned his neck.

"Spooky," he said.

"Full of bats, vato," said Bobo. "Snakes and stuff."

"So," Mike said, "the gold played out—"

"And they found copper. Copper all over the place up here. P-D moved in quick and became king of the hill."

Bobo pointed at a little gully.

"A band of Apaches whaled the shit out of some Mexicans up there one time."

"Good deal," said Mike.

"Not for the Mexicans."

Mike said, "Bobe? You get any snow up around here?"

"Sometimes . . . Hey, what's that fool doing?"

A distant, almost familiar pickup truck swung across the road ahead. It slowly backed partway into their lane, forcing them over onto the shoulder as Mike braked hard and swerved. They squeezed past and saw a stark arm rise from the driver's window, its fist extending one finger.

Bobo said, "That guy's flipping us the bird!"

Mike shook his head.

You just couldn't figure some people.

They shot back onto the road in a scattering of pebbles and continued down. Ramses Castro sat in his truck and watched them go. He scratched himself and softly sang, "Roly Poly—Daddy's little fatty." He had a rash from driving for so long sitting on the sweaty plastic seat. The gearshift was a little sticky, but he wrestled it back into first and headed up into the hills.

Mike and Bobo were heading for the company store. They'd made up their dream list of goods that the García family simply couldn't live without: ice cream, thread, beef, noodles, bread, pies, soda, stockings. "Sliced bread," Bobo had cried. "They love sliced bread!" Jam, sugar, flour, peanut butter. Bobo had slipped into Garcíaspeak and called it "peanah battah." Crayons and underpants were major items of concern. Mike, overwhelmed with family feelings, had grabbed Bobo's arms and shouted, "Let's buy up the whole damn store!" into his face.

Bobo was going on about things that barely penetrated

Mike's reverie. Those cliffs! Those abandoned mines! Cornflake pie! Mexicans!

". . . so Almita," Bobo was explaining, "has been seeing Angel Apodaca." He shook his head, spit out the window. "Pinche Angel, what a jerk! Pops been trying to stop her. . . ."

Mike was going to build a small cabin at the rear of the Garcías' yard. He was going to go back for his books, get Mr. García to help him build some shelves, and then he'd teach Umbelinda the fistfight speech from *Life on the Mississippi.* In his mind, he was setting the books up in alphabetical order: *Dickens, Faulkner, Hemingway, Ruark. No, wait. Crane, Dickens, Faulkner, and Hemingway. Then Melville. Then Ruark. No, wait. First Brontë, then Crane, then Dickens. . . .* This inane pastime kept him happy for long minutes at a time.

". . . Angel is head clerk at the P-D store. His dad's the boss—real company men. Pops says to me, 'First they screw us when we work for them, and I won't have them screwing our women too.' How do you like that Pops anyway? . . ."

Mike was thinking he'd marry one of the twins. Why not!

He had a brief sexual fantasy featuring great upheavals under a sheet and the transported cry of "*Favajuuu!*"

He'd find a romantic trinket at the store.

However, the Copper Penny presented itself on the way.

It was a little miners' bar about a half mile from the Motor Lodge as they swung up toward Morenci. "I believe a libation is in order," Bobo said.

"A brief snort," Mike agreed.

"Brew shall be quaffed," promised Bobo.

It was one of the twelve million forgettable box-shaped bars that figure so prominently in many an American outskirt. The kind of joint that had antlers over the door and no sweet drinks. Grainy pictures of long-dead miners crowded whiskey bottles before the mirror. Far back, peeking out like a spy, was a photo of Mr. García in his prime, holding up a pick with one arm and laughing out loud. A trout was bolted to the wall, and several still-living copper miners were screwed tight to their stools, glowering at their beers 'n' shooters. Most of them were wondering *What in the Hell.*

Bobo and Mike made straight for the bar.

"Hiya," said Mike to the bartender.

"How do," said the man. Mike was astonished at the length of the man's ears—his earlobes were wattles that depended beside his face like saddle bags.

"Beer," Mike said. "And another for Pancho."

The barkeep glanced at Bobo.

"Hey," he said. "You're the García boy."

"That's right," said Bobo.

"How's the wrestlin'?"

"Gave her up," said Bobo.

"Don't tell me that!"

"Hung up my shorts."

"I'll be."

"Nothin' lasts forever."

"Tell me about it."

"But I got no complaints."

"Hell no," the barkeep proclaimed. "Don't look back."

"Early retirement," Bobo said, raising his hands helplessly.

"Kee-rist," the barkeep sympathized.

He started away, then stepped back and said, "What kind of beer you boys want?"

"Big and cold," said Mike.

"Them's the best kind, I always say," quipped the bartender.

He delivered two frosty mugs to them and said, "You lookin' for work? 'Cause if you're lookin' for work, you might as well turn her around and drive back on down to the flats!"

"That bad, huh?" said Mike.

"That bad and worse," said a miner.

The barkeep said, "See this fella?" pointing at Bobo. "He's the Butcher of Burundi."

"The hell you say," said the miner, and returned to his beer.

"War's over," the bartender said to Bobo. "Copper demand is way down."

"Bullets!" the miner cried. "No more Gott-damned bullets." He shook his head, took another drink.

Mike was suddenly struck by an immense vision. Arizona copper made pennies; the pennies bought bullets also made from Arizona copper; the bullets flew through the air and plugged themselves into German, Japanese, Chinese, Korean bodies. This was the worst imaginable form of continental drift.

"It's okay," said Bobo. "Just visiting."

The miner reached over and slapped a penny on the bar before Mike.

"Look at that," the miner said.

Mike looked at the penny.

The bartender said to Bobo, "How's the family?"

"Fine. You know. Making do."

"How's the old man's leg holding up?"

"Kinda stiff, I guess."

"That's a shame, you know it?"

"I know it."

The miner said to Mike, "This penny comes right out of that hill behind you."

Mike made an appreciative face that looked like he was saying: *Wooo!*

"And here it is," the miner continued, "right back in Clifton."

"How do you like that," said Mike.

The bartender leaned one elbow on the bar in front of Bobo and asked, "How're them girls?"

"The little ones or the big ones?"

"Little ones! They got little ones up there?"

"Got a herd of little ones up there."

"Wow—and how 'bout them twins?"

"They're fine."

Mike's miner half turned and said, "Leave them twins out to run wild, and you'll have some more Gott-damned little ones, that's for sure."

The miner on the other side of Bobo snorted.

"What's that supposed to mean?" said Bobo.

"Now, Pat," warned the barkeep.

"No, I really want to know," Bobo said. "What's that supposed to mean?"

"Jesus, kid," said Pat. "It's not a secret or nothin'." He turned back to Mike and said, "This penny here has come home to roost. And I'll tell you what—it ain't worth a plug poo!"

Bobo turned Pat around.

"What are you saying?" he asked.

"Go ask that Apodaca boy up to the big store." Pat glanced sideways at another miner and snickered.

"Okay, boys," the barkeep reasoned.

Bobo smiled vaguely. Mike watched his face go pale.

"He knocked one of them up," Pat said. "Don't look at me. I din't do it!"

Bobo turned to the bartender.

"That's what they're sayin'," the bartender said. "Ol' Angel left town last night in a big hurry."

"Burnin' rubber." The miner behind Bobo smiled. "If you catch my drift."

Pat guffawed.

"Service with a smile," he said, "and now I'll run a mile."

"Gave her a poke," the other miner chimed in, "now watch my smoke."

These subterranean imbeciles chortled in chorus.

Bobo turned back to Pat. He gawked at him as if he were the weirdest spider he'd ever seen.

"You damned beaners," Pat said, suddenly maniacally brave and performing for the other miners in the room. "You oughta learn to keep it in your pants."

Mike threw a vast punch into the side of Pat's head and blew him right off the stool. Bobo seemed as startled as Pat. The barkeep jumped across the bar, reaching for Mike, and Bobo clipped him one on his giant ear. He yowled and dropped behind the bar. Two miners piled on Mike, and Bobo started launching them in body flips—bodies flew to and fro like sacks of beans, toppling tables and chairs. "Boys!" the bartender hollered from behind his fort. "Boys!"

Pat had risen, apparently thrilled at the chance to punch somebody, and he and Mike stood toe-to-toe, throwing punches at each other and grunting. Then, as if by magic, they were out on the street, rolling in the dirt. They each had dirt in their mouths and eyes as Mike shoved Pat's face into the ground and tried to erase his nose, and Pat managed a yogic twist of the body and delivered three blows to the side of Mike's head with his knee. *This old son of a bitch,* Mike thought, *got mule legs on him.*

Bobo exploded out the door in pursuit of two miners, and they receded in the distance, diminishing in size like an optical illusion. The bartender followed and came over to Mike and Pat and kicked Pat a couple of times on the ass. "Pat, get the hell outa here. I called the cops." Pat was apparently more worried about jail than he was about Mike, for he extracted himself from the clench, gave Mike a sharp kick in the back, and trotted off. Mike lay gasping in the dirt. "Jeez, buddy," said the barkeep. "Weren't none of *us* knocked that gal up." He went back inside, tenderly fondling his swollen earlobe.

A deputy sheriff slowly rolled up to the curb in a gleaming Plymouth patrol car. The car idled beside Mike, and as he lay there looking up at the insignia on the car's door, he thought: *That engine's running smooth—they must keep it tuned up.* The window rolled open, and a pair of aviator shades peered down at him. They were dark as strong coffee.

"What's your name, friend?" the sheriff said.

"McGurk. Mike."

The sheriff wrote it down. Then he swung his gaze back on Mike.

"Mr. McGurt," he said, "this is not the way you comport yourself in Clifton, Arizona."

47

BOBO WAS CAUGHT IN AN ABANDONED BUILDING BY A photographer for the Clifton *Copper Era.* The panicked miners had run at full gallop right past the newspaper office, and Bobo, with a wide grin on his face, had flown along behind them, arms pumping rhythmically. The photographer grabbed his camera and charged after them and snapped a shot of Bobo in midair, about to deliver a flying body slam to one cringing miner; the second photo caught him in full swing, a roundhouse right flying at the other, already bloodied man. This picture would run on the front page, under the headline RAMPAGE. The body slam and a third, muddier picture of one desperate miner waving a plank in Bobo's face would run on page 2 with the legend: MEXICAN STANDOFF.

The next morning, everyone would be reading about it. Bobo was well aware that he had brought more unwelcome attention to his family. He was thinking about his father's face as Mr. García pondered the photographs. The sheriff was tapping him on the chest with his pencil as he spoke, but Bobo didn't hear a word. He imagined his father's brow wrinkling as he worked his way through the words.

Mike stood behind the sheriff and off to the side, dirt smeared all over his shirt and a little blood on his lip. He was thinking about how he'd started the fight and now Bobo was going to be in the paper. His knuckles were swollen, and his gut was killing him. The ear that received Pat's knee kicks felt as hot as if it were being broiled. And the sheriff was busy writing citations by the stack—they were just barely avoiding a jail term, which the sheriff was more than happy to inform them of: "You're just barely avoiding a jail sentence, boys. Do you understand?" said the sheriff.

"You bet!" said Mike when Bobo said nothing.

"Let's hope so," said the sheriff. He handed out his flimsy tickets and documents. Then he settled his gunbelt more solidly on his hips and strode away. He folded into his car, glared at them again for good measure, then drove around the corner, where he lurked, eager as a coyote watching a pack rat.

"Gimme the keys," said the Butcher of Burundi. "I'm driving."

Mike handed him the keys.

They pulled out. The sheriff, tingling all over, burst out of the shadows and fell in behind them. They kept to the speed limit, and the sheriff followed them at exactly three car lengths' distance. His fingers strangled the wheel.

"We're being followed," said Mike, looking in his side mirror.

"Escorted's more like it," said Bobo.

Mike turned around in his seat: the sheriff actually shook one finger at him.

"Naughty naughty," Bobo said.

"I told you I screw everything up," Mike said.

"You didn't do nothing."

"I started the ball."

"That peckerwood did it."

"I threw the punch, and don't tell me different."

Bobo switched into his sophisticated accent and said, "Nonsense." Then: "Dear boy."

"I guess I gave old Pat a big surprise, though."

"I guess you did."

"But still," Mike said, watching the sheriff fall back, stop, do a three-point turn, and head back down to Clifton, "I'm always getting into something." The sheriff's disappointment that they hadn't gone on a shooting spree was so strong that his car seemed to slouch as it fell away.

"It was that pinche Angel Apodaca who got this fight started," Bobo said.

Mike watched the muscles ripple in Bobo's cheek, and he thought: *Oh-oh.*

When they got to Morenci, Bobo pulled into the sloping parking lot of the company store and set the brake against the hill. "One time a car let go," he said. "Almost rolled right through the big window." They sat and stared at the window. "Now," he continued, "if you want to screw something up, do it big. Blow the mines up." He got out and slicked back his hair with his palms. "Derail the ore trains."

"Be cool," Mike said.

"I'm cool."

"You don't look cool."

"Cool as can be."

"Yeah, but you don't look cool."

"Mike," said Bobo, "I'm cooler than a dead man's ass."

They walked down the slope and pushed through the doors.

There were aisles crammed with items, and more items hung from the ceiling. Bobo pushed through a few garlands of garlic and bellowed, "Where's Angel?"

Mike busied himself with the shopping. He took a cart and began piling in the goods. Bubble bath looked good. So did canvas work gloves.

"Estoy buscando al hijo de su chingada madre del Angel," said Bobo.

Mike grabbed an obscenely overpriced five-pound bag of oranges. He told himself Bobo would maintain his composure. A packet of big pink combs caught his eye. He dashed to the cooler and bought beer and ice cream.

Bobo's voice was joined by another Mexican voice, and they chattered. Bobo's voice rose; the other man's crooned placatingly. Bobo spit curses. The other man reproached him. Mike followed the tones of voice.

A bag of jacks. No, *six* bags of jacks! Cheese, milk, eggs, bacon, sliced bread (ten loaves—they could freeze it), jam, peanah battah. Doughnuts. Socks. Needles. He was giddy.

The voices rose: *Rraccatta-rraccatta.* Faster, higher in pitch, Bobo saying, "*Rracca-rracca* Angel!" and the other voice saying, "No!" Mike heard a shuffle. He listened carefully. A slight rip of cloth.

He peeked around the canned soup shelf to find Bobo throttling a chubby Mexican. Bobo's body was halfway across the counter. The Mexican had hold of Bobo's pocket and was slowly pulling it free of his shirt as his own face went purple.

"Gleet," the Mexican said to Mike, eyes bulging. "Pleet."

"Bobe?" Mike said.

Bobo pulled the man back and forth.

"Where," he demanded, "is . . . An . . . gel!"

The man pointed out the window.

"Zrff," he said.

A woman came from the back room with a broom and launched into Bobo. Mike watched her wind up and swing a home-run hit into Bobo's backside. He let go of his victim and turned on her. "Ow!" he said. The Mexican behind the counter picked up a sack of flour and hit Bobo. Bobo fell forward in a white cloud, catching up the woman and cascading with her into the bread rack. The Mexican leaped up on the counter, yelling, "*Chingatta rraccatta* Angel!" and dove onto Bobo and the woman. Mike galloped forward and piled on. The four of them rolled down the aisle, wrestling and kicking cans free from the shelves: creamed corn's trajectory carried it into the bottles of soda pop.

The woman extricated herself from the tangle and staggered to a telephone and dialed. "Estan locos!" she was hollering. "*Policía! ¡Quieren matar a mi Angel!*" She slammed the phone down again and ran to Mike. Grabbing the back of his belt, she gave a mighty heave. He was startled to find himself rising off the dog pile and being carried backward. She butted the door open with one knee and his head and tossed him out. An unbelievable crashing emanated from the store, accompanied by her screeches. And, in the distance, the inevitable siren of the sheriff, who was speeding up the hill, no doubt eagerly telling himself a thrill killing was under way in the P-D company store.

Mike made a passing attempt at cleaning himself up and realized it was futile. He thought fast. *Shopping!* came to him as a safe pursuit at the moment, so he crept back into the store—Mrs. Apodaca had her back to him. She was apparently engaged in an attempt to sweep Bobo into the meat locker with her deadly broom. Bobo had a handful of Mr. Apodaca's hair. Mike busied himself with his cart and was pushing his way past the marshmallows when the sheriff charged in and threw himself behind the detergent racks.

"Mr. McGurt!" he said. "What's my situation here!" He peeked cautiously around the Ivory Snow boxes, hand near his gun.

Mike said, "Sheriff, it's a fight over honor."

"Mexicans," the sheriff said.

"We have a pregnancy," Mike confided, "and a missing father."

"No!"

"Angel Apodaca skipped town and left Bobo's relative in a compromised position."

The sheriff didn't like this one bit. He straightened up and glared around the store. Mike could tell he wanted to shoot something. His lips were thin as a paper cut. He hitched up his belt and strode toward the combatants, muttering, "Damned Mexicans anyway."

He pulled Mrs. Apodaca away and started yelling at Bobo and his adversary.

"Hey! *Hey!* I said, Hey!"

Mike pushed his cart to the cash register and stood smiling at Mrs., who was noisily crying behind the counter. As she held the tissue to her nose with one hand, she rang up sales with the other. "Cash," she said. "We don't take checks."

"Yes, ma'am."

"Hey!" the sheriff bellowed.

Mrs. Apodaca looked at a large can of dog food and said, "We got a special sale—buy six, get one free."

"Sounds wonderful," Mike enthused, and went for the extra cans.

"Mr. García," the sheriff was intoning, "I have reason to believe you are a menace to the populace of our community."

"Animal!" cried Mr. Apodaca.

"Mr. Apodaca," the sheriff said, "the only thing I find lower than Mr. García's behavior here today is the behavior of your son—if you know what I mean."

Mrs., at the register, wailed, "Angelito-o-o!"

Mike looked down the aisle at the men. They were gathered with heads bowed, almost like a prayer group. *Boy,* he thought, *wish Lily could see this!* The two Mexicans, tattered and panting heavily, looked sheepish as the sheriff rose to an indignant height of twenty feet four inches.

"Now, I don't approve of hanky-panky at a young lady's expense," the sheriff said. "And, Mr. García, judging from your comportment earlier today, I shouldn't let you go, but this here's a general assault on decency. So I'll let you go if you shake hands."

Bobo shook his head.

Mr. Apodaca crossed his arms and pulled the corners of his lips down toward his chin and stared at the ceiling.

"Boys," the sheriff said, "you shake hands now, or I drag your asses down to the jail and lock you up for a week and let you two fight all you want. Comprende, amigos? Now shake."

Bobo and Mr. Apodaca shook.

The sheriff adjusted himself, put his hands on his hips, and said, "Mr. García, I am compelled to escort you toward your own town. And I will urge you to remain there until you can either behave or leave our region."

He followed Bobo down the aisle like a disapproving school teacher.

Bobo stopped to pay for the goods, then everyone went to the truck and loaded them. The sheriff tucked the bag of oranges behind the toolbox. "This your truck, Mr. McGurt?" he asked.

"Yes, sir," said Mike.

The sheriff stood to one side and stroked his chin.

"You're on my bad side, son," he said.

"Yes, sir, I know that."

"I been thinking."

"Sir!"

"You could maneuver yourself back into my good graces," said the sheriff.

"You name it," said Mike.

"I need a truck towed."

"Your truck, sir?"

The sheriff nodded.

"Where at, sir?"

"It's parked behind the station down in Clifton," said the sheriff. Bobo was sulking beside the tow truck. Mr. and Mrs. beat it back inside the store. "It's a quarter-ton Ford, given to me by my father in nineteen hundred and fifty. It broke down coming up the grade from Safford just yesterday."

"Sir."

"Blue."

"Sir!"

"And I want it treated as tenderly as a baby, do you understand?"

"I'll treat it like my own child," said Mike. "I'll tow it to your door."

"Free of charge," said the sheriff, hand magically levitating near his holster.

"My pleasure," said Mike.

The sheriff handed Mike one of his cards. It showed a Morenci address. "Can you find it?" the sheriff said.

"I'll do my best."

"Fine," the sheriff said absently. He pointed at Bobo.

"But first," he said, "get this piece of shit out of my community."

48

THE SCENE AT HOME WAS SOMBER.

Bobo, Mike, and the elders gathered in the living room. The men sat with their elbows on their knees, bending in toward the story, heads bowed. Mrs. García sat well back in her corner of the sofa, crocheting a doily and listening, making *tsk-tsk* sounds and shaking her head. Unseen listeners gathered at all the good listening places in the corners and the bedroom walls.

Almita first heard that she'd been abandoned when Bobo told Mr. García in hushed tones. She'd been loitering in the hallway. She came out into the light and said, "What?" She put her hands over her mouth and stared, tears starting down her cheeks. Bobo blanched and said, "Alma." Mike half rose, reaching to her. She looked at his hand with what appeared to be horror, then ran back to her room, unleashing the saddest cry Mike had ever heard. Mama hove to her feet and followed her, enlisting Umbelinda and Chata and sending Mike to get a pitcher of cool water. Florita, clearly shaken by all this cataclysm, followed after Mike. She sniffled as she ladled water into the pitcher.

Mr. García leaned in toward Bobo, the couch creaking beneath him. He addressed his son in Spanish.

"Is she really pregnant?" he asked.

"Yes, Father. I believe she is."

Mr. García rubbed his face.

He looked at his hands.

He shook his head.

"Fortunately," he said, "I'll enjoy being a grandfather."

Bobo chuckled a little.

Mr. García poked him in the knee.

"And that Angel Apodaca ran away."

"Yes."

"What a coward," Mr. García said.

"I will kill him," Bobo said.

"No you won't," said Mr. García, and Bobo knew instantly that he would not.

"I can't believe this," Bobo said.

"It's hard to believe, my son. But what I hear about you fighting in town—this is also hard to believe."

Bobo hung his head.

"I—" he said.

"Who did you fight?" his father asked. He pushed Bobo's head up and said, "Eh?"

"Miners. I don't know—they insulted her."

"They all knew about Alma and Angel?"

"Yes, Father."

"And they spoke indelicately?"

"They did."

"In that case, Bonifacio, I hope you taught them respect."

Bobo smiled.

"I think I did."

"However," said his father, "beating up Angel's father . . . I see no wisdom in that."

Bobo nodded sadly.

"And," Mr. García said, "fighting with *Señora* Apodaca? Bobo?"

"I know," said Bobo.

"Gentlemen don't fight with women."

"No, Father. I know. There was no honor in that, I admit, and no wisdom, either. But I had to kick somebody's ass."

Mr. García spat into his spittoon.

"That's an interesting philosophy," he said.

They heard firm footsteps coming down the hall, and they looked up.

Mama came into the room and said, "She is pregnant, and I don't want to hear any comments about it. Say nothing critical to her. I expect us to have love in this house."

Bobo and Mr. García looked at each other and grinned.

"Say yes, boy," Papa said.

"Yes, Mother," said Bobo.

She nodded once, took the water from Mike as he carried it in, and went back to comfort Almita.

"I've got to go for the sheriff's truck," Mike said.

"I'm going," Bobo said.

"Do you think that's a good idea?" Mike said.

"I'm going."

"You're already in trouble with him," Mike warned.

"I'm going, I said."

Mr. García told Bobo, "Keep out of trouble."

"Sí," Bobo replied.

He and Mike got into the tow truck and sat for a minute, looking at the García house. Against the dark, salted with pale stars, it was solid, its windows glowing yellow. The dogs barked far down in the yard. Shadows fluttered before the shades. One of the girls came out on the porch and waved at them, backlit in the open front door. "Blanca," Bobo said. They waved back, not sure if she could see them in the gloom of the truck. She turned and went back inside. Suddenly, Mr. García's laugh erupted from the doorway: Ha-*hah!*

They couldn't pull away, nor could they pull their eyes from the bulk of the house. Mike fancied he could see through the walls, could see Florita heating pots of food, see Almita lying across her bed and Mama patting her hand with those small canary palms of hers, see Umbelinda trying on one of his shirts, see the birds in their tiny nests in their cages settling down on their eggs. Beside him, Bobo could see both through the walls and through time. He took out a cigarette and handed it to Mike. Mike took it without looking at him. Then Bobo took one out for himself. They lit up, and they smoked together, just watching the dark pull tight around the García spread.

"I put paint in the back of the tow truck," Bobo said.

"No," said Mike.

The engine whined and surged as they pulled the big blue Ford up out of Clifton. There were no cars on the road at all. No lights, either. They drove up the old Coronado Trail in pitch blackness, their headlights throwing a pale gray wedge ahead of them.

"Come on," said Bobo. "Won't nobody catch us."

"Bobe!" said Mike, and he felt this was a perfectly adequate response.

"Just five minutes. You don't even have to do nothing. Just stop at the P-D store, vato."

Mike gritted his teeth. This . . . this . . . *savage.*

"Bobo, listen to reason. You almost got arrested twice today. You can't just . . . *traipse* back to the scene of the crime and paint obscenities all over it!"

"Just, like, 'Angel Apodaca Is a Shithead,'" said Bobo. He was positively beaming. "'Angel Eats Dog Turds.'"

"Stop it."

"'Angel Apodaca Puts Carrots in His Butt.'"

"Stop!"

"Ah, Mike. You're such a chicken."

"Am not."

"Coulda fooled me."

"I'm no chicken, let me tell you."

"Just five minutes, ese. We hit the store and we're gone. Nobody's wise till morning, and we'll be laughing our asses off in bed—perfect alibi: we was takin' the sheriff's truck home!"

Well, he had a point.

"Okay," Mike said.

"All right!"

"Five minutes is all you get."
"Yes!"
"And I am not a chicken."
He looked at Bobo.
"Let me tell you!" he said.

49

THE STORE WAS PERCHED ON THE EDGE OF A RAVINE. IT dropped fifty yards to a small rubble field where the effluvia of a long-forgotten mine shaft formed a small half-cone of jagged boulders.

Mike eased the tow truck into the lot; the tow chains on the sheriff's Ford clanked loudly as he scraped over the hump in the drive. He flinched—sure everyone for miles around could hear them. One bright lamp shone on a high pole. Mike swung the truck around so its nose was pointing uphill; hence, the Ford wouldn't roll forward into the back of his tow truck. He set the brake, hopped out, and kicked two wooden blocks against the back tires so the trucks wouldn't creep backward. He checked the chain, the tow hook pulling the Ford's front tires off the blacktop. Everything was in order. The only sound was a distant dog's barking.

"Here goes," said Bobo.

He picked up a can of paint and one of Mr. García's ancient brushes and giggled.

"Oh, yeah, Angelito . . . here I come," he said.

"I don't know about this," said Mike.

"Chic-ken," taunted Bobo.

"I am not!" Mike said, following him toward the front of the store. "I'm wondering how I get myself into these things is all."

"Just lucky, I guess," Bobo said, then started to whistle tunelessly, exactly like his father.

❦ ❦ ❦

The other vehicle crept up the hill and stopped. It had been following them with its lights off since they'd pulled away from the station, towing the big blue Ford. The driver turned off the engine and watched them move across the lot toward the store. "They going to rob it?" he murmured. Then he cracked his door and eased it open and slipped out into the night and moved in their direction.

"Let's see," said Bobo, regarding the shadowed wall of glass.

He put a tentative splash on the glass.

"Hurry up," Mike said. "I've got a bad feeling."

"You would," Bobo replied.

He painted a big A. "A is for Angel," he said. He added NGEL. "Now what?"

"Whatever," said Mike, scanning the lot nervously.

"How do you spell *comply?*" Bobo asked.

"Comply!" said Mike, turning to him. "Wow."

Their observer took that moment to scoot to the side of the tow truck. It was hot from the drive; its metal was still ticking. He crept along its flank and lay in the gap between the front of the sheriff's truck and the back of Mike's truck. He looked between the tires of the Ford. And he looked up. And he looked back at the slope. And he looked up at the chains again.

ANGEL APODACA COMPLY WITH YOUR

"With your what?" Bobo said.

"Pretty classy so far," Mike said.

"What did you expect," sniffed Bobo. "I'm classier than shit, vato."

Mike regarded the message.

"Responsibilities?" he suggested.

"Too long."

"Yeah, but it's the only thing that makes sense."

"How about Duty?" said Bobo.

"Duty. Duty. Duty doesn't make sense."

"Sure it does."

"No it doesn't."

"What you talkin' about?"

"Believe me, Bobo."

"Pinches gabachos think they know everything."

"I'm telling you, it doesn't make sense."

"Oh, Mr. English Teacher all of a sudden!"

"You'll sound like an idiot is all I'm saying."

"Who you calling an idiot, pendejo?"

He arose. He smiled. He offered his actions to the ancestors, to the grandfathers—except Grandfather Sneezy, who had beat him up, then gone to Disneyland.

He breathed in the air. It was good. Cold and thin.

He looked at the various control levers and figured out which one released the chains.

"McGurk!" he cried.

Both of them spun around.

"Hi!" Castro shouted, then yanked the levers.

"No!" Mike cried.

The winch whined, then unloaded the chains with a loud clanking. The Ford fell hard and bounced once on its front springs.

"Castro!" he shouted.

The Ford began to roll back, the sharp pitch of the lot accelerating its backward plunge.

"Ayiii!" Castro called. "Yip! Yip!"

Mike put his hands up, as if to catch the truck as it hurtled toward them.

"I win!" Castro yodeled. "I win! I win!"

Bobo said, "You ain't stopping that truck, Mike."

But Mike was wild-eyed, crouching just a bit as if awaiting a fastball pitch. Bobo could hear the tires on the blacktop. Castro was dancing around above them, laughing idiotically.

Bobo picked Mike up and scurried to one side as the huge Ford backed through the front window of the P-D company store at forty miles an hour. Glass exploded around it, and it made a hideous riot of crashes and shatterings and booms and pows as it backed all the way through the store, overturning and bursting can after can and package after package. And, it seemed almost immediately after it entered, it made a massive crash as it backed out through the far wall of the store and plunged down the ravine in a vast whirlwind of dust, flour, sugar, cornmeal, soda foam, socks, notebook paper.

Mike was frozen to the spot. He was utterly paralyzed.

"Dang!" Bobo crowed. "Castro done killed the sheriff's truck!"

He darted to the wrecked front of the store and hooted.

"Killed the store too!"

Castro ran to his truck, started it up, drove into the lot, and spun doughnuts while honking his horn.

Mike said, "Oh, shut up."

"What's his problem?" Bobo said.

Then he walked into the shattered maw of the store and put his hands on his hips. Castro tore up the drive and flew out of the lot, swerving insanely as he vanished back down the mountain. Mike joined Bobo.

"Oh, jeez," he said.

"This is some statement," Bobo said. Cans rolled around on the floor; light fixtures hung loose and sparking. "I don't know," he continued. "Maybe I shoulda written something shorter."

Once he started laughing, he couldn't stop.

It even got to Mike. He was angry at first, felt betrayed that Bobo would laugh at this catastrophe. But then it started to seem funny to him too.

After a moment, Mike really got into the spirit of things.

He dug in the glove compartment of the tow truck and found one of Turk's old service station courtesy cards. They used to leave one tucked under the windshield wipers of each car they repaired. Bobo, seeing it, snorted and started laughing again.

They affixed the card to the remains of the front door and

drove away. It fluttered there in the breeze all night. Dawn would reveal its message:

YES!
Another FINE JOB
Compliments of—
McGURK!!!

50

Mr. García didn't think it was funny.

"You must go," he said.

"But I don't want to go," Bobo said.

"You must go. The situation obligates you, Bonifacio."

He turned to Mike. "My," he said, "you gotta go. Far go away."

Mike knew it was true, but he couldn't believe he was hearing it.

Mrs. García sat on the couch, wringing her hands.

She reached out for Bobo and he went to her and she squeezed him hard.

"I wakee you up in morning pooty soon," said Mr. García. He patted Mike's shoulder. "You go away." He pointed at the two of them. "Two. Together. Pooty quick."

He nodded at them.

"Too much trouble come here now. Maybe you come back more time."

Mike hung his head. Bobo hung his head. Mr. García hung his head.

"Ay, qué vida," he said.

And Mike understood, because he was thinking the same thing. *What a life, what a strange life.*

Eyes all over the house watched them as they made their way to their rooms. Mama García was already thinking up what she would say to the sheriff when he came. Mr. García was thinking about money—now that Almita was pregnant and Bobo fleeing, how was he going to pay their bills? Florita and Almita lay in their bed, clutching each other; Almita imagined the life within her as a small red light, pulsing with each heartbeat.

Bobo lay on his bed in the dark and let silent tears roll out of his eyes.

Mike just sat on the edge of his bed and hung his head and felt cursed. He was always going to screw things up—he could feel it. He looked up when his door opened. It was Umbelinda. She stared at him with huge eyes.

"Chata said you pushed the sheriff off a cliff," she said.

He smiled.

"No, honey. I, uh, I pushed his truck off a cliff."

"He wasn't inside?"

"No."

She entered the room and closed the door.

"Are you going to jail?" she said.

"Not if I get out of here," he said.

"Out?"

"I have to go away."

She watched him carefully.

"You can't go," she said quietly.

"I don't want to go, believe me," he said.

"Then stay here. You can hide under my bed!"

"I have to, Belinda," he said.

She held her little hands before her, as if she were holding something, or holding something away from herself.

"Mike . . . ," she said, tears filling her eyes. "Don't go."

He patted the bed beside him.

She dragged herself across the room and climbed on and sat beside him. She stared up at him with brimming eyes and said, "No!" He took her hand in his. His hand seemed vast to him, rough and brutal.

"I'm sorry," he said.

She started sobbing.

"P-please," she said. "You can't go away. You can't you can't!"

He put his arm around her small shoulders.

"I'm sorry."

She cried with her mouth open, hitching and wringing the bedspread. It lasted for several minutes, Mike feeling lost, wishing someone would come in and tell him what to do.

"I have to go, kid. Just for a while," he offered.

She pushed away from him.

"I hate you!"

She tried to break free from his grasp, but he wouldn't let go.

"No you don't," he said.

"I hate you! I hope you die!"

She hit him.

"No you don't, Belinda. Don't say that, because you'll hurt my feelings."

He turned her face toward him. Tears plastered her hair to her face. He was going by instinct—he smoothed the wet hair away from her cheeks.

"You know why I'll be hurt?" he asked.

She glared at him, furious.

"Why," she sulked.

"Because . . . " His voice stopped. He couldn't say it.

"Why?" she repeated.

He cleared his throat.

"Because I . . . because I guess I love you," he said. "That's why."

The child stared at him, and the stare seemed to be endless. Mike watched her face work through several emotions as what he'd said sank in. She blinked. She fell against him slowly. He kept his arm around her. She nodded against him.

"Me too," she said.

"You scrawny little kid," he said.

"Mike," she whispered. "I want you to be my daddy."

He had no idea what to say.

"Come back," she said. "Come back and be my daddy."

He kicked off his boots and lay back on the bed and wrestled her up beside him and held her. She rested her head on his chest, feeling him breathe, holding her palm flat against his heart.

"Promise," she said.

He held his breath.

"My daddy."

He touched her hair.

God, God, God.

"Promise?" she insisted.

"I," said Mike, so quietly that he almost couldn't hear it himself, "promise."

She snuggled in close to him. She closed her eyes. Soon she was asleep. He stroked her cheek, then he bent to her and kissed a child for the first time in his life.

"Good night, kid," he said.

And against his ribs, she stirred a little and mumbled, "Papa."

51

THE MORNING CAME TOO SOON. BOTH ALMITA AND FLORITA sniffled into wadded tissues, red-eyed and miserable. Bobo patrolled back and forth between them, kissing and hugging and saying good-bye. The little girls collapsed in heaps on their beds, wailing and gasping. The canaries were asking "Pete?" in their cages, which made Mike even more miserable. Mama García dragged Bobo down onto the couch and held him and wept.

Mr. García gestured to Mike.

"Come," he said.

Mike followed him through the dark house. Outside, the dawn was graying the eastern sky. Mr. García led Mike to a table, covered with white cloth. Mounds and lumps were visible under the cotton.

"Pick up," said Mr. García.

Mike lifted the cloth off the table.

Mr. García had arranged platters of food for him. Thick slices of tomato and avocado on a blue plate, fat radishes all around them. Beside it, a bowl of olives, and a plate with slices of cauliflower, red onion, and jicama. Lemon and lime slices. Goat cheese. Machaca. Hard-boiled eggs. Two bottles of wine. Cinnamon tea. Leaves of romaine lettuce with salt and lemon juice on them. Tortillas.

Mr. García spread his hands out over the food, as though in blessing, and said, "Everything García."

Mike nodded, sat down. A fat ant rushed around the edge of the plate of cheese. Mike pointed to it.

"Farmer," he said. "Like you."

Mr. García nodded once.

"By Gah," he said.

They were all lined up at the fence, waving. Mike went from cheek to cheek, planting kisses. Then they marched up to his cheek, and he received kisses. Mr. García hugged him. Umbelinda never let go of his hand. When Florita kissed him, she whispered in his ear: "Favajú, bad boy!" It sent a tingle right down to Mike's boot.

They climbed in the truck.

"North," Mr. García said. "Go over."

"Yes, sir," said Mike.

Umbelinda came up to his door and handed him a crayon drawing. In it, a big figure stood holding the hand of a small figure. Behind them, a house with smoke rising from a chimney. Under the figures, she'd written: YOU ME.

He reached down and scooped her up and planted a kiss on her face.

"Remember," she said.

"I will," he said.

They waved as he put the truck in gear, Bobo beside him on the rumbling motorbike. They waved without ceasing until they had shrunk to the size of ants as he pulled away. The adults waved above the fence, and the girls waved through the fence. The dogs leaped and gamboled in the background. Mike saw haloes of butterflies sparking in the air above their heads. Crows lifted off from the phone lines. Mama García's glasses glinted in the sun. He watched them until he went around a curve and they vanished.

For two days, as he drove, Mike thought of ants, and dogs, and little girls.

52

GRANDFATHER SNEEZY WAS SITTING IN FRONT OF THE GAS station when they got there. He wore his old cowboy hat and a pair of Ray-Ban sunglasses. His old .22 rifle lay across his legs. Mike jumped out of the truck and ran up to him. "Grandfather!" he cried. "You're back."

"I am," said Mr. Sneezy.

"What are you doing?"

"Working. Got me a job guarding your station." Mr. Sneezy shifted in his chair, adjusted his hat. "Couple weeks ago, some sons of bitches broke in here and ransacked the joint. Cut the chains and all."

"That was me and Bobe," Mike said.

"I know that," said Mr. Sneezy.

Bobo parked his bike and got off. He shook his leg and walked up to them, peeling off his gloves. He smiled down at the old man.

"Hey, old-timer," he said.

Mr. Sneezy touched the brim of his hat.

"We had a time up to McQueen," Bobo said.

"Got in a little trouble," Mike said.

"Cops?" said Mr. Sneezy.

"Probably," said Mike.

"I'd say so," said Bobo. "Definitely."

"How about yourself?" Bobo asked.

"Ask me about Disneyland," said Mr. Sneezy.

"How was Disneyland?"

"It's the goddamnedest thing I ever seen." He reached down for a paper bag and rustled around in it. "I brought something to show you," he said. He removed his cowboy hat and took out a cap with Mickey Mouse ears. He put it on. In yellow thread, it said: *DELBERT.* Bobo sat down on the ground, he laughed so hard.

"You don't like it?" said Mr. Sneezy.

"I like it! I like it!" Bobo wheezed.

"Lookin' sharp, Grandfather," said Mike.

"I got you two a pair of pirate hats," Mr. Sneezy said. "You want 'em or not?"

"Oh!" gasped Bobo. "I do!"

"Got some mail," said Mr. Sneezy.

"Mail!" said Mike. "Like what?"

Bills.

A catalogue of wrenches.

A letter from Lily.

More bills.

A letter from Lily!

Mike tore open the envelope. The paper was flimsy, and it smelled of perfume. "Yum-yum," said Bobo. Mike blushed.

Lily had sent a coded message from Love Central.

"Cuz," she wrote, "I am the saddest shore. Your tide leaves my stones dark. In spite of myself, I am a lone gull's cry in the fog. . . ."

And she signed off: "Without You,

XXX Lily."

Grandfather Sneezy peered over Mike's shoulder.

"What in the hell," he wanted to know, "is that there supposed to mean!"

Mike folded it up and slipped it in his shirt.

They sat around the kitchen table, wearing their hats. Mike brewed a pot of coffee, and they blew into the cups and squinted through the steam at each other as Bobo and Mike told their story. Mr. Sneezy nodded, listening. He poked Mike in the arm when he got to Umbelinda. "You got a child now," he said. "You got to shape up."

Bobo said, "Umbelinda McGurk. Kinda ugly, but I heard worse."

When Mike got around to the slaughter of the company store and the Ford, Mr. Sneezy grinned and said, "Shoo-ee!" He said to Bobo, "You saved Mike!"

"Ain't I always doing it," Bobo said.

"Here," said Mr. Sneezy. "I got something to give you."

He reached into his bottomless paper bag and surprised Bobo with a rubber pirate sword.

"That's your reward."

Bobo loved it—he waved it around in a threatening fashion. "I figured you was enough of a dumbshit to love that thing," Mr. Sneezy noted.

Then he told them his fabulous tale: submarines that went underwater and found sea monsters; a little rocket ship you could fly in the air; a castle; a jungle boat ride with giant cement animals attacking it; Peter Pan's boat flying in the night sky. Mike and Bobo kept saying "No!" to everything. Their imaginations were doing jumping jacks as they tried to picture these things.

"We got to go!" said Bobo.

"Hell yes," said Mr. Sneezy. "Hundreds of women, screaming."

"Let's head out," Bobo said.

"I'm game," said Mr. Sneezy. "Long as you're driving."

"I have things to look after," said Mike.

"Like what?" said Bobo. "Like stayin' out of jail?"

"Like"—Mike spread his hands—"right here. Texaco Turk's."

Mr. Sneezy said, "Mike, I hate to say this, but it ain't Turk's no more. It's Central Arizona Title and Trust's."

"Damned right, baby," said Bobo, slamming his cup down.

"You're stealing this here coffee right now," said Mr. Sneezy. "I could shoot you where you sit."

"Come on," said Mike.

"Repossessed, vato," said Bobo.

"This is home," Mike protested. "I can work it out."

"They done took it," said Bobo. "Grapes of friggin' Wrath!"

"I'll work off what we owe."

"From jail?" said Bobo. He looked around and wrinkled his nose. "No offense, partner, but this place stinks. I personally wouldn't want to be sitting in it when the sheriff comes for me."

"He's got a point," said Mr. Sneezy.

"Yeah," said Mike. "It's kind of depressing."

"Kind of!" said Bobo.

"I thought you hated it," said Mr. Sneezy.

"I do," said Mike. "But it's home."

"Not now it ain't," said Mr. Sneezy.

"Mike," said Bobo, "we ain't got no home."

Mike said, "I've been robbed."

Mr. Sneezy crossed his arms and did his ferocious Geronimo look. "Sons of bitches," he noted.

"Screw it," said Bobo. "Let's go to L.A."

L.A.! Lily rose in Mike's mind, grinning sweetly. She turned slowly, lit by a heavenly pink light, as she recited verse and her hair flew in a soft wind. *I am a lone gull's cry,* she confided.

"L.A.?" Mike said.

"Where the hell do you think Disneyland is?" said Mr. Sneezy.

"L.A.," Mike said.

Bobo hopped to his feet and pointed his rubber sword at Mike. "I ain't waiting. I'm going. Me and Grampa Sneezy. You in or out?"

"I suppose," said Mike, "I can't stay around here and wait for the cops to find me."

"You can't stay here anyway," said Mr. Sneezy. "If I don't go with you boys, then I have to run you out. It's my job."

"How can you take off for Disneyland?" asked Mike.

"Early retirement," Mr. Sneezy replied. "I don't owe nothin' to the man."

"Think of snow," said Bobo.

"You like that snow," said Mr. Sneezy. "They got the Matterhorn right there in Disneyland."

"No!" said Mike.

"It ain't as big as I thought, but they got it there, all covered with snow. You ride little sleds all over it."

Bobo waved his sword at Mike.

Mike smiled. He imagined one of those silly mouse hats with *Belinda* written on it. And five more with whatever their names were. Maybe one for Mama and Papa too. And one that said *Lily,* though he suspected Lily wouldn't be caught dead wearing it.

"It's done," he said. "You don't have to ask me twice!"

Mr. Sneezy stood guard outside in his Mouseketeer hat, his .22 held at chest height. Bobo and Mike boxed books and keepsakes in oily Pennzoil crates. They tromped back and forth through the house, weighed down with memories. Bobo had replaced his pirate hat with Turk's WWI helmet.

"This isn't right," Mike said.

"Nope," said Bobo.

"This is rotten as hell," said Mike.

"Right-o," said Bobo.

"This is *my* house. I've got a right to hate it if I want to."

"You said a mouthful there, brother!"

"I have the right to abandon the whole deal if I feel like it."

"Empty," Bobo agreed.

"But I don't think I appreciate being *put out!*"

"Be it ever so humble," Bobo hollered from the back rooms.

"There's no place like home," Mike muttered, as he boxed Turk's forlorn 78s.

Mike stepped up to Mr. Sneezy.

"I'm mad," he said.

"'Bout time," said Mr. Sneezy.

"This whole thing—it torques my crankshaft," said Mike.

Mr. Sneezy said, "Do something about it."

"Like what?" Mike said.

Mr. Sneezy said, "Don't ask me. You're a young man. You're a warrior."

"I am?"

"It's up to you to make the decisions. We'll follow you."

"You will?"

Mike thought he'd been following somebody.

"Dang rights," said Mr. Sneezy. "You're the leader. We're your soldiers."

Mike snorted.

"Aw, come on," he said.

Mr. Sneezy turned away from him and stared at the horizon.

"Grandfather?" said Mike.

Mr. Sneezy said, "You're the man."

Mike stood there and watched the horizon with him. *I'm the man?* he thought.

"They can't have it," said Mike. "I've decided."

Bobo and Mr. Sneezy looked at each other.

"Okay," Bobo said.

"Okay," said Mr. Sneezy.

"What are we gonna do?" asked Bobo.

"We're blowing up the station," said Mike.

Bobo and Mr. Sneezy smiled.

"I like it," said Bobo. "I really do."

"Just like a dipshit McGurk to think of something like that," said Mr. Sneezy, but Mike could tell he was pleased. "I swear—it's something so numskulled that Turk coulda thought of it."

"Don't give me a hard time about it, Grandfather," said Mike, "or I'll tie you to that chair and blow your ass up too."

"I'd like to see you try, you little soft-handed toad," said Mr. Sneezy.

He was thinking: *Now you're talkin'!*

"I'll be damned if I let some freebooting agency steal my gas station!" Mike announced.

Bobo slapped the table.

"Exactly!" he said.

"Let them repossess a half a pound of shrapnel!"

"Egg-zackly!"

Mike leaped up and showed them his ass.

"As Bobo once said, Repossess *this!*"

"Hear, hear!" said Bobo.

Mr. Sneezy smiled. "I'm thinkin' about a Viking funeral. It's Turk's final send-off, when you think about it. Burn his ship to the ground."

"Men," said Mike, "let's do her."

They were overcome with the need to shake hands, and they turned to one another in sequence and pumped and pumped.

53

THEY STOOD IN THE DARK, WATCHING THE MOON RISE, frosting the glass and steel of Turk's Texaco with cold light. "We'll take the bike," Mike said. "You move the truck down out of the way."

"Okay," said Mr. Sneezy. "You can count on me."

Mike grabbed his arm.

"I always could, Grandfather," he said.

The old man puffed up and marched to the tow truck. He tried to start it with the gearshift in first, and the truck lurched and stalled.

"Buy a horse!" Mike called.

"Kiss my ass," said Mr. Sneezy.

He got it going and got it in the wrong gear and howled and jerked down the drive and into the dark.

Bobo laughed.

"What a codger," he said.

Mike was fingering the cigarette lighter, making peace with all the evidence of his life that was about to explode. He ran through lists in his mind, a repetitive catalogue of every item that had caused him grief and that now, on the verge of disappearing, took on an aching poignancy. It was all there, picking up or losing fresh details in each run-through: *My Life.*

He felt his photographs tucked in against his shirt, slick against his belly, Lily's letter leaking scent.

"Bobe?" he said. "After Disneyland, you want to help me find my mom?" He shuffled his feet. "I'd like to take her some flowers."

"Sure, Mike," Bobo said. "I got nothin' better to do. Tú sabes."

Mike nodded.

The smell of gas was overpowering.

Suddenly, Mike thought of something.

"Wait a minute," he said.

He trotted back up to the station. He went into the kitchen. An old mantel clock was ticking on top of the icebox. He had felt a wave of guilt over executing the clock. He pulled the clock down and tucked it under one arm, and as he turned, he saw the Texaco Home Lubricant can on the table. He nabbed it too.

He stopped in the living room and stared at the spot where Turk had died. There was no mark on the mongrel carpet. He was standing exactly where Turk had lain. No sign whatsoever that the eternal Turk McGurk had passed into another world. He looked around him. To be honest, there was not much sign that *anyone* had ever lived there. Just empty, ramshackle little rooms, grease-stained and dim.

He walked out slowly, walked down to Bobo.

"What's that?" Bobo said.

"Clock."

"Oh."

"I had to save it."

"Uh-huh."

"Felt like I was killing it or something."

"Huh!"

Mike set the clock beside them on the road.

"Well," Mike said.

He flicked the lid on the lighter.

Bobo nudged him and pointed at the moon.

"Rabbit," he said. "Ain't no man there."

Then they blew up the station.

❦ ❦ ❦

Late in the night, leading Bobo on his motorcycle, Grandfather Sneezy squat as a troll in the sidecar, Mike smiled. He had all the gas he could use. Maybe Lily would like to go to Disneyland. He imagined finding her in the air, piloting one of those little spaceships. Or better yet, she'd be on the Matterhorn, riding down through the snow, great white fans rising to each side of her sled, cascades and explosions of powdery snow glittering in her hair, and Mike, shivering, tasting the sugar sweetness of snowy air, would reach out as she hurtled past and touch her once. And she'd know—just from that one touch. Mike was the man. Their breath, in his mind, formed twin whirlwinds, silvery in the moonlight, and it closed over their heads. He was so immersed in the dream that it took him a minute to hear the clock begin to chime. It sounded its bell in the seat beside him twelve times in a row, and it seemed to take all night to finish.

54

FIVE MILES BEHIND, RAMSES CASTRO WATCHED THE fragments of Turk's Texaco settle back into the desert and burn. He was having trouble getting his pickup started. He had to tap the gas pedal just so, or the thing would wheeze and gag all night. Finally, it caught. Castro couldn't believe Grandfather Sneezy hadn't brought him a hat. He worked the shifter into first and rolled out, whistling Bob Wills, lights off, six candy bars piled beside him, feeling good, feeling happy, trailing Mike's rapidly dwindling taillights, ready to go anywhere.